Deception

SUSAN M BAER

Deception

Copyright © 2017 Susan M. Baer

All rights reserved.

Published: April 18, 2016
Cover Photo: iStock by Getty Images
ISBN: 978-0-9979631-0-6
Publisher: Susan M. Baer

Find out more about Susan Baer and her upcoming books online at www.susanbaerauthor.com

DEDICATION

This story is dedicated to all the men in this world who think their career is enough. Boy! Do you have a lot to learn. LOL

CONTENTS

ACKNOWLEDGMENTS

Technology and Social Media Advisor:

Nolan Overton

Editors:

Robert Baer
Mary Jo Baranko
Peggy Brown

Technical Content Research:

Robert Baer

One

Dr. AJ Carrington sat in his Jaguar XJ and silently scolded Fate for persecuting him. The last thing he needed was to give the hospital administrator, Dr. Douglas Jameson, one more thorn to stick in his side. Yet a half a car length stood between him and the entrance to the parking garage of his office at Central Valley Health and Wellness Center. He was going to be late for his nine o'clock meeting with Douglas.

He looked at the clock on his dashboard, 8:51 a.m. He had left his 7:30 a.m. meeting with Charles Anderson, the president of the board of directors, in plenty of time. But Fate had been stalling him at every opportunity, and now that he was so close to his destination, she couldn't resist throwing one more obstacle in his way.

He had planned to already be in his office

gathering what he needed for his meeting, because he knew his sorry excuse for an executive assistant certainly wasn't going to have it ready for him. But a youthful looking businessman, no doubt with a superiority complex, decided to make his own lane to the right of a city bus before it pulled over to exchange passengers. The young man didn't quite reach his lofty goal and the bus rerouted him through the lawn next to the parking garage entrance. So instead of preparing for his meeting, AJ was sitting in his car waiting for the authorities to clear the way.

A flash of red in his rearview mirror caught his eye and he watched the city of Lincoln police cruiser slowly drive up the center left turn lane as it navigated the rush hour traffic. A crowd had gathered to gawk at the carnage and the officer triggered two short whoops of the siren to clear his path to the accident.

As AJ waited he blew out a heavy sigh and thought about his meeting with Douglas. He tried to mentally prepare himself for the verbal abuse he was sure to endure. He had come to expect Douglas to exploit every opportunity to revile him, but recently the hospital administrator's attacks were more personal and borderline vindictive. This was not the way AJ wanted to end his week.

The officer exited his cruiser just as the tow truck pulled the sports car from the driveway of the parking garage. The young man who had wrapped the once beautiful red Dodge Charger around the light pole sat in the grass and leaned up against a tree while the trauma team evaluated his condition.

Fortunately for him he picked the light pole just around the corner from the Central Valley ER. He had the best of the best working on him.

The line of cars crept forward and AJ was finally able to turn into the garage. He took a quick glance at the team attending to the driver. Dr. Collins, the head surgeon, was directing the others. AJ smiled as he made his way to his parking spot. Collins was the best in his field but his bedside manner was non-existent. That young man's physical health was being treated by leading edge medicine, but after dealing with Collins, he'll probably never want to drive another car as long as he lives.

AJ found his spot and was genuinely surprised to see Fate hadn't directed someone to take it so that he'd have to search the garage for an empty one. He made it inside and weaved his way through the maze of hallways and elevators. When he stepped into the administrative offices in the mental health wing he could feel a knot forming at the base of his neck.

"Good morning, Suzanne." He walked past his administrative assistant's desk, looked at his watch instead of her, and headed straight for his office.

"Good morning, Dr. Carrington," she whispered.

He rolled his eyes at her barely audible voice and set his briefcase on his desk. He really wished she would grow a backbone. He was damn tired of her soft demeanor. Most days it made it difficult to deal with her incompetence because she always looked like she was about to burst into tears. But today wasn't one of those days.

He started sifting through the papers on his desk

looking for the ones he needed.

"Suzanne, where is the hardcopy of my Las Vegas presentation? I emailed it to you this morning with very explicit instructions to have it printed on the grey, twenty pound stock, and to have it sitting here on my desk."

"I have it here, Dr. Carrington. I just printed it." She hurried through the door to his office.

"It should have already been on my desk. I am meeting with Dr. Jameson in five minutes."

"I'm sorry. I was on the phone with your publisher. I didn't think the call was going to take as long as it did."

"You need to be more prepared, Suzanne, we have talked about this before." He grabbed the report, separated the top sheet and rubbed it between his fingers. He restacked the pages and placed it in his briefcase.

"What did you work out with the publisher?"

"They are sending the corrected copies of your textbook right away," she said.

"Are they sure my latest research was added to Appendix D this time?"

"Yes. That was the first thing she told me was corrected."

"And are my credentials correct?"

"Yes, Dr. Carrington. I had her read them to me. I wrote it down so I could show you." She reached into the pocket of her suit jacket and retrieved a folded piece of paper. She held it out to him like a proud child showing her report card to her father. "She said they listed your MD in neurology."

He ignored the paper in her outstretched hand.

"That was in there before. Did they remove the degree in psychiatry that I do not have?"

"Yes, Dr. Carrington. I referenced the notes you gave me."

He whispered, "I wish I could feel more confident about that."

"What?"

"Nothing. Are they reprinted yet?"

"I think so. They had an editor look over the entire book and they assured me there are no other missing pages or mistakes. The new books will be here in four to six weeks."

He sighed. "Suzanne, the London lecture is in *three* weeks not four to six. Call them back and tell them to print them NOW and to ship them directly to the hotel in London. This was *their* mistake, not mine." He shook his head and looked at the papers on his desk. "I do not have time for this."

"Do you need me to reschedule your meeting with Dr. Jameson?"

"Why the hell would I want you to do that?"

"Well...you said you don't have time—"

"I was referring to the fact that I do not have the time to do your job in addition to mine!" He pinched the bridge of his nose. "Where is the budget report for my meeting with Dr. Jameson?"

"It's done. I just...need to print it."

"Then get it printed. Now!"

She turned and ran to her desk. When she returned she handed him a packet of papers.

He grabbed the report from her hand. It was still warm from the printer.

"Did you verify the flight and hotel reservations

for the Las Vegas conference for Monday?" he said.

"I was just about to do to that."

He dropped the papers into his briefcase and rubbed the ache slowly growing in his temples.

"Suzanne, where is the To Do list I emailed to you last week?"

"It's on my desk, Dr. Carr—"

"Go and get it."

She scurried out of his office. He could hear her shuffling papers around then slam a desk drawer. When she returned she held it out to him.

"I do not need to look at it, Suzanne. I know what is on it. Why did it take you so long to locate it?"

"I, uh, I forgot which drawer it was in." The paper quivered when her hand started shaking.

He turned to her and glared. "It should be ON your desk not in it. I have a meeting that I am going to be late for because you were not following the list I gave you. Everything I need for this meeting should have been on my desk, in a stack, waiting for me when I got in. Furthermore, I should not have to give you a list to follow. That is your job!"

She took a step back and hunched her shoulders.

He followed her as she continued to back towards the door.

"You have been working for me for six weeks and you are just as incompetent as the first moment you walked through that door. I expected to see improvement by this time and I see none. When I get back from my meeting with Dr. Jameson that list in your hand had better be completed or I suggest you update your resume. Am I making myself clear?"

Her entire body shook so hard he couldn't be sure, but he decided she had nodded her consent before she ran back to her desk looking like she was going to be sick.

He ran his hands through his hair and growled in frustration. The urge to throttle the little mouse scurrying out the door nearly had him chasing after her. For the last six weeks he had been training her and he couldn't help but feel it had all been a colossal waste of time.

With a sigh he went through the list of executive assistants he'd had since Marie quit last year. This latest disaster was number six. He had interviewed the first three himself and after he fired the third one because of what he felt was total incompetence, he decided to give HR the task. But they hadn't done any better, and Suzanne gave new meaning to the term "airhead".

Where the hell were all the smart ones and why couldn't he find one of them? Surely Marie wasn't the only one who could keep his life moving like a well oiled machine. He growled again as he sorted through the files on his desk looking for the ones he needed.

"Hey, no running in the office," Warren said.

AJ looked out into the reception area and saw Dr. Warren Jackson trying to hide his smile as he watched Suzanne rush out the door into the hallway. AJ grunted and returned to organizing the paperwork for his meeting.

He glanced at Warren when he stepped into his office. The guilty expression on Warren's face hadn't faded much over the past twelve months. AJ knew he should let him off the hook, but Warren was the reason he was having so much trouble finding a decent assistant. After all, Warren was the one who had turned Marie into a stay-at-home mom.

"Is it safe to come in?" Warren smiled.

"Probably not. There is a good chance I could become homicidal." AJ threw another file across his desk.

"Come on, AJ. It can't be that bad. You're just being too hard on her." Warren lounged back in the soft leather chair in front of AJ's desk.

"I will pay for a fulltime nanny. Hell, I will pay for an army of nannies if you let Marie come back to work."

"She would love that. It would get her out of the house, but you know it's against company policy to have spouses working in the same department." Warren grabbed a pencil from AJ's desk and twirled it in his fingers. "Besides, if she were here all day neither one of us would get any work done. I come to work so I can get some rest."

AJ grinned. He thought for a moment as he considered his best friend. Warren was the Chief Trauma Psychologist for Central Valley, and the best one AJ had ever seen. Warren was truly gifted when it came to soothing someone's soul who had survived a tragedy. But more importantly, AJ was profoundly grateful that Warren could run his department on his own. The last thing AJ needed was someone else to babysit.

He and Warren had been friends since grade

school but had lost touch after he left for medical school. By the time he returned to Lincoln, Warren was gone. Then about a year ago Warren had moved back to Lincoln and took his position at Central Valley. That was when AJ's well-ordered life had started to unravel. Just when he had found the perfect executive assistant, Warren came along and stole her heart, turning her into a wife and mother instead of AJ's longed for assistant.

"I am really happy for the two of you, Warren. Despite the inconvenience it has caused me." AJ closed his briefcase and sighed. "You and Marie are good together. And you definitely make good looking children. Speaking of which, how is my godson?"

"Vocal as ever. I think he's either going to be a rock star or a politician. He definitely has the lung capacity for both." Warren shivered.

"Good. My curse of revenge is working perfectly." AJ smiled and picked up his briefcase. "I have a meeting with Douglas." He glanced at his watch. "Actually, I should have been there five minutes ago. But my executive assistant, who you seem to think I am too hard on, did not have everything ready for me when I got in." He paced to the door.

"Don't forget about tonight, AJ. I've been planning this party for months." Warren rose from his chair and followed him to the door.

"I will not forget." AJ sighed. "Five-thirty sharp. Parillo's private dining room. Park down the block."

The instructions for Marie's surprise birthday

party were tattooed on his brain from the repeated reminders from her doting husband. AJ couldn't stop the laughter as he shook his head and stepped through the door.

"Good God, you are pussy whipped."

****

"No. You listen to me, you piece of shit. You're nothing more than a little messenger boy for your boss. We have an agreement and I expect to get exactly what I am paying for." Dr. Douglas Jameson snapped the pen he was holding in half. He ignored the sharp stab of pain when the splintered cylinder pressed into his palm and he dropped the broken pieces to his desk.

"There is no need to get nasty good doctor. I simply pointed out if your next payment is late the contract is void. Vasquez prefers his deals to be precise and clean. Your next payment is due tomorrow. I suggest you have it transferred by noon. Otherwise, you might find yourself in need of the morgue."

"How dare you threaten me. I can have you eliminated—"

"You overestimate your value, Dr. Jameson. Vasquez is not known for his patience and I would not make him wait too long for his money if I were you."

Douglas opened his mouth to speak and the line disconnected. "Prick!"

He threw his cell phone onto his desk and paced to the window. He stared at the view without seeing it and took a deep breath. Vasquez needed to move faster. Douglas' patience was wearing thin and it was past time to make the final arrangements to his plan. Carrington was leaving town on Monday and everything else was in place. Vasquez needed to step it up.

Douglas rehearsed the conversation to come. It always took more effort than he cared to exert when dealing with *Dr.* Carrington. No doubt the arrogant bastard would be late again.

He turned back to his desk and glared at the glistening, solid gold pen as it rested in the velvet lined case. He picked it up and rolled the cold, heavy, metal barrel between his fingers.

A droplet of blood eased down the crease in his palm and he closed his eyes on a soft moan. The illusion of Carrington's blood dripping from the tip of the pen triggered a tsunami of ecstasy through his body. He sighed when the glorious sensation reached the very ends of his extremities and rippled back toward his chest. He inhaled slowly and opened his eyes. His vision focused once again on the pen and the engraved words of praise halted the wave of pleasure like an impenetrable wall of stone.

He seethed at the memory of the day it was delivered.

'The pen the board ordered for Dr. Carrington is on your desk, Dr. Jameson. Mr. Anderson's secretary dropped it off this morning.' Samantha followed Douglas into his office. 'It's beautiful but rather heavy. I wouldn't want to use it very often.'

Douglas opened the gold box and lifted the engraved accolade. The board had decided to show its appreciation to the great and wonderful Dr. Anthony Joseph Carrington for his years of service to the hospital.

Douglas glanced at Samantha. She was busy reading through a report and he took the opportunity to run the barrel of the pen along the stone paperweight on his desk. He examined the pen and smiled to see the scratch running diagonally through the word "appreciation".

He placed the pen back into its box and Samantha turned to face him. She folded her arms across her chest.

'I'm still waiting for the budget report from pharmacy,' she said. 'Renee promised me she would bring it up before noon. That's the last piece I need and I will have the full budget report ready for the board meeting tonight.'

'Call her and tell her you want it by eleven. We have lunch reservations at The Red Door.'

She scrolled through her calendar on her PDA.

'I'm sorry, Dr. Jameson, but I don't have that meeting in my schedule and Mr. Rosenfeld called and requested the quarterly financials this morning for the new orthopedic wing. He asked me to have them delivered to his hotel at twelve-thirty. All the runners are booked for the day so I told him I would bring them personally.'

'Really?' He slid his leer up her body. 'Don't you think your boss should take priority?'

'Mr. Rosenfeld writes rather large checks to this hospital, Dr. Jameson. I think that makes him a little more important.'

'Daniel would wait for you and you know it. So

tell me, Samantha, what makes him preferable to me?'

She sighed. 'I don't mix business and pleasure, Dr. Jameson. Mr. Rosenfeld doesn't expect anything more from me than a stack of papers and that's what makes him preferable to you.'

'We have discussed this before, Samantha.' He stepped close to her. 'You need to be more concerned about making your boss happy. I should be your priority.'

'Central Valley is my priority, Dr. Jameson.'

'Exactly. Keeping the administrator satisfied makes the hospital run smoother. It all trickles down from the top.' Douglas reached for her cheek.

She slapped his hand away and stepped back.

'I've warned you, Dr. Jameson, I'll go to the board if you don't stop harassing me.' She lifted her chin. 'Maybe I'll just stop at Mr. Anderson's office on my way back.'

He raised his eyebrows and smirked. 'That threat has gotten old, Samantha, and you know damn well the board will side with me, especially Anderson. He's from the old school, when secretaries knew better than to resist.'

'I am NOT your secretary, Dr. Jameson. I am the Assistant Administrator. That makes me a bit higher on the food chain. If I don't like what you are doing, I can go to the board. I don't have to answer to anyone else.'

'Except me.' He paced to his desk and sat on the edge then crossed his arms. 'When you're done sucking his dick, tell Daniel I said hi."

'Your day is coming, Dr. Jameson, and I can't

wait to watch you fall.' Samantha turned and slammed the door on her way out…

Douglas could feel the vein in his temple throb. Samantha had rejected him once too often.

"Stupid bitch, you could've had it all."

He opened the drawer to his desk and carefully placed the engraved pen back into the gold box. In his private lavatory he washed the half-dried blood from his hand. The small clock on his desk chimed the hour and he snarled at his reflection in the mirror.

"Late again," he whispered.

He took a deep breath and focused on his objective. Carrington's days were numbered, but the closer he got to the end, the more impatient he became. He straightened his shoulders and smiled at the man staring back at him.

"Patience, my good man." He adjusted the knot in his tie. "One step at a time. You will be rid of him soon, one way or another."

Douglas treated the small wound in his hand and covered it discreetly. He was drumming his fingers impatiently on his now empty desk when AJ walked into his office.

"You're late," Douglas said.

"Thank you for noticing, Douglas. I am so glad you appreciate everything I do for Central Valley."

Douglas leaned back in his chair. "Yes, of course, how could I forget? Well, I would hate to waste your precious time so I'll get straight to the point. I have a scheduling conflict with the Las

Vegas conference next week. Samantha will be going in my place." Douglas turned his chair toward the window behind him and avoided eye contact with AJ.

AJ would have laughed if he wasn't so annoyed by the way Douglas treated him. He knew how Douglas felt about him, the professional jealousy was no secret. Dr. Jameson's contempt for him was known by every employee at the hospital. In fact, AJ wouldn't be surprised if the janitor knew about it.

Douglas made it quite clear that he felt AJ was not qualified to be one of the hospital's department heads and frequently questioned his research. But each time Douglas had tried to discredit him AJ was able to prove Jameson's claims to be false.

In the past six months Douglas' attacks were becoming more frequent, and more personal. AJ was beginning to question Douglas' sanity and had thought about the best way to approach that particular problem.

As the director of the Neurological Disorders and Spinal Rehabilitation department, HR was always looking to him to evaluate hospital employees who displayed any behaviors the administration deemed questionable. It wasn't unheard of for him to recommend some type of intervention, but suggesting a psychological or neurological evaluation of your boss could be seen as a power grab rather than a necessary step to prevent harm to the hospital.

Maybe it was time to file a formal complaint with the board. But even that was risky since

Douglas was stacking the board with supporters.

Shortly after taking over his position, Douglas started accusing the board of directors of favoring AJ, and in the six months that followed three board members had resigned. In the last two months three more board members had resigned and all six positions had been filled by close associates of Douglas. There was a good chance AJ's complaint would be viewed as retaliation and he was getting the feeling his time at CV was coming to an end.

"Your secretary?" AJ said.

"Samantha is the Assistant Administrator and she knows enough to assist you. She will present my report at the conference."

"I see. So this is one of those days when she is conveniently qualified to do your job?"

"Filling in for me *is* her job and she is more than qualified to do it!"

"Since when? Everyone knows her only job requirement is to warm your bed. You have made that abundantly clear and now you expect me to believe she can fill in for you when millions of dollars are on the line?"

Douglas sneered. "I'm sure with your expert guidance she'll do just fine."

"The investors are expecting you, Douglas, not Samantha! We will never get the funding if you snub them like this!" AJ took a deep breath and tried to slow his growing anger.

The presentation they had planned to give at the conference was a pitch for funding for a new wing of the research center on the hospital campus. The addition would house AJ's research projects.

"Then I guess you will just have to do without your new playhouse."

"Do not make this personal, Douglas. This deal is good for Central Valley. My research has been proven again and again. You need to be there!"

Douglas leapt out of his chair. He stopped inches from AJ and glared.

"Your arrogance is nauseating," he said. "I'll never understand why I'm the only one who can see it. My decision has nothing to do with you. I am the hospital administrator. I tell you what is going to happen and you accept it without question." He walked to the window and looked at AJ through the reflection in the glass. "Samantha will schedule a meeting with you for Monday morning. You can make any necessary changes to the presentation then."

"Douglas, we—"

"This conversation is over. Shut the door on your way out."

AJ hesitated for only a moment then without a word turned on his heels and slammed the door.

He glanced at Samantha as she sat at her desk in her office. He stopped when she looked at him. A sudden feeling of uneasiness rushed through him when he looked at her face. He saw the hurt in her eyes and watched her swallow hard. The gesture left him with an uncomfortable feeling.

His gaze wandered to her features, her emerald green eyes that looked too perfect to be real, her long blond locks that gently curved under her chin and around her neck, the slender oval shape of her face and pouty lips. She was beautiful but he found her flawlessness unsettling. She looked manufactured, like a Barbie Doll.

AJ blinked to clear his vision and looked at her again. This time he saw the hurt etched in her face and he sighed in disappointment. If she couldn't handle a few harsh words from him, the investors would tear her apart. This deal was dead.

Two

Marie's party was in full swing when AJ snuck away to a dark corner of the room. He needed the momentary isolation to recharge his patience. Most of the guests knew him, but more than half of those he barely recognized, and his preoccupation with his current dilemma was seriously hampering his ability to make nice with strangers.

He nursed his bourbon and rubbed his hand along his chin. He had to figure out how to make this presentation work. He frowned. Life was such a pain in the ass sometimes.

Losing Douglas' presence at the conference was a devastating blow. It would appear that the hospital didn't support his research. And showing up with Samantha, Jameson's arm candy, clad with her reputation of sleeping her way to the top, would make his pitch for funding look like a cheap carnival act.

He rubbed his throbbing temples. There was no way Samantha was going to be able to pull off this presentation standing up. Her best chance was to sleep with a few of the corporate investors in exchange for their financial support. He frowned when he pictured her seducing a man while he slipped a money clip full of bills into her cleavage. That was definitely not how he wanted this deal to go.

He blew out a heavy sigh. Her presence was going to be damaging. Not only to the presentation, but more importantly to his reputation, which was probably why Douglas was sending her. AJ had made it a point to always surround himself with nothing but the best and the brightest. Everyone looked to Dr. Carrington for answers. They accepted his word without question and he liked it that way. He was respected.

But all that had started to change. With the exception of Warren, AJ was beginning to feel disconnected from his colleagues. Not that he considered any of them as friends, but the respect they had for him was apparent. That was until about a year ago.

After Jameson's first attack on his research, AJ felt a small shift in the atmosphere at Central Valley. That was when the balance of power had begun to swing. He had been forced to work harder to keep the administration's backing. Before Dr. Jameson was promoted to hospital administrator, AJ had the full support of the administration as well as the board of directors. Now it seemed Douglas was using his position to make AJ's life as difficult as possible. Somehow he knew Douglas would be elated if he suddenly resigned.

"Good, God, old man," he whispered. "You are such an idiot."

How could he have been so blind? Douglas was trying to force him out. All the signs had been there, plain as day, but he'd been too busy to see them.

AJ slid his hand around to the back of his neck and squeezed the aching muscles. So far he'd been able to defend himself against Douglas' attacks on his work. But eventually the board would side with Douglas. And once the word got out, the details wouldn't matter, the industry leaders would start to doubt his work too. He needed to make an exit before Jameson did real damage to his reputation.

He never thought he'd have to consider leaving Central Valley. He'd spent the last seven years building his career and molding his reputation, as well as the hospital's, as the leader in treating brain dysfunctions. He hadn't planned to retire from Central Valley, but somehow he just thought he would.

He sighed and looked into his glass. He swirled the amber liquid and inhaled the rich aroma of aged oak. When the bourbon settled he noticed the tired look in his reflection. It made him feel...lonely?

"Jesus, you must be tired, old man," he said with a smile.

He took a quick swallow and scanned the crowd. He stopped when he saw Warren kiss Marie and his son affectionately as they talked to a small group of well wishers. He would have never thought Warren would settle down and he certainly never thought he would mature enough to be a father. But AJ had watched Warren change his goals and priorities over the past year and his best friend never looked happier.

AJ never thought about having a family of his own. He only had one brother and they weren't particularly close. Their parents were strong and independent, not showing much affection for each other or their two sons, so it never occurred to him that a family would provide more than the basic needs of food, shelter, and clothing. Yet when he looked at Warren he felt a strange sensation. He couldn't quite figure out what it was, but it left him with a sense of loss, as if something was suddenly missing from his life.

He dismissed the idea. The only thing that mattered was his career. He could provide his own basic needs, and when his body demanded physical release he had an abundance of secretaries to choose from who were willing to help him take care of it without any strings attached.

A few tables away another couple sat close enough to be Siamese twins. The young man tucked a strand of hair behind the woman's ear and raised her chin with his fingertips. He kissed her tenderly and the young woman nearly melted into his lap.

AJ raised his glass to his lips and whispered, "Get a room."

He took a sip of bourbon and watched the catering staff replenish the hors d'oeuvres. He'd seen less fuss with events Central Valley hosted for big shots. Warren had spared no expense with this party, yet AJ was not surprised. He had never seen his best friend so much in love with a woman before. And Warren seemed to truly enjoy spoiling her. The twinge of loneliness AJ had felt just a moment ago returned and he grunted in denial.

He turned his gaze back to the Siamese twins and saw Marie had joined their table. She was smiling as she talked to the couple. She looked truly happy. He knew she was, but it still surprised him. When Marie had worked as his Executive Assistant he had thought she was just like him, all business. She had never given him the impression her personal life even existed. But somehow Marie had found a way to have both, that was until Xavier had come along.

'Maybe that's what you're missing old man.' AJ laughed to himself and smiled. For now he was content to watch.

He tossed back the last of his drink and leaned into the soft cushion of his chair. He decided to enjoy a little more of his favorite hobby, people watching.

He looked around the room and stopped at each couple to study their faces for clues. How many of them were truly happy and how many of them were putting on a show for the rest of the world to see? When he was younger he would fantasize about married life being full of love and happiness, just like all the TV shows. But then his parents would walk into the room looking, for all the world, as if they were just acquaintances. So he grew up thinking marriage was a duty and a responsibility, not something anyone really wanted to do.

He laughed to himself when he thought about how naïve he had been. His education and a "close call" had taught him that there was more to it, but what exactly the *more* was he had no idea.

Warren dropped into the chair next to him. "Who is she?"

"Who's who?"

"The woman you're thinking about."

AJ couldn't help the sheepish grin that crossed his face. "No one in particular...just wondering."

"Why don't you jump in? The water's great."

"I know I'm not the most knowledgeable about that sort of thing but doesn't it still require two? I am currently unattached."

AJ's gaze roamed the crowd and settled on a familiar figure. Samantha turned to greet Marie and his good mood disintegrated. His body reacted to the sight of her in that little black dress that hugged every curve, and he scowled. Despite his distaste for being forced to work with her, he could feel the blood rushing to his groin and he had to shift his weight to accommodate the change.

She flicked her hair over her shoulder and a sense of recognition flashed through his mind. Then it hit him, he was aroused by her because she was his type...tall, blonde, and a reputation of 'no strings attached'.

"She could do the job. Marie likes her."

AJ laughed out loud. "Okay, first of all, I'm not getting married and second, if I was I would hope it would be to someone a little less experienced."

"I thought experience would be a plus for you. You don't have much patience when it comes to training a woman."

AJ smiled. "You do have a point."

"So, how about it?"

"A woman is a complication I don't have time for right now. I have more important things to worry about."

"Like what?"

AJ clapped Warren on the shoulder. "This is a party. Let's not spoil it."

"Since when has that ever stopped you? You were always throwing a wet blanket on me."

"You know damn well if I hadn't you would have spent a small fortune on bail and probably still be working on your undergrad."

"Stop bragging." Warren smiled. "Tell me what's going on."

AJ sighed. "It's complicated."

A waitress stopped at the table and placed two glasses of bourbon in front of them.

"Thanks, Sophia." Warren smiled.

"Sure thing, cuz," she said and turned to pick up two empty glasses on the table next to them.

Warren picked up his glass and took a sip before he turned to AJ. "Then give me the simple version. What's the problem?"

AJ waited until the waitress was out of earshot. "This deal for the research wing."

"I thought it was pretty much in the bag. Jameson's been bragging about what good buddies he is with the investors. I figured it was a slam dunk."

"That's what has me worried...Douglas backed out this morning. He's sending the Assistant

Administrator in his place."

"Samantha? Geez…I mean, Marie likes her but I heard she was a bit of an airhead. Why the hell would he send her?"

"I don't know. When I met with Jameson this morning he told me he had a scheduling conflict. I think it has more to do with trying to make me look bad."

"What the hell is his beef with you? I know he doesn't like you but this could hurt the hospital."

AJ scrubbed his hands over his face then scanned the party guests.

"Since he never showed any concerns with this project that would house *my* research and waited until the last minute to back out, my guess is he's trying to hurt my reputation not the hospital's. I'm sure he's got another attack against my work ready to go. He's probably planning to take it to the board while I'm conveniently out of town at this conference."

"Surely he's smart enough to realize putting you two on opposite ends of this deal is going to look bad. The investors could assume the administration is ineffectual or that your research is flawed or controversial. Central Valley is asking for a lot of money for Douglas to be casting that kind of doubt into the mix. Even if they are such good buddies of his, that's going to make them question their involvement. After all, business is business."

"Apparently he's not that smart…maybe I can talk to the board when I get back. I tried to reach Anderson and Smith this afternoon but they're both out of the country until sometime next week. Their secretaries were uncharacteristically vague about that." He looked at Warren. "They're the only two left I feel comfortable discussing this with right now. The rest are either in Douglas' pocket or sitting on the fence with no indication which way they might fall."

"So what are you going to do?"

AJ looked back to where Samantha was still talking with Marie. He had never let a woman intimidate him before, especially one who couldn't think her way out of a paper bag. But then again he never had to deal this closely with one who was intimately involved with an adversary.

"Keep my fingers crossed." He threw his bourbon to back of his throat. "And hope she isn't going along to put the final nail in my coffin."

Three

AJ walked into his office and found Samantha sitting in his chair. She was dressed in a low cut, short, red dress. Her gentle curves were displayed beautifully in the sexy satin. The dress was familiar, he'd seen it before.

He walked behind his desk and reached across her body to set his briefcase down in front of her. He brought his hand back and brushed her hair from her neck.

She turned her head into his palm and whispered, "Do you ever think about me?"

He spun the chair around and yanked her to her feet. He swept his desk clean in one stroke and pushed her to her back. He covered her with his body and kissed her with a feeling of desperation.

She moaned then pushed at his shoulders and broke the kiss.

"Do you like what you see?"

A flash of red caught his eye and he looked at his phone. Suzanne's line was blinking with an incoming call. AJ realized the position he was in and jumped to his feet. He wiped Samantha's lipstick from his mouth with the back of his hand and fought to catch his breath. He put more space between them and clumsily pointed at her.

"That dress is not appropriate for this office." He crossed his arms over his chest and watched her closely.

She rose slowly and sensuously off his desk. She walked around it, her fingertips glided along the polished wood. She bit her bottom lip and smiled coyly.

"Is it really the dress you object to or is it me you don't want in your life?"

He closed his eyes and groaned. The need to possess her, cover her with his body and thrust into her softness was strong. But he couldn't do that here...could he? What if Suzanne walked in?

His heartbeat thundered in his ears. He swallowed hard and opened his eyes. Samantha stood close to him and he could feel the cool satin of her dress as the material settled on the fine sprinkling of hair on his torso. His shirt hung open and when he gasped in surprise his chest pressed against her breasts. He took a step back and stopped abruptly when his back hit the wall behind him.

She ran the tips of her fingers along the neckline of her dress and toyed with the material where the two sides met between her breasts. She tipped her head to the side, a pouty frown on her lips.

He let his gaze roam her body before he looked at her eyes. They flashed with a familiar spark. He'd seen that look before. She was challenging him.

"What I do or do not like is not the point," he said. He pulled the sides of his shirt together and fastened the button at his waist. "You do not work for me and that dress belongs somewhere other than my office."

"I think it's exactly what your office needs." She ran a glossy red fingernail along his jaw. "Maybe if you weren't afraid to admit it, you'd see I'm exactly what you need in your life."

She pressed her body to his and tipped her head up.

He could feel her warm breath on his neck and waited for her to kiss the vein he could feel pulsing in his throat. He clenched his jaw and willed her to bite him.

She stepped to his right side and whispered, "You know you want me. It's time to admit it."

He grabbed her hand and brought her palm to his lips. He licked her warm skin and turned around to follow her.

Samantha spun and *her hair turned dark as it swayed across her face. Her features blurred and when he blinked his stomach knotted. It wasn't Samantha in that damned red dress, it was Jackie.*

She was just as he remembered her. Dark, wavy, long hair, full figure and lips so inviting arousal shot through him like a lightning bolt.

Her expression changed and his heart constricted. The look on her beautiful face was tortured and full of pain.

Suddenly, Jackie was standing a few feet away under the oak tree. The wind was blowing her hair wildly as the leaves stirred around her.

'I thought you wanted me. Why did you make me come here?'

The howl of the wind became deafening and he struggled to hear her voice. A tear ran down her face and disappeared under her chin.

AJ tried to move but he was paralyzed. The more he struggled the more his heart ached. He had to reach her. He needed to hold her, to ease the emptiness consuming him.

The tear reappeared and rolled down her neck. Inch by inch it made its way down her silky smooth skin until it was nestled in her generous cleavage. The image made him dizzy with desire. He tried to move his arm, to brush the backs of his fingers along her cheek, but he still couldn't move.

She turned around. The wind tugged at her long hair and his vision blurred.

'Jackie! Don't leave me!'

The distance between them was growing, he was losing her.

'NO!'

He finally broke free from his paralysis and lunged for her, but Jackie faded from his view and he stumbled forward, falling into darkness.

AJ woke with a start and bolted upright, his breathing was labored as if he had just run a marathon. He ran his hands through his hair and looked around trying to make sense of his surroundings. He found the clock on his nightstand. It was barely 5:00 a.m., Saturday morning. He exhaled.

"It was just a dream, old man, ancient history."

He flopped back down onto his bed. He was still sweating but his heart rate had slowed. He closed his eyes and tried to see her face again.

He hadn't dreamt about Jackie in so long he'd almost forgotten about them, the dreams that had consumed his life for nearly three years. Before, his dreams of her had always been pleasant, filled with love and passion hot enough to burn the sheets. But this dream was different, this one was a nightmare. Her heart was breaking and it was all because of him.

He blew out a heavy sigh and sat up on the edge of his bed. The real world had returned and the details of his dream were already fading.

"She's gone, AJ. It's over. It wasn't meant to be." He took a deep cleansing breath. "It's time to get to work. You have a presentation to get ready for."

He paced to the shower and turned it on. He stared at his reflection in the mirror. The few strands of silver at his temples suddenly made him feel old and the lines jutting out from the corners of his eyes seemed deeper, longer. He rubbed his face with the heels of his hands and looked again.

It had been thirteen years since he'd last seen Jackie and he wondered what she looked like. Was she still as beautiful as he remembered her?

With a sigh he stepped into the shower. He closed his eyes and pictured Jackie's smile, the smile he loved, the smile that reflected the beautiful soul within her.

He remembered the smell of her perfume and his body hardened. The thought of her soft breasts pressing against him sent an urgent pulse rushing through his veins. He reached down and squeezed his shaft.

"Jackie," he whispered. "I miss you."

He laid his left hand against the cold tile and leaned against it. He massaged his cock with slow, firm strokes. Her face came into view again and her smile began to fade.

"No, Jackie, smile for me. I love you."

A single tear rolled down her cheek.

'I thought you loved me, AJ.'

"Stop it!" He opened his eyes wide to block the memory and increased his strokes. "Show me her smile, damn it. I want to see her happy. She was happy once."

He could feel the tension building in his muscles and he tightened his grip. He closed his eyes and tipped his face up to the spray of the hot water.

Another face flashed in his mind. Samantha was staring at him, her face unreadable. The red dress hugged her sensuously and he concentrated on the gentle curve of her breasts. Her face appeared again. He dropped his head and opened his eyes.

"Remember Jackie, damn you. Come on, AJ, remember her smile."

His strokes became forceful and angry, almost painful.

"You made her happy once. Remember it!"

He stroked his shaft faster and his body

tightened. The muscles in his legs tremored and he pressed the fingertips of his left hand against the tile. An instant later he exploded.

He closed his eyes and breathed deeply while the trembling in his limbs subsided. Jackie's face appeared again and the tear dropped from her chin. The look of pain he couldn't help but remember each time he thought of her was unchangeable. It was a reflection of the pain he had inflicted before she walked away from him thirteen years ago.

AJ groaned and leaned his forehead against the steam coated tile.

"God, help me. I can't do this again."

****

AJ walked into the office well before 6:00 a.m. The suite was quiet and dark. This part of the medical center was usually deserted on Saturday, unless a special fund raising event was in the works, and he was counting on the solitude to help him get his mind back on track.

He shut the door behind him and didn't bother to turn the lights on. Residual light from the hall outside gave enough illumination through the windows in the waiting room so he could see the way to his door.

For the first time he just stood there and looked around the waiting room, slowly scanning the space from left to right. How many times had he walked into this place and never really saw it? He was always in a hurry, always someone to see or somewhere to go, quickly gathering reports or other paperwork necessary for whatever meeting he was rushing off to next. But this time it felt different. This time it felt like there was something missing.

After Marie's birthday party last night he had gone home to find his townhouse suddenly felt cold and empty. The sensation was so strong he had actually looked in each room to see if anything was missing and checked the windows for any sign they had been pried open.

Uneasiness lingered and he decided a good night's rest would solve the problem. He had fallen asleep to the thought of having a family to come home to, while trying to convince himself he didn't need one. He'd built his life around his career and thought he had everything he could ever want. But then he saw Warren with his small family at the party and something shifted inside, like a hole had opened up.

He replayed a scene when he had held Xavier in his arms and talked with Warren, and a pang of jealousy pricked his heart. Something about holding Xavier was energizing and he found he hated relinquishing him back to the arms of his father. Next to Warren and Marie, AJ was Xavier's favorite person. He could feel the connection every time he held him.

The desire to be a father suddenly surfaced, catching him by surprise. He pushed his thoughts away with a quick laugh and headed for his office.

"Well old man, you have to find a woman willing to help you with that first." He shook his head with a smile and stepped through the door.

A chill swept over him when he put his briefcase on his desk. He opened it and pulled out his presentation to the investors for Wednesday. The pages felt warm to the touch and he realized just how cold his office was. It was a particularly chilly, late October morning and the drizzle of rain outside made it feel even colder.

He overrode the weekend settings on the heat. In the dead silence of his office he could hear the warm air rush through the ducts. He stepped to the windows and looked through the rain speckled glass. Less than a dozen cars sprinkled the parking lot and none were familiar. Good. He could work without interruption.

His phone vibrated in his pocket. He checked the number and connected the call from Warren. He looked back out at the rain and spoke.

"You're up early," he said.

"Yeah, not by my design. The X-man is more of an early riser than you."

AJ smiled. He could hear Xavier talking in the background, not that a four month old could utter anything comprehensible, but he sounded like he was intent on being heard anyway.

Warren continued. *"I knew you'd be up already so I thought I'd catch you before you headed into the office."*

"Well, tell the X-man he has to get up a little earlier next time. I'm already in my office. I have to figure out a way to get this funding." He blew out a sigh and walked to his desk. "I wish I could just scrap the whole thing and look at moving my work. But if I back out on this deal now it will look like there is something wrong with my research."

"Maybe, maybe not. Jameson's been around the

circuit. Most of the power players know him so I'm sure his reputation reaches beyond Central Valley."

"I can't rely on that." AJ dropped back into his chair. "So what did you need?"

"Marie is headed over to Janet's place later and I've got the X-man for the day. I thought you might be in the mood to stop by for a good cigar and bourbon. Maybe we can figure out what Jameson's game is."

"I just might take you up on that, but I doubt we can figure out what's going on in that man's head. His accusations are so farfetched they never cease to amaze me." AJ looked at his watch. "I'll give you a call when I'm done here."

"Don't wait too long. I'm beginning to understand the X-man's language."

AJ laughed. "I'll be there as soon as I can."

"Thanks. I knew I could count on you."

"No. You just know I'm a sucker for the X-man."

"Whatever works. Later."

AJ slid his phone into the breast pocket of his shirt and picked up the copy of his presentation. He had been through it a million times but he knew if he wanted that funding without Douglas' support it had to be perfect.

He stared at the papers without seeing them, his thoughts drifted to the dream he'd had this morning. Suddenly it made sense. He had dreamt of Jackie because of his frivolous thoughts about wanting a family, wanting what Warren had.

AJ puffed out a sigh of relief when he realized the dreams weren't starting over again. It was just a fluke. He had dreamt about Jackie because she was the only woman he had ever loved, still loved. His subconscious had brought her back when he was toying with the idea of having a family of his own. So, it was a sign. He needed to get back to work. That was his life. He didn't need a family to feel whole, his work did that for him.

The office phone rang. He ignored it and refocused on the reports on his desk. Suzanne could deal with whoever wanted him on Monday. Hopefully she could actually do something to earn her paycheck. She had been leaving a great deal to be desired, as far as he was concerned.

He thumbed through the pages and sighed. The presentation was good, actually it was more than good, but something didn't feel quite right. Maybe it was just the fact that he couldn't shake the bad feeling he got about Douglas backing out on him. There was more than a scheduling conflict keeping Douglas from going to Vegas but he'd be damned if he could figure out what it was. He knew how Jameson felt about him but this deal was good for the medical center. Douglas should be able to set aside his personal feelings for the good of Central Valley.

AJ dropped the papers on his desk and turned to watch the rain hit the window. The presentation would have to be good enough. No matter how many times he reviewed it there just wasn't anything he could change to make it better. And once he got the statistical and financial reports from Douglas on Monday he would have all the information he needed.

His cell phone vibrated against his chest and he pulled it out with a disgusted groan. So much for no interruptions today.

He checked the caller ID and recognized the number. It was the main line for the medical center. He wanted to ignore this call too, but when the hospital called after hours it was always important. With a grunt he answered the call. "Dr. Carrington."

"Dr. Carrington, this is Samantha. I apologize for calling so early on a Saturday, but I wanted to meet with you concerning the Las Vegas conference as soon as possible. Unfortunately, my schedule doesn't allow for anything else before we leave. I was hoping I could meet with you today, preferably this morning."

AJ exhaled a disgusted sigh and looked at his watch. The minute hand jerked forward and hit the twelve, indicating the six o'clock hour precisely. He really didn't think she could add anything to the presentation, but he would feel better if he knew she was at least familiar with it.

He also wanted to know whose side she was on, Douglas' or Central Valley's. He didn't think she was smart enough to sabotage him, as her reputation inferred, but her involvement was Jameson's doing…and that made her a possible threat.

"Fine. How quickly can you get everything together?"

"I'm in my office. I can meet you here or in your office. Just call me when you get in."

"I am already *in* my office, Ms…Samantha."

AJ realized he didn't know her last name and it annoyed him. He would prefer to use it, to keep any interactions with her professional, but he'd only ever heard her referred to as Samantha.

He continued. "Considering we are leaving on Monday for the conference and I have a tremendous amount of responsibility to this hospital, I fail to see how you can assume I would not be working in my office today."

"I do apologize, Dr. Carrington. I had no intention of implying you would have the audacity to waste time considering your 'tremendous amount of responsibility'. I was simply trying to help as best as I can. If you would prefer to wait until we get to Las Vegas to review Dr. Jameson's portion of the presentation, as well as his financial and statistical reports, I will write summaries for you. The documents are rather extensive and there will not be enough time for you to review them once we get to the hotel."

She had Jameson's presentation? That he definitely wanted to see. And she had his other reports, too. Maybe she did have something to add after all. He decided to soften his approach.

"No, Samantha. I am the one who should apologize. Apparently I have misplaced my manners this morning. I would very much appreciate it if you would bring Dr. Jameson's reports to my office. As you pointed out, it would be best if I started reviewing them today." He smiled to himself. "And it would be unfair of me to ask you to go through the trouble of summarizing them for me."

"Your generosity is immeasurable." She paused. *"I'll be there in five minutes."*

"Good." AJ disconnected the call. Once he got those reports in his hands he would feel a lot better.

Samantha heard the dial tone as she opened her mouth to speak. Her comeback was on the tip of her tongue. She smothered the stab of pain that pierced her chest. No matter how many times her reputation of being "unqualified" preceded her, the disappointment when people failed to give her a chance to prove them wrong never diminished.

Plus, Dr. Carrington's tone was aggravating to say the least. His reputation as an arrogant hard-ass was apparently not an exaggeration. She had hoped they could be friendly with each other considering the fact that they would be working together on this presentation, but apparently he had other ideas. She shoved her phone into her briefcase with a growl.

"Men!"

She gathered up the financial reports and shoved them in as well, not caring if the pristine papers got mangled in the process. She was done trying to impress the stuck up, male chauvinist, department heads at this hospital. Even their executive assistants weren't very friendly to her. To her face they were cool and polite, but more than once she caught them whispering behind her back.

The only person who had been nice to her was Dr. Carrington's former assistant, Marie. In fact, they were still friends, but now that she had married Dr. Jackson and was no longer working at the hospital, Samantha didn't have any friends at the office.

After Dr. Jameson had dumped this presentation

on her desk Friday morning, she had spent the afternoon talking to some of her contacts. One in particular, Daniel Rosenfeld, seemed rather eager to obtain a copy of her résumé. Samantha made sure the email went through before she had left for the day.

The path to Dr. Carrington's office was quiet and dark in some places. She tried to avoid the office on Saturday because the eerie silence normally bothered her, but today the gloomy hallways fit her mood perfectly and fueled her determination to hold her ground with him.

Samantha blew out a heavy breath and stopped at the door to the suite of offices that housed the departments of Neurology and Psychology. Dr. Carrington's office was the first one on the left. She grasped the doorknob and hesitated. She had hoped Dr. Carrington would be different.

Marie had told her that despite his reputation he was a good man, a little on the demanding side, but a good man nonetheless. But Samantha's first conversation with him today was no more hopeful than the last time she had spoken to him. His opinion was obvious in his tone. He believed her reputation was accurate. She straightened her spine, tugged on her suit jacket and stepped through the door.

AJ checked his schedule for next week and noticed Suzanne hadn't rescheduled his meeting with the staff at Greenhill Estates for Monday morning.

"Damn it."

He'd have to fit it in somehow. He heard a knock on his door and closed his calendar.

"Come in, Samantha."

The door swung open immediately and Samantha marched across the threshold. She spun around and closed the door with enough force he could almost believe she had intended to slam it. She walked with confidence and purpose past his desk to the conference table next to the windows and set down her briefcase.

The lack of pleasantries on her part irritated him and he sighed loudly.

She pulled a stack of papers out and marched back to his desk. She set them down forcefully in front of him and smiled sarcastically.

"I do apologize for making you wait while I retrieved these reports from my briefcase."

He looked into her eyes and saw something there he hadn't expected. Despite the fact she was passed around more often than the gravy boat at Thanksgiving dinner, she looked fresh and untouched, even with the daggers shooting from her eyes.

He dropped his gaze and scanned the pages. He spoke without looking up.

"No need to apologize. It was unfair of me to expect a pleasant greeting from you, such as 'Good morning'."

He heard the leather creak as she sat in the chair in front of his desk.

"How rude of me. But then again, what can you expect from a dumb blond? Unless I'm doing something fun, like prepping for a colonoscopy, I sometimes forget to utter pleasantries."

AJ had to bite the inside of his cheek to keep from smiling and kept his eyes on the reports in front of him. He rather enjoyed her sarcasm.

He scanned the numbers in the financial report. They looked legitimate at a glance, but he'd have to go over those figures more closely later. The report looked more detailed than the other financial reports he'd seen from Douglas. It would be easy to kill the deal if Douglas was asking for too much unnecessary funding.

He heard Samantha stand from the chair and looked up to watch her pace slowly to the windows. He stared for a moment at her watery reflection in the glass. A drop of rain ran down the window and for a brief instant she looked as if she was crying. Their eyes met and he tried to read her thoughts.

She was different than what he had expected. Nothing about her indicated she was anything like her reputation. But if she wasn't an airhead, why would she tolerate the way Douglas treated her?

And why did she contact him today when Douglas told him she would contact him on Monday? Douglas obviously wanted him to have as little time as possible to prepare for his absence. She had to be doing this on her own. But she seemed less than thrilled to be here. Not that he had given her a reason to be happy about it, but the fact that she was working on this presentation on a Saturday indicated she had something to gain from a particular outcome, hopefully a successful one.

"Everything seems to be here, Samantha. I will read over these more closely and let you know if I need any further information."

She turned toward him and leaned back against the window sill, a curious look on her face. She was silent for a moment before she spoke.

"You have quite an impressive office, Dr. Carrington. Even on a dreary day like today these windows and the skylight let in quite a bit of light."

"They also let in quite a bit of cold air in the winter."

"Adding another layer of clothing solves that problem. I'd rather have the light."

"What a brilliant idea. I should write it down so I can try that instead of turning up the heat the next time I feel a chill." He leaned back and crossed his arms over his chest.

She started walking a path around the conference table and brushed her fingertips along the top of each chair as she passed it.

"Despite popular opinion I do experience moments of intelligence every now and then," she said.

He watched her move to the bookcase on the far wall and pull a book from the top shelf. Apparently she felt the need to demonstrate her claim of possessing a higher IQ.

She presented the front cover of 'Dreams' by *Carl Jung* to him, then looked at it herself. "What do you think of Jung's dream interpretations? I hate to admit I find him a little difficult to follow." She opened the book and fanned the pages slowly. "You didn't make any notes in here. I was hoping to gain some insight from someone as knowledgeable as yourself."

AJ hesitated. He wasn't in the mood for a friendly chat and he certainly wasn't going to discuss dreams with her.

"As stimulating as this conversation may seem, I have a presentation next week that is a bit more important than my professional opinion of Carl Jung's theories on dreams."

"Yes. Of course. How presumptuous of me to waste your time. I really must practice better manners." She put the book back in its place and hesitated a minute before she gathered her briefcase and headed for the door.

AJ cleared his throat when she got to his desk and she stopped to look at him.

"Am I forgetting something, Dr. Carrington?"

"One more thing before you go. I am afraid I do not know your last name and I would prefer to use it instead of Samantha. I think it would be best if we maintained a professional tone with each other."

"Samantha will have to do. I am not in the habit of using my last name and I have no problem keeping my professionalism without it. If you are concerned about your ability to maintain your professionalism," she cocked her head and smiled, "I'm afraid that will be your problem."

AJ stayed silent as he watched her march to the door and disappear behind it. He couldn't stop the smile from creeping across his face. Her spunk was intriguing.

Four

AJ pulled into the driveway at Warren's home and saw him slouched in a wooden Adirondack chair wrapped in a wool blanket. He had a glass of bourbon in one hand and a baby monitor in the other.

AJ shook his head and laughed as he walked from his car to the porch. He ascended the steps and stopped at the top.

"I never thought I'd see the day."

"Go ahead. Laugh it up, Golden Boy. I can't wait to return the favor." Warren stood and led AJ into the house. "If you had rung that doorbell I would have lost my mind. You have no idea what it took to get that momma's boy to go to sleep without her here."

AJ followed him into the den. "How long has he been asleep?"

"About twenty minutes and not nearly long enough to be manageable." Warren tossed the blanket onto the overstuffed couch and poured AJ a drink. "If it's okay with you we're going to skip the cigar. Marie doesn't want me smoking in the house and it's too damned cold to sit out back."

"No. That's fine." AJ sat with a heavy sigh and ran his fingers through his hair.

Warren handed him his drink and sat in the chair on the other side of the coffee table. "Still worried about this deal?"

AJ rolled his sore shoulders. "Maybe…"

"Jameson?"

"No. I'll find out sooner or later what he's up to. I don't have the energy to try to figure him out right now."

"Then what's going on? You look exhausted. Rough night?"

"You could say that."

AJ stood and paced to the window. The rain had stopped but it was still overcast and the window was speckled with water. He looked at the wooded backyard decorated with fall colors and spoke.

"Do you remember Jackie?"

"Jackie who?"

AJ looked into his glass and swirled the liquor and ice. "Jackie Dean."

"Your Jackie?"

"Yes."

"Yeah, I remember her." Warren paused. "What made you bring her up?"

"I don't know." He turned to face Warren. "I haven't thought about her in years."

"You mean, dreamt about her in years. I bet you *think* about her a bit more often than that." He leaned back against the soft cushion. "You loved her AJ. Any fool could have seen that. The bitch of it is you probably still do."

"It doesn't matter. She walked out of my life and never looked back." He sipped his bourbon and smiled. "So how's Marie?"

"Marie's fine and I'm not letting you change the subject. You brought Jackie up for a reason. Spit it out."

AJ sighed. "I dreamt about her this morning." He set his drink down on the minibar next to him.

"Oh, man. You gotta tell me about it. Those dreams were always hot as hell."

AJ shook his head. "Not this time. I dreamt about the last time I saw her…I think. There were some things that didn't make sense."

"Did you remember anything new?"

"No. But it was bizarre as hell. It started out with Samantha in my office. She was wearing the red dress I bought for Jackie and she was coming on to me."

"Did you at least get to have sex with her?" Warren wiggled his eyebrows.

"No." AJ looked down at the floor. "I was about to when she turned into Jackie."

"And if you say this dream was *not* hot as hell, then I know you didn't get to have sex with Jackie either. Sorry man, that just sucks."

AJ took a swallow of bourbon. "Yes, it does. Because then I had to watch her walk away from me again."

The room fell silent and AJ could hear the clock ticking on the mantel. He closed his eyes. He could feel Warren's sympathy and he hated it.

The dreams he'd had before had haunted him mercilessly and Warren had seen how they had all but destroyed his sanity. He'd had one every time he closed his eyes. And Warren was right. They were hot as hell. So damn hot that AJ got a hard-on at a mere glimpse of any woman who resembled Jackie.

He followed a few of the women until he saw their faces and realized they weren't Jackie. The day he drove fifty miles out of his way to get a better glimpse of a woman he thought might be her was the day he realized her memory had consumed his life. Nothing he tried worked and he and Warren were out of ideas when one day the dreams just stopped.

Eventually he was able to put Jackie's memory behind him. Well, not exactly behind him, but at enough distance that he could think about her occasionally without having his heart ripped from his chest. Jackie walked out of his life and took his will to love with her. He had learned to survive without it and he wasn't about to let it back in.

AJ swallowed the last of his drink and filled his glass with fresh ice. He watched the bourbon trickle down the frozen cubes as he poured it and Warren spoke.

"Do you think the dreams are starting again?"

AJ shook his head. "No." He looked at Warren and smiled. "I think it was a fluke because my bastard of a best friend made married life look so good I was momentarily jealous." He snorted a laugh. "That was until I saw you on the front porch today."

Warren smiled back and raised his glass in a toast. "You just wait, you son of a bitch, your day will come."

****

Samantha drove up the long tree lined drive of Greenhill Estates and continued around to the parking lot in the back. Her mother's apartment was situated in a nice quiet corner of the assisted living complex. At least her mother could still feel like she was independent, living in the country like she had most of her life.

Samantha called to her when she walked into the kitchen.

"Mom. It's me." She could hear voices coming from the living room.

"Now Sarah, that's why you need to use this organizer when you take your medications. It's the only way we're going to be able to make sure you take them on time." The young nurse turned to Samantha when she appeared at the doorway. "Hi, Sam."

"Hi, Nancy. Hi, mom." Samantha leaned down and kissed her mother on the cheek. "How are you doing today?"

Sarah wiped her cheek in disgust and ran her hand along her robe. "What the hell did you do that for? Stop slobbering on me."

"I'm sorry, mom. Why don't you just tell me about your day." Samantha stacked the puzzle books on the end table next to Sarah while Nancy refilled her medication organizer at the small dining table at the far end of the room.

Sarah smacked Samantha's hand.

"Put those down! They're mine."

"I know they're yours, mom, I'm just straightening up for you."

Sarah mumbled and scattered the books. One of them fell to the floor and Samantha stooped to pick it up. When she stood Sarah was glaring at her.

"Give that back," Sarah whispered.

She snatched it from Samantha's grasp and clutched it to her chest.

Samantha sighed and smiled weakly. "Mom, you look tired. Why don't you take a nap?"

"I'm not tired." She tightened her grip on the book and Samantha could see her knuckles turning white.

"Mom, let me—"

"Stop calling me that, I'm not your mother. I would have taught you better than to walk into someone's home and just do as you please."

Samantha held her tongue and walked back into the kitchen to wait for Nancy. Her mother was obviously having a bad day today. And it was days like this when the best thing she could do for her mother was leave her alone.

She looked out the window above the sink and stared blindly at the cattle grazing in the field beyond the fence. She suppressed the ache rising in her chest with a deep breath. Each time her mother forgot her it hurt a little less. She knew it was the early onset of dementia brought on by her traumatic brain injury, but Samantha also knew the pain would never go away completely. A small part of her still held out hope that she had meant too much to her mother to be forgotten, even when a disease was attacking her mind.

She heard Nancy enter the room, but she didn't turn to greet her. If she did she wouldn't be able to stop the tears she was fighting to hold back.

"I'm sorry, Sam. She forgot to take her medicine this morning and I suspect she forgot to take it last night too."

Nancy stopped beside Samantha and stared out the window with her.

"The treatment team wants to move your mom to The Acres. We could watch her more closely there and she would still have the feeling of being in the country. We're going to request authorization from Dr. Carrington on Monday."

Samantha continued to look out the window. She knew this day was coming. Her mother had been declining faster in the last couple months. Still, she wasn't as prepared to hear those words as she thought she would be. She turned to Nancy.

"I understand...I should go. I have a lot to do before I leave for Las Vegas on Monday and I can't miss this trip. Dr. Carrington has to get that funding. His research might be the only chance I have to help her." She wiped a tear as it escaped. "Should I come back later?"

"That's up to you, but if you're asking me if she'll remember you...I doubt it. This is a bad day, Sam, and she usually doesn't improve until she's had her medication and a good night's sleep."

"I know…you're right."

"Maybe tomorrow will be a better day. But to be honest she's been bouncing back slower each time she does this. Why don't you just worry about your trip? We'll take care of things here."

"Okay." Samantha sighed. "I'm not scheduled to be back until next weekend but if you need me, if anything happens…"

"Don't worry. We'll call you right away. She's in good hands, Samantha. You know we'll do everything we can to make her comfortable."

"I know…thanks…"

Samantha walked out knowing what she had to do. Sarah had suffered a traumatic brain injury (TBI) in a car accident when she was forty. Her recovery was quick at first and her medical team had started hoping for a full recovery. But then her progress seemed to hit a brick wall, and soon afterward she had started to decline.

Sarah was diagnosed with Dementia brought on by the TBI. That was when Samantha started searching for the best doctors in the field of brain trauma. It didn't take long for her to learn the very best one was right in her own backyard.

Dr. Carrington was strictly research but she had somehow managed to convince her mother's treatment team to persuade him to take on Sarah's case. Whatever it took, she had to make sure Dr. Carrington got that funding. It was the only thing she could do to help her mother. If there was a chance his research could help find a cure she wasn't about to sit back and wait for it to happen on its own.

So no matter how much it hurt, she had to accept Dr. Carrington's rejection and disapproval. Some things were just too important, and her mother needed her now more than ever.

Five

AJ looked at his watch and walked at a brisk pace down the hall toward the meeting room. Running late on a Monday morning was always a bad omen for him. But maybe flying to Vegas this afternoon would bring him luck. He was glad this meeting was with the nurses at Greenhill Estates because they were more forgiving on tardiness than Jameson. He reached the room and burst through the doors.

"I apologize for my time ladies. My assistant was supposed to reschedule this meeting since I am catching a flight in about three hours. But apparently it slipped her mind."

He looked up and, as he had expected, each one was smiling. Nancy spoke for the group.

"No need to apologize, Dr. Carrington. We all know how busy you are and we appreciate the time you are donating to Sarah's case."

"Thank you. But that does not excuse the fact that I am wasting your time by running late."

Nancy placed a cup of coffee in front of him and handed him a form.

"This shouldn't take long, Dr. Carrington. The only thing that has changed is Sarah's rate of decline. She is forgetting to take her medication even with all the memory aids we have in place for her." She sat across from him. "We think it's time to move her to The Acres."

"Yes, I would agree. My last visit with her was disappointing. But, there is one more treatment I would like to try. As soon as I can get the study results compiled I will put together a regimen for her.

AJ scanned the page. It was a standard referral form for insurance purposes. The information had been typed in the appropriate boxes and all that was needed was his signature. He signed the paper and handed it back to Nancy.

"Have all the mirrors removed from her room in The Acres before she gets there. It will be easier than trying to remove them later if she loses her short term memory completely and starts remembering herself as a younger woman."

"I have added that to the list of preparations for her move. The only glitch is the antique mirror in her bedroom. She is very attached to it. Apparently it has a strong sentimental meaning for her." She looked at the other nurses. "But we have a few ideas on how to get around that."

AJ sipped his coffee. "I do not doubt that. I can

always count on all of you to get done what needs to be done." He quirked a smile and continued, "If any of you decide to change your career path let me know. I am in the market for a new assistant."

A wave of light laughter rose from the ladies seated at the conference table. Edna, the eldest of the group, spoke up.

"We've heard about you, Dr. Carrington. I'd take a sea of bedpans over a week as your assistant."

The laughter raised a notch and AJ smiled. He could always count on Edna to be as blunt as possible.

"Well then, if you do not need anything further from me I will let you get back to your sea of bedpans."

Edna winked at him when he rose to leave.

"Thank you again, ladies, for your time. I know it is as valuable as mine." He nodded to Nancy and turned to leave. He couldn't stop the grin when he heard them speak in unison like a class of grade school children.

"Goodbye, Dr. Carrington."

****

AJ felt a bead of sweat ease down his skin in front of his ear. He arrived at the gate just as the plane was being boarded and pulled a handkerchief from his pocket.

"Delta flight 3794 to Las Vegas now boarding all passengers at gate G2."

He scanned the crowd for Samantha and wiped the moisture from his face. She wasn't in the long line of people waiting to board the plane so he kept checking for her to appear at the boarding area. He still hadn't seen her by the time he handed his ticket to the agent.

"Wonderful," he whispered. Now Samantha was backing out. What a fitting way to end his miserable day. He should probably make sure his hotel reservation hadn't been cancelled. He pulled out his cell phone as he walked down the Jetway and called the hotel in Las Vegas.

"Good evening. Thank you for calling the Las Vegas Oasis Resort Hotel. How can I help you?"

"This is Dr. Carrington. I need—" AJ stopped dead in his tracks as he stepped into first class.

Samantha was seated in the first row, her PDA in her hand. She met his gaze momentarily before she looked down at the screen and tapped her stylus against her chin.

"I'm sorry Dr. Carrington. I didn't get that. What can I help you with?"

"Nothing. I am sorry to have bothered you." AJ disconnected the call.

"Having trouble with your assistant? Shouldn't she be making those calls for you?" Samantha kept her attention on the report she was reading.

"And what calls would those be?" AJ put his briefcase in the bin above his seat.

"The ones where you start with announcing your name and follow with 'I need'." She looked up at him. "Suzanne knows who you are so you weren't talking to her and anything you need should already be in place. Maybe she really is as useless as the other EAs claim."

"EAs?"

"Executive Assistants."

"Hmm. Well, I do not participate in the chatter amongst the Executive Assistants, but I can validate your hypothesis on Suzanne's lack of usefulness." AJ pulled his suit jacket off and handed it to the flight attendant.

"What is it you need arranged?" she said. "I can call my assistant and have her take care of it."

"Nothing. I just thought…" He fell silent and loosened his tie minimally.

"That I was going to miss this flight?" She paused. "I was a good little girl and got to the airport on time, Dr. Carrington. I didn't see you at the gate before I boarded or I might have waited for you." She looked back at her PDA. "This presentation is important, Dr. Carrington, and I am completely dedicated to making this trip a success, even if that means meeting with the investors alone."

"Are you implying I am not taking this project seriously?"

"I wouldn't dare make such an implication," she said.

AJ sat down hard in the seat next to her and loosened his tie further before he undid the top button of his shirt.

"I was one of the lucky winners of the TSA lottery today," he said. "Apparently I hit the jackpot. They not only searched my bags but I was treated to a complete physical as well." He paused. "The only thing they did not do was a full cavity search."

"What a shame. I would have paid a fortune to

see that."

"I do not find it the least bit amusing. I will have you know I am a very busy man with a tremendous—"

"Amount of responsibility. Yes, I know Dr. Carrington. You mentioned that already."

He straightened the cuffs of his shirt. "I am pleased to know you were paying attention. Hopefully, you remembered a few more things."

"I remember more than you realize," she whispered.

"What?"

She hesitated. "I said I remember more than you realize."

"I hope so." AJ tapped the flight attendant's arm as she walked by. "I would like a shot of Maker's Mark, no ice…on second thought, make that a double."

"Of course."

He watched her take one step backwards and turn toward the tiny space used to store the food and beverages for the plane. He couldn't help but be annoyed at the inescapable lack of privacy and personal space. Given the option, he would choose solitary confinement over an airplane right now.

Samantha kept her gaze on her PDA and smiled.

"Having a bad day?"

"Would it please you to hear that I have been?" He plucked a piece of lint from his trousers.

"Not really. I need you at your best. I have no intention of wasting an entire week in Las Vegas attending a conference if this deal is dead before it takes its first breath."

"I am sure you can find plenty of enjoyable activities to occupy your time. After all, what happens in Vegas stays in Vegas. Is that not what they say?" He leaned back and closed his eyes.

When she didn't reply he opened his eyes and looked at her. The thin line of her lips and her hooded gaze told him he had crossed a line.

"I apologize if I offended you, Samantha. That was not my intent."

"Maybe you should get some sleep, Dr. Carrington. You look quite tired."

"I said I was sorry. Do you not believe me?"

She glared at him. "And I said you look tired. Do you not believe me?"

He locked his gaze with hers. "Yes, Samantha, I do believe you."

She looked away and he dropped his head against the back of his seat. He didn't have the energy to spar with her. The flight attendant handed him his drink and he downed it in one swallow. He handed the glass back to her and closed his eyes. Hopefully they would be in Las Vegas when he woke up. Otherwise this was going to be a very long three hour flight.

****

AJ walked down the long hall to his hotel room. He slid the keycard through the reader and the light flashed red. He looked up at the door and a sign read 'Authorized Personnel Only'.

Samantha hooked her hand in his elbow and tugged lightly.

"One more door, Dr. Carrington." She pulled

him along and pressed her breasts against his triceps.

He reached across his chest and slid his hand over hers. The red satin of her dress was thin and he could feel the heat of her body when he pressed the backs of his fingers into the warm, soft flesh of her breast.

They reached the door to his room and she turned to lean her back against it.

"You know you want me, AJ. What are you waiting for?"

He caressed her torso from her waist to her breasts and kissed her hard. He pressed his body against hers and pulled the skirt of her dress up in the back to massage her ass.

"Take me," she whispered.

He slid his fingers under the silk of her panties and a *burst of wind and mist slammed into his side. The salty taste of the ocean reached his tongue. He let go of her and turned to his right.*

He was standing at the edge of a cliff. The angry sea, hundreds of feet below, battered the jagged rocks of the shore. His legs felt weak and he stepped back to steady himself. A voice called to him from behind.

'Dr. Carrington.'

He spun around and the hall stretched on. He turned to the door and tried his key. The light flashed red and the voice called to him again.

'I'm right here.'

AJ turned to his left and Samantha pressed her bared breasts against his chest. The red satin dress hung loosely from her waist.

She wrapped her arms around him and whispered, 'I've been waiting for you.'

He grabbed her hair and kissed her hard. He ran his open mouth down her neck and massaged the smooth flesh of her breast.

Samantha twisted his shoulders and spun him around. His world tilted and he blinked his eyes to steady himself.

When his vision cleared Jackie was standing under the oak tree. A driving rain had soaked the satin of her red dress and it clung to her beautiful curves.

'How could you do this to me? Why did you make me come here?'

'I wanted to be with you. Jackie, I miss you so much.'

'I saw what you did with her. How could you do that to me?'

'With who? What happened? Tell me what I did, Jackie. Please.'

The wind howled and blew against his body. He tried to go to her but the rush of air was too strong.

'Jackie!'

The leaves swirled around her and tugged at her long hair as she turned away from him.

'Jackie, don't leave me. Jackie!'

The wind ceased in an instant and AJ fell forward into darkness.

AJ opened his eyes on a sharp intake of breath. The flight attendant stood next to him holding a freshly opened bottle of club soda over her beverage cart.

"I'm terribly sorry, sir, are you okay?"

Samantha leaned over him and whispered to the woman.

"Dr. Carrington could use a hot towel if it wouldn't be too much trouble."

"Yes, of course. I'll be right back."

The flight attendant pushed her cart forward and AJ turned to Samantha. Samantha's gaze followed the woman until she was at her station then she looked at him.

"Are you alright?"

"I am…I am fine…I think." He massaged an ache in the triceps of his right arm. He felt a sticky film on his sleeve. "What happened?"

"You were sleeping when she ran her cart into your arm. We hit some rough turbulence after she opened the club soda and she nearly landed in your lap." Samantha lowered her voice. "Your dream must have been interesting, though. I couldn't tell if you were excited or terrified." She nodded toward the flight attendant as she approached.

"Here is your hot towel, Dr. Carrington. Please don't hesitate to let me know if there is anything else I can get for you." She smiled politely and turned away.

AJ covered his face with the towel and held it there. The moist heat relieved his tension. If only it could wash away the humiliation. Did Samantha know he was dreaming about her?

The image of her breasts, plump and perfect, made him hard. He groaned softly into the warm towel and willed his body to apathy. He dragged the towel down under his chin and ran it around to the back of his neck.

"Did I say anything?"

"Nothing coherent and nothing anyone could hear. Except for…"

"Except for what?" His heart dropped to the pit of his stomach and he looked at her.

"Well…You gasped rather loudly and I don't think it was because the flight attendant bumped in to you. Do you remember the dream?"

AJ dropped the now cooling damp towel to the armrest of his seat. He folded it and avoided eye contact with Samantha. "No."

"Nothing?"

"No."

AJ handed the towel to a passing flight attendant and pulled out his iPad to check his calendar. Anything was better than continuing this conversation. The details of the dream were fading but the pain of the past was resurfacing, and with this new twist of involving lustful thoughts of Samantha followed by a healthy dose of heartache ala Jackie, he knew he wouldn't last long. This time his dreams might literally kill him.

He swallowed hard and tried to concentrate on the agenda for the first day of the conference. He heard Samantha sigh and watched her out of the corner of his eye pull out her PDA. He turned to her and spoke softly.

"Thank you."

Samantha lowered her PDA to her lap and looked at him for a moment. The look of surprise on her face was obvious before she smiled.

"You're welcome."

Six

The pilot announced their decent into McCarran International Airport and somehow AJ doubted Samantha had even heard him. She had been staring out the window of the plane for the past hour. She looked completely engrossed in her thoughts, as if she was in another world altogether.

In that time he had found that he couldn't stop looking at her. She was quite captivating, and something about being this close to her made him feel…complete.

He looked at her face. Her expression was vague but her eyes betrayed what she was feeling. She was worried about something. He wanted to place his hand over hers and squeeze gently, just to let her know he was there. He looked at her hand as she held onto the end of the armrest. He lifted his hand and stopped. What the hell was he doing? She was sleeping with Douglas.

He looked at her face again. That thought seemed a bit surreal. The Samantha he had expected from her reputation didn't exist. The Assistant Administrator for Central Valley was known as a woman who had slept her way to the top. But this woman most definitely got to her position on merit, even if that merit consisted mainly of a strong will and a desire to prove her self-worth. She was definitely a woman to be reckoned with. There was no doubt in AJ's mind about that.

As for whose side she was on, well, that still remained to be seen. He had serious doubts she was here to do Jameson's bidding. Most likely she had her own agenda, but so far she seemed determined to secure the funding for Central Valley. Whatever her motive may be was irrelevant, as long as she was working toward the same happy ending he was.

He looked across the aisle when a man cleared his throat. He thought he'd been caught staring at her but realized the gentleman was directing his attention to the flight attendant. AJ pulled his phone from his pocket to check his calendar and remembered he had turned it off for the descent into McCarran. He nervously looked for something to hold his attention and avoided the strong urge to look at Samantha again.

Since he'd woken from his nightmare he'd been thinking about how she had covered for him. He would have expected her to enjoy watching him embarrass himself in front of a plane full of first class passengers. But instead, she had minimized the situation.

The pilot came over the intercom to report the weather conditions in Las Vegas as the flight attendants made a final check of the cabin. The plane landed and he and Samantha gathered their items and debarked in near silence, speaking only pleasantries to the flight attendants before they headed up the Jetway. Samantha kept her attention on her PDA and avoided eye contact with him. She seemed more comfortable keeping her distance from him and that soured his mood, especially since he was more comfortable with closing the distance between them. They were in the limo on their way to the hotel when he finally spoke to her.

"I am grateful for what you did for me earlier, but I cannot help but wonder why."

"Why what, Dr. Carrington?" Samantha kept her eyes on her PDA.

"Why you did not embarrass me on the plane earlier."

"And what would that have accomplished?"

"At the very least some personal satisfaction."

She looked up at him and crossed her arms over her middle. "And what makes you think I would enjoy embarrassing you in front of a plane full of people?"

"You do not like me very much, Samantha, that point is clear." AJ poured himself a drink from the mini bar. "And I suspect the other administrators at Central Valley treat you with nowhere near the respect you deserve. Therefore, I would expect you to relish the chance to watch one of us topple, especially when I made it so easy for you."

She hesitated and bit her bottom lip as if she was

considering her response then sighed.

"One of the investors was on the plane," she said. "It could have hurt the deal if I discredited you in front of him."

"There were not any investors on that plane. I do not usually attend these…fund raising events, but I have seen the list of men who Douglas invited and I do know them all personally. I would have recognized any one of them."

"First of all, this is not a fund raising event, Dr. Carrington. It is a presentation to investors. One that will hopefully convince them to financially support much needed research, your research. Secondly, there *was* an investor on that plane."

"You are obviously mistaken. If one of the investors was on that plane and I did not greet him, he would have greeted me. That is how things work in these circles. Pleasantries are expected."

"Unless neither of you knew the other."

"I told you—"

"The investor was David Wisenthall and he was sitting in the seat directly across the isle from you. I'm sure you don't know him because he was a last minute substitute for Grant Wisenthall, his grandfather, who apparently became ill over the weekend. I was cc'd in an email Dr. Jameson received this afternoon. It included a photograph of David Wisenthall. I would have told you sooner, but I haven't had an opportunity until now."

AJ downed his drink in one swallow and fought the uncomfortable feeling of embarrassment creeping into his gut. He needed to stop underestimating her. Hopefully she wasn't waiting for him to acknowledge he was wrong, because he wasn't about to. Instead, he changed the subject.

"Why do you care one way or the other if this deal falls through? I doubt you would lose your job over it considering Douglas appears to be doing his best to kill it."

"Because I am a professional, Dr. Carrington, and I am very good at what I do. It's important to me to do my best. I have a reputation to protect."

AJ smiled. "Letting this deal fall through could not possibly hurt your reputation, Samantha."

"Why you arrogant, son of a... I was hired as the Assistant Administrator because I was the most qualified candidate for the position. I realize you and Dr. Jameson, as well as most of the other administrators, believe otherwise, but I assure you the gentlemen we will be speaking to over the next several days feel differently. They know I am more than capable of carrying out my responsibilities. *That* is the reputation I am speaking about. And *that* is the only one I care about."

AJ waited until she finished and swallowed the foot he had so eloquently shoved into his mouth. He looked down and stared at the empty glass. For once in his life he truly didn't know what to say.

She was right, she wasn't incompetent at all. In fact, he suspected she was quite brilliant. After he had reviewed the reports she had given to him early Saturday morning, he decided Douglas hadn't written them. They were too well organized and far more detailed than anything he had received from Douglas before. He suspected Samantha was their true author.

He looked up to find her still staring at him. She appeared to be waiting for him to respond, probably waiting for him to apologize. He decided not to disappoint her.

"I am sorry, Samantha. That was unfair of me, not to mention exceedingly inappropriate."

She crossed her arms tighter. The action pushed her breasts up and brought his attention straight to her cleavage. A vision of her dressed in the red satin dress flashed through his mind and a sudden pulse of arousal shot through his veins.

"That's it? No promise to be more professional from this point forward? How disappointing."

"I…yes. I will do my best to be more professional." AJ cleared his throat. "I like to think I form my own opinions of people without making assumptions based on what others have said about them. I realize now I failed to give you that consideration. I apologize."

Samantha slowly lowered her arms to her sides and whispered, "Thank you."

****

Samantha had gone straight to her room after they had checked in. She had claimed to want a good night's sleep before their first meeting in the morning, but AJ suspected she was simply avoiding him. He couldn't blame her considering how he had spoken to her.

He let her go without an argument but couldn't help the disappointment of being left alone. It was late and he should be calling it a day as well, but sleep was the last thing he wanted. If he thought he'd get some rest he would be in his bed right now, but he'd dreamt about Jackie for a second time on the plane after he had decided the first dream was just a fluke. Seeing the hurt etched into her features wasn't something he wanted to revisit.

He paced in the sitting room of his suite looking for something to keep his mind occupied. He had tried the television but nothing interested him enough to keep his mind from drifting to thoughts of Jackie. Finally in desperation he decided to head for the casino. It was the last place he wanted to be, but maybe all the noise and activity would be enough to keep him distracted.

AJ hated casinos. Just walking into one gave him an instant headache. All the addictive and destructive behaviors of the "regulars" were so predictable. He couldn't stand to watch people waste their lives while they spent their hard earned money on a game that was designed to make them lose. So, he promised himself he'd concentrate on the tourists and the other patrons who were only there for entertainment, the ones who weren't counting on the game to make them instantly rich. They usually outnumbered the regulars anyway.

A group of young women rushed through the isle and knocked him off balance. He grabbed the edge of a poker table to steady himself. He turned to apologize for interrupting the game and recognized the gentleman he had nearly landed on. Daniel Rosenfeld was Central Valley's biggest investor and the one AJ most wanted to impress with his presentation.

"Hey there, Doc. I didn't know you were a poker

player. Have a seat." Daniel indicated the empty chair next to him.

"Thank you Mr. Rosenfeld but I am not a gambler."

"Really. Then what the hell are you doing in a casino?"

AJ hesitated. "Research."

"Well then, have a seat. Maybe you can bring me some luck while you conduct your *research*. Right now I need all the help I can get." Daniel turned to the dealer and wiggled his eyebrows. "One card, darlin'."

AJ sat down and scanned the faces of the other players. The young man at the other end was drumming the pads of his fingers on the soft felt of the table. There weren't many chips in front of him so he either didn't start with much or he didn't care that he was losing his shirt, or maybe his luck was about to change. He was anxious but he wasn't sweating. AJ spoke quietly to Daniel.

"I would pay close attention to the young one. He's got a good hand."

Daniel shifted his gaze to look at the young man. "It's about time," he whispered. "The young buck has had shit for luck the past hour and a half. I've been trying to donate to his college fund but the shifty bastard next to him is winning big tonight."

The dealer handed Daniel another card and AJ looked at the "shifty bastard". A bead of sweat ran down his hairline and AJ smiled.

"I think the shifty bastard just ran out of luck," he whispered.

"I would have to agree with you there, Doc.

Even the best poker players can't sweat on demand."

AJ glanced at Daniel's cards, a pair of aces and three kings.

The young man pushed the remainder of his chips to the center and said, "All in."

"Call," the shifty bastard said and shoved his chips into the pot.

"Fold," Daniel said.

He placed his cards face down and slid them toward the dealer as she called for a show of cards. The young man smiled as he laid three lovely ladies down in front of him and the shifty bastard groaned.

"Congratulations, son. Well played," Daniel said. He gathered the last of his chips and tossed a five hundred dollar chip to the dealer then turned to AJ with a smile.

"Come on Doc, let's get a drink."

He clapped him on the shoulder and headed for the casino's lounge. A scantily clad waitress met them as they settled down at a table in the back.

"What can I get for you gentlemen?" she said.

"Your best scotch darlin', and just bring the bottle." Daniel smiled when she winked at him. He watched her sashay up to the bar. "God I love this town."

AJ followed his gaze. "It is definitely interesting."

The waitress was attractive but not quite his type. She was a bit too thin and her flaming red hair was so bright it hurt his eyes. She definitely complimented the flashing lights in the casino.

"It's funny I ran in to you here, I was expecting

to see Douglas strutting around trying to pretend Samantha is the love of his life," Daniel said.

"I beg your pardon?"

"Oh, I didn't mean anything by that. I just know she's too smart for the likes of him. Or does their absence mean he finally convinced her he *is* the love of her life?"

"Mr. Rosenfeld—"

"Now don't get all upset. I suppose you and Douglas are friends. I was just making an observation."

"Mr. Rosenfeld—"

"Please Dr. Carrington, call me Daniel. My father is Mr. Rosenfeld. That name makes me feel like my old man."

AJ smiled. "Then please call me AJ."

"AJ, huh. I like it."

"Thank you." He paused. "Daniel, Douglas and I are not friends."

"Really? I would think a money whore like Douglas would be licking the crack of your ass considering you are the biggest attraction for investors that Central Valley has to offer."

AJ huffed out a laugh in spite of himself. Daniel Rosenfeld was definitely a breed of his own.

"I appreciate the compliment but the truth of the matter is Douglas and I do not see eye to eye."

"Well that's not a surprise. I never thought Jameson possessed an adequate amount of class to properly swim in these waters. Come to think of it, I don't think anyone else has either. But you're both here representing Central Valley, surely that means you both agree this new wing is a good idea."

"It would appear that way. However, Douglas is not always forthcoming with information and as a matter of fact—"

"Well don't worry about that old coot I can get anything I want out of him, including the time and date he shot his last wad." A devilish grin crossed his face. "When you write big checks people will tell you just about anything, especially a money whore." Daniel raised his glass to AJ and took a swig.

"Daniel, I think—"

"Too much probably. Am I right? Now look, Douglas may be a nincompoop when it comes to social skills and proper etiquette, but he's got a good enough head for business when this kind of money is on the line. As long as he's in favor of this project I can almost guarantee you I'll get on board with it."

AJ watched Daniel's gaze follow a very curvy redhead that had just walked in with a couple of friends. He turned to get a better look at her.

"Sorry, AJ, I saw her first." He looked back to AJ. "I hate to be rude but this lone wolf just found himself a nice little filly to keep him warm tonight. Take care of this scotch for me, would ya?" Daniel dropped a couple large bills on the table and winked at the group of ladies.

AJ couldn't stop his grin as he watched Daniel practically running across the bar. When the billionaire playboy was gone with his new pet, AJ downed the last of his drink.

Shit! He had his work cut out for him. He was afraid Douglas' absence was going to be a problem and apparently, he was right.

****

AJ heard the elevator doors open and he stepped through without looking up. He turned the corner to head to his room and nearly flattened Samantha. He wrapped his arms around her and caught her as she stumbled.

She gripped his shoulders and pulled herself toward him as she steadied her feet under her. She dropped her gaze with a soft sigh and slowly slid her hands down his biceps where she firmly wrapped her fingers around his arms.

He held her and looked at her eyes, her body was warm and soft against his. Time stood still and a comforting warmth enveloped him. Her body molded to his and she met his gaze with a shy expression. Their forms fit perfectly together and a feeling of home fluttered through his senses. It was familiar, just like in his dreams.

AJ looked behind her and the hall stretched on. He looked to his right and a sign on the door read 'Authorized Personnel Only'. His heart started pounding and he looked at Samantha.

"Are you okay?" she said.

He let go of her and stepped back when she released her hold on him.

"Yes. I am sorry. I didn't…did not mean to do that. I should have been looking where I was going."

"It's alright. I'm fine." Samantha straightened her blouse.

AJ wrapped his hands around the bottle to give

them something to do.

"I thought you were asleep," he said.

"I tried, but I couldn't. I thought maybe a drink would help me relax." She looked at the bottle of scotch in his hands. "Did it work for you?"

He shook his head. "Not yet."

"Maybe you should have another." She smiled.

"Are you suggesting I get drunk so you can take advantage of me, Miss Assistant Administrator?"

Her smile faded. "Have a good evening, Dr. Carrington."

AJ grabbed her arm when she stepped past him.

"Samantha, it was a joke. I did not mean to offend you. I am sorry. I...I wasn't thinking."

He looked into her eyes and a sudden desire surfaced. When she didn't pull away from his grip it made him want to pull her closer. Instead, he turned to face her.

They stood in silence for several minutes and he continued to hold her arm. He knew he should have let go of her by now but, he just didn't, and since she wasn't pulling away he decided it was allowed.

She squared her shoulders and lifted her chin.

"Maybe I overreacted," she said.

"I should have expected as much from you."

"Excuse me?"

He raised his other hand in surrender fashion and nearly knocked himself out with the bottle of scotch.

She snickered and he finally let go of her arm.

"What I meant is my jest was ill-mannered," he said, "considering what you obviously tolerate at the office."

He could tell by her expression she wasn't sure how to respond to him.

He scratched his chin. "I'm not doing this right, am I?"

She smiled. "That depends on what you're trying to do."

"Can we start over?"

"Sure," she said.

"Okay. Let me see…you suggested I try another drink. What if I say, 'Would you like to join me?'"

"I don't think that's such a good idea." She crossed her arms. "I wouldn't want to bruise your ego when I drink your ass under the table."

He smiled. "Don't be so sure of yourself, madam. I've been known to hold my own with the best of my fraternity brothers."

"Really? Then what happens if you drink me under the table? Are you going to try and take advantage of me?"

"Somehow I do not think you would let me get away with that."

She turned and hooked her hand around the crook of his elbow.

"You're absolutely right. Besides, I'm limiting you to one drink." She winked at him. "I can't afford for you to have a hangover tomorrow."

"No. That definitely would not be a good idea."

She walked with him toward his room.

"I thought you were a bourbon man," she said.

"I am. This," he looked at the label, "belongs to Daniel Rosenfeld. He gave it to me when he spotted a little filly, as he so eloquently put it, to keep him warm tonight."

She laughed. "That sounds like Daniel."

"I decided to head back to my room because everyone down there seems to be either well on their way to passing out or getting more out of control than I care to be a part of. I felt a bit out of place."

"I hadn't thought of that. I'm not a fan of bar crowds either."

He stopped at his door and looked at her. "Somehow that does not surprise me."

AJ stepped through the door and sighed in relief. A small part of him was afraid he was going to find Jackie standing under an oak tree in the rain.

"What's your poison?" he said.

"Scotch on the rocks." She sat in the wing backed chair and smiled. "I don't think Daniel would begrudge me a glass of his finest."

AJ poured their drinks and joined Samantha in the sitting room. He handed her the scotch and sat across from her. He sipped his drink and looked at her over the top of his glass.

Her face was so beautiful. She made him want to steal her away from the world and keep her for his own forever. Her deep green eyes drew him and he found he didn't want to look away. He wanted to study them as if the secret to life could be found there. He looked away when she fidgeted.

"Have you been to Las Vegas before?" he said.

"Yes. Several times on business."

"What kind of business?"

"This same thing, actually. I worked with the administrator for Mercy Hospital before coming to Central Valley."

"Really? I don't know Dr. Johnson personally but I have heard he can be a real bastard to work with."

Samantha paused. "Something like that. My move to Central Valley was not *up*."

"Is Douglas any better?"

Samantha took a healthy sip of her drink. "He's different."

AJ huffed out a laugh. "You can be honest with me, Samantha. You know as well as anyone Douglas and I are not friends. You can trust that anything you say to me will not get back to him."

She took another big sip. "I've learned the hard way you can never be too careful with trust."

He looked down and stared into his glass. "I am sorry to hear that. Was it someone you cared about or just a friend?"

Samantha stood and walked to the window. The bright lights of the Vegas skyline filled the tinted glass and her reflection was camouflaged, her expression unreadable.

"Both," she said.

A mirror hung on the wall to her left and AJ could see her profile reflection. She turned toward the mirror and their gazes met, the pain in her eyes was deep. Betrayal was such an ugly business.

Samantha turned to him. "I'd better go. It's getting late." She hurried past him and opened the door before turning to him once more. "I'll see you tomorrow."

He watched as she closed the door behind her and he sighed. He knew the pain she felt. It was the same pain he'd been running from for the past thirteen years.

AJ paced to the balcony and stepped into the night air. He took a deep breath and wondered what Samantha had gone through. Did she at least know the whole story or was she left to try and fill in the blanks like him?

He thought about Jackie and wondered if she knew how much she'd hurt him. She had accused him of betraying her, but he couldn't remember what had happened that night. When she had walked away without an explanation he had felt the betrayal was hers. He thought she had loved him too much to just walk away. He sighed. The thought that she could leave him so easily still cut like a knife because he had never stopped loving her, and despite everything he knew he always would.

For the millionth time he thought about tracking her down to see how she was. It wouldn't be hard to find her. But then the fear of what he might find always put an end to that thought. He didn't know if it would be worse to find she was unhappy or to find she was living happily without him.

"Stop torturing yourself, old man. If she had wanted to come back she would have."

He looked at his watch, 1:00 a.m. He had five hours to try and get some rest. He threw the rest of his bourbon to the back of his throat and headed inside. Hopefully he'd had enough to drink to keep his dreams at bay.

Seven

AJ woke to the sound of his voice screaming Jackie's name. He looked at his hands and found two halves of what used to be the top sheet on the king size bed. His fists still clutched the linen so tight his knuckles were white. He threw the material off his body and sat up on the side of the bed.

He closed his eyes and recalled the end of the dream. Jackie had been safely in his arms. Despite her accusations that he loved another woman, he wasn't going to let go of her until she believed him. He needed to convince her she was the only woman he had ever loved. But then, just as before, she vanished and only the red dress hung heavy in his grasp. The agony was too much and he tore the satin down the middle.

He looked at the ruined top sheet crumpled at the foot of the bed and a heavy weight settled in his gut.

These dreams had to stop. He couldn't let them rule his life like they had before. With a sigh he grabbed his cellphone and called Warren.

"That was fast," Warren said. *"He didn't waste any time getting there."*

"What? Who?"

"Anderson."

"Charles Anderson is coming to Las Vegas?"

"Isn't that why you called?"

"No. I need a script for Trazodone," AJ said. "If I don't get some sleep I'm going to blow this whole deal. Send it to a pharmacy here in Vegas. I don't care which one."

"You had another dream?"

"Two," he said. AJ ran his fingers into his hair and leaned his head on his hand, his elbow rested on his knee. "Now tell me why you think Anderson is in Vegas."

"Later." Warren sighed. *"Let's deal with your dreams first. You never do anything without a reason, so I think it's safe to assume your subconscious isn't any different and this is something that can't wait."*

"Well, it is going to have to wait. This is a complication I do not have time for right now."

"AJ, you know I'll write you the script. But you also know it's not going to help if you don't deal with this. Tell me what you can remember."

AJ looked at the clock on the nightstand. He had two hours before his first meeting. He rubbed the ache at the back of his neck and tried to recall as much detail as he could.

"Samantha is wearing Jackie's red dress. She

looks so damn hot in it I can't keep my hands off her."

"Any sex this time?"

AJ could hear the amusement in Warren's voice and couldn't stop the smile from spreading across his face.

"I try. She sure as hell is interested. But…" His smile faded. "But then she turns into Jackie and the guilt starts. I go back to the night she left."

"Anything new?"

"Yes but nothing that is a memory. They start off with Samantha. In fact, the one I had on the plane was almost like a premonition. I dreamt about this hotel, and last night when I ran into Samantha in the hallway it was like déjà vu."

"What about the other one?"

"This morning I dreamt I was running late for my first meeting. I couldn't find the room and then when I got there Samantha was surrounded by investors." He smiled. "I started walking toward her and Daniel Rosenfeld spun her into a slow dance. When I got to them he spun her into my arms and he told me that I had seen her first." He shook his head. "The next thing I knew I was on top of her."

"And?"

AJ closed his eyes. "I almost forgot how good she felt."

"Samantha?"

"No. Jackie. It was Jackie I was making love to." He opened his eyes and exhaled. "Anyway, that's when she accuses me of cheating on her."

"Does she tell you who this time?"

"No."

"Anything old?"

"I have to watch her walk away again." He took a deep breath. "No matter how hard I try to hold on to her she always walks away."

"Okay. Give me a couple days. I want to look up a few things. In the meantime—"

AJ's phone beeped and he checked the caller ID.

"Hold that thought, Warren. I have to take this." He switched the connection. "Dr. Carrington."

"Dr. Carrington, this is Charles Anderson. I apologize if I am inconveniencing you but I must speak to you concerning an urgent matter. I will be waiting for you in the Chancellor's Room."

AJ swallowed hard. Charles Anderson was supposed to be in Europe. What the hell was he doing in Las Vegas?

"Yes, of course. I will be there in twenty minutes." He switched the connection again and paused before he spoke to Warren. "Charles Anderson is waiting for me in a conference room of my hotel. What the hell is going on?"

"I don't know all the details, but I bet he's not alone. The rumor is Mercedes is with him. I was in the ER all day yesterday but I heard Jameson left early with three board members in tow."

"Let me guess, Jorgens, Davis, and Watson."

"And if Anderson and Smith caught the redeye to meet with you first thing this morning, I would bet the board is split right down the middle on whatever Jameson is trying to pull."

AJ rubbed his temples. "Well, hopefully my instinct is right about Samantha and it will work in my favor that she is here with me. I seriously doubt she is in Douglas' camp."

"I hope you're right. Let me know if I can do anything on my end."

"Get me that script, and anything you can find out about what happened the night of the formal would be helpful."

"That would be a lot easier if you let me track her down. I think her mother still lives in Lincoln."

"She does but I don't want her involved in this. Jackie made her choice thirteen years ago. If she wanted to work things out she could have contacted me. I am easy to find."

"I'll see what I can do."

AJ headed for the shower. "Look, Warren, I just want these damn dreams to stop. Track down anyone you can, just not her. I'm not sure I could handle that right now. I have to go, they are waiting for me."

AJ disconnected the call and stepped into the shower. Fifteen minutes later he was in the elevator heading for the Chancellor's conference room trying to convince himself his life wasn't about to start unravelling.

****

AJ opened the door to the Chancellor's conference room and stepped inside.

"Dr. Carrington, thank you for meeting with us on such short notice." Charles spoke for the group.

AJ stopped dead in his tracks. He scanned the faces of the people seated at the table in the middle of the room.

Charles Anderson and Mercedes Smith

represented the Central Valley board and sat at the far end, their faces unreadable. Next to Mr. Anderson sat Daniel Rosenfeld and David Wisenthall, they too had their best poker faces on. The only face he could read was Samantha's. She was seated next to Mercedes and her expression could kill a man at ten paces. Thank God she wasn't looking at him.

"Please have a seat." Charles indicated the chair closest to AJ.

He sat down and realized he was the only one at his end of the table. He would have laughed if not for the serious expressions all directed at him.

"Something tells me this is not going to be pleasant for me."

Mercedes leaned forward. "This is not pleasant for any of us, Dr. Carrington. I can assure you." She stood and gathered the papers lying in front of Samantha. She handed them to him and said, "Do you recognize these documents, Dr. Carrington?"

AJ glanced at them. "They are department authorization forms for funding."

"Are they authorizations you signed?"

AJ took a closer look. The items listed were for his department and they looked legitimate until he saw the miscellaneous item. The handwriting looked similar to his but he couldn't remember requesting the money. He never asked for miscellaneous funds. Every cent had a purpose and he made damn sure it was documented. He turned the page over and saw his signature on the bottom. His heart rate increased.

"This is a forgery. I have never requested

miscellaneous funds and I certainly would never have requested such an exorbitant amount."

Mercedes' expression was cold and emotionless. "Jameson claims you did."

"He is lying. This is nothing more than another attempt to discredit me." AJ dropped the papers to the table and leaned back in his chair. "I can prove these are forgeries. I have copies of every authorization I have submitted in the five years I have been the director."

Charles cleared his throat. "Yes, well unfortunately your office appears to be missing some documents. I had it searched yesterday."

"You searched my office? Who the hell authorized that? It certainly was not me. I am required to protect any and all confidential information that is housed in my office." AJ leaned forward and jammed his index finger into the table. "And I would never authorize access to my office without my presence."

"There is much more at stake here, Dr. Carrington, than someone's history of memory loss. As president of the board, I am only required to notify the hospital administrator of any justified search and seizure involving Central Valley."

"I took an oath to care for and protect those who have put their trust in me. I am legally responsible—"

"That oath will be worthless if you are found guilty of embezzlement," Charles said.

AJ could feel his insides vibrate with anger. Embezzlement? How could they even think he would do something so immoral?

Charles continued. "Therefore, I called Douglas and directed him to unlock your door and let my security officers in."

"Which gave him time to remove files from my office." AJ could feel the muscles in his jaw tighten.

"My security officers were standing at your door when I called Dr. Jameson. He, of course, was denied access during the search despite his arguments to the contrary. Several files were confiscated for review. But, as of an hour ago, nothing useful has been discovered."

"Those copies exist. Your men obviously missed them."

Mercedes crossed her arms. "Your office was searched thoroughly, Dr. Carrington. Every file even remotely tied to a fiscal matter was removed. I oversaw the task personally."

AJ stood and leaned over the table toward her. "Then you missed something. I did not take that money."

She countered his posture and spoke softly. "Then prove it."

"This is fiction!" AJ grabbed the copies of the forged documents and flung them across the table. "Douglas' history of false allegations against me indicates his word is unreliable. So why do I have to prove myself trustworthy, AGAIN?"

Mercedes rubbed her temples and sighed. "Dr. Carrington, no one in this room is a fan of Dr. Jameson but he is still the hospital administrator of Central Valley. That does carry some weight."

"And I do not?" AJ shook his head and huffed out a sarcastic laugh. "I have dedicated the last seven years of my life to making Central Valley the Goliath it is today. Everything I have done was through and for that medical center. My reputation is synonymous with Central Valley's reputation. So tell me, Ms. Smith, why the hell would I risk everything I am for any amount of money?"

"We're not talking about just any amount of money, Dr. Carrington. Dr. Jameson claims to have found a ledger showing miscellaneous funds being transferred to you. He claims the ledger shows a total of more than six million dollars. I believe the exact amount was six point two five million."

The air left AJ's lungs and he took a step back. He whispered, "Six million dollars?"

Mercedes drummed her fingernails on the table. "Is your life worth more than that, Dr. Carrington?"

AJ squared his shoulders.

"Yes, Ms. Smith, it is. Every life is priceless, mine included, because every life is precious." He pointed at the forged documents. "Even his. But if Douglas chooses to throw his away because of some twisted sense of hatred there is nothing I can do about it."

Mercedes sighed. "That is a beautiful sentiment, Dr. Carrington, but with the hard evidence on Dr. Jameson's side I'm afraid it won't be nearly enough. So, until such time as hard evidence can be produced to counter Jameson's claims you have been placed on administrative leave."

"What?" AJ looked at the two board members hoping this was a sick joke. "You can not do this. My research is at a critical point. If I stop now it could jeopardize everything I have done in the last three years."

"We will assign another researcher to oversee your work for now," she said.

"And what about the London lecture? Central Valley will lose the European contract if my textbook is not presented to the investors before the end of the year."

"Dr. Hanson will be sent in your absence," Charles said.

"The research is mine, damn it, and Hanson is a moron! He has never been able to comprehend even the simplest of my theories."

"Then the lecture will be postponed." Charles sighed. "The board will negotiate an extension to the contract."

"That's not good enough!" AJ shoved his chair backwards and it skidded several feet before it hit the wall behind him. "You cannot let Douglas put lives at risk over some personal war he has waged against me!"

Charles rubbed his jaw. "Dr. Carrington, we have no intention of putting anyone's life at risk."

"Then you cannot do this. You can not keep me from my research."

Mercedes gathered the authorization forms and stacked them neatly in front of Charles.

"I'm sorry Dr. Carrington but effective immediately you are on administrative leave," she said.

"No! Damn you! Find another way to handle this."

"You will surrender your keys, security badge, and any other Central Valley property you have in your possession," Charles said.

Samantha stood and looked at Charles. "Mr. Anderson, Dr. Carrington's work is too vital to be stopped. You have to find a way to let him keep working."

"I have done all I can. My hands are tied at this point."

She turned to Mercedes. "You know Dr. Jameson is lying, Mercedes. You know as well as I do what kind of a man he is. Those authorizations would have gone through his office. He would have had to approve them. If anyone was embezzling money then Dr. Jameson would have known about it. And if he didn't say anything that makes him an accessory."

Charles rubbed his brow. "Jameson claims you had those authorizations in a separate file, Samantha. He claims to have found them in your office while searching for something else."

"He planted them. He would have no reason to be searching my office. His secretary has copies of everything."

"It doesn't matter, Sam," Daniel said. "No one will care how he found them. As for whether or not he planted them, that's a matter of his word against yours."

Mercedes looked at Samantha. "And he's done a fantastic job of painting you as a brainless office whore, so who do you think people are going to believe?"

Daniel tapped his pen on the table. "I'm sorry, Sam, but they will only care that millions of dollars have been embezzled."

AJ ran his hands through his hair and paced to the window at the end of the room. Nausea crept into his gut and he looked at the people enjoying the pool several stories below. They looked happy and he envied them. His own happiness was slipping through the sieve he was trying to hold it together in. He turned and leaned against the sill.

"Now I know why he backed out of this presentation on Friday. He needed me out of the way."

Charles spun to face AJ. "Yes. I am curious about that myself. I couldn't get a straight answer from him. What reason did he give you for not attending?"

"He said his reasons were personal and none of my damn business."

Charles and Mercedes exchanged a look that communicated a message. What exactly the message was, AJ didn't know.

Mercedes turned to Samantha. "I assume Dr. Jameson gave you the same reason for sending you in his place?"

"No, actually, he told me that since I was so fond of Mr. Rosenfeld's…" Samantha stood and paced to a smaller table behind her. She turned around and leaned against it. "He told me that since I was so fond of his *company* that I had a better chance of securing the funding than he did."

Mercedes swiveled her chair toward Samantha.

"I find something very puzzling about you, Samantha," she said. "You are right about Dr. Jameson. I do know what kind of a man he is. The difference is I do not tolerate his behavior. You, on the other hand, do. Would you care to tell me why that is?"

Samantha crossed her arms and straightened her spine.

"I need this job. What Dr. Jameson says, about me or to me, doesn't matter."

AJ knew she was lying. He could see it in her eyes, and if he was right, everyone else in the room could see it too. He watched Mercedes consider Samantha's response then she turned to him.

"Dr. Carrington," she said, "you have also tolerated a number of false accusations from Douglas. Why haven't you filed a formal complaint with the board? Is he holding something over your head?"

"No." AJ gestured to the documents. "I never thought he would go this far. Looking back it was a serious error in judgment on my part." He shook his head. "I did consider recommending a competency evaluation based on the personal nature of his most recent attacks, but I thought the board members in his pocket would accuse me of attempting a power grab." He sighed. "I wanted to do what was best for Central Valley. I did not want to drag the hospital through the mud."

Charles stood and paced the length of the table then spoke directly to AJ.

"The board had voted to place you both on administrative leave. However, Mercedes and I were able to bargain for simple probation for Samantha. She will be allowed to work but her access to certain offices will be closely monitored."

AJ nodded his understanding.

Samantha shook her head and smiled sadly. "That seems rather generous considering I outrank Dr. Carrington. I suppose the board members feel he manipulated Dr. Jameson's naïve little office whore."

Charles turned and looked at Samantha. "Since you brought it up, yes, that was the gist of the conversation."

Samantha swallowed hard and looked at AJ. His chest constricted with a mixture of pain, anger, and guilt. Just a few days ago he would have been one of those men making that same assumption about her. It was excruciating to see her try to hide the pain in her expression, but he forced himself to watch. The least he could do was try to share the pain he was guilty of condoning.

When the last of the pain drained from her face and her expression became hard and determined he walked back to the table and stood alone where he had been sitting. He pulled his keys from his pocket and tossed them into the middle of the table.

"The rest is at home." He looked at Charles. "So, what happens now?"

"The board will meet again tomorrow to appoint an investigative committee to look into Dr. Jameson's accusations. In the meantime, I will be conducting my own independent investigation."

AJ shoved his hands into his pockets. "Is this another privilege afforded to the board president?"

Charles slid his hands into the pockets of his trousers. "The board wants a quick resolution. I want the truth."

"So do we, AJ." Daniel rose and walked toward

him. "David and I would like to know where our money was spent so we're going on a little hunting expedition."

David Wisenthall paced to AJ and extended his hand in greeting.

"Dr. Carrington? I'm David Wisenthall. Grant Wisenthall is my grandfather and the money is actually his. I believe you know him."

AJ shook his hand. "Yes, Mr. Wisenthall, I have met your grandfather. Please tell him I will cooperate fully with both investigations."

David smiled. "Call me David. And don't worry, Dr. Carrington. Papa has already expressed his faith in you and he has never been wrong in judging a man's character that I'm aware of."

"I want to thank both of you gentlemen, for believing in me. Your support means a great deal."

"Don't mention it, AJ." Daniel said, "I know your dick points north."

AJ huffed out a laugh. "I will take that as a compliment."

"Like I said last night, Douglas is a money whore. My bet is he's got the money hidden somewhere."

Charles picked up the papers on the table and put them in his briefcase.

"Dr. Carrington, I suggest you and Samantha start packing." He turned to him and continued. "Mercedes will be accompanying you both back to Lincoln on the six o'clock flight."

AJ straightened his spine. "Will there be anyone waiting for me?"

"No. The board members did agree unanimously

on that point. We want to conduct our own investigation before the authorities are involved. Mr. Rosenfeld and Mr. Wisenthall have agreed to those terms and Dr. Jameson has been warned that any leak to the public would be considered a serious breach of his contract. He was not happy but he has agreed to keep quiet for now."

"Thank you, Charles, for everything. I can only imagine how difficult it must have been to convince the others not to press charges immediately."

"You're welcome, Dr. Carrington. But it truly wasn't as difficult as you might think. I believe you may have more allies than you realize."

AJ took a deep breath and noticed he was breathing a little easier. It was a relief to know he had such powerful men in his corner. Now if only he could get some sleep he just might survive this ordeal.

Eight

Samantha watched AJ walk out with Mercedes before she approached Daniel Rosenfeld. She had known him for many years. In addition to the last two years she had been working with Dr. Jameson, she worked with Daniel on other investment deals for Mercy Hospital.

"Mr. Rosenfeld, may I speak with you… privately."

"Of course, Sam." He led her to the other side of the conference room. "Sam, why didn't you tell me what Jameson said to you?"

"Why would I?"

"Because it is unprofessional to say the least and I sure as hell don't take that kind of accusation sitting down. I respect you as a business associate, Samantha, and I do not tolerate potshots to my character, or to anyone else's for that matter. "

"I'm sorry, Mr. Rosenfeld, I don't take his insinuations seriously and I never thought about the fact that you might take offense to his remarks."

"You shouldn't tolerate that from him, Sam. Hell, I'll make a place for you in one of my divisions—"

"Mr. Rosenfeld...I need your help with something."

"Well, of course Sam, that's what I'm trying to tell you."

"No. I mean, I need your help with something. I have to find a way to keep Dr. Carrington working. His research is too important. He's on the verge—"

"Now just a minute, Sam. He's in a hell of a mess right now. We need to get to the bottom of this. Maybe he should take some time off."

"No... His work is helping so many people and they don't have time to wait for this to blow over."

"They have other researchers who can pick up where he left off. They won't let it stall. That would create more losses than the money that's gone AWOL."

"Mr. Rosenfeld, please... Dr. Carrington is the best in his field. People need him."

"Sam, what's going on? This isn't like you. You know how this business works."

She bit the inside of her cheek to stop the tears.

Daniel turned and looked at Charles and David talking at the other end of the room. He turned back to her and said, "Give me a minute."

Samantha watched him pace to the other men and talk quietly. When he returned he grabbed her elbow gently and led her to the door.

"Let's finish this conversation in my suite. We have a few hours before your flight."

She nodded her consent and followed him. She knew he was right. The accusations Dr. Jameson had made against AJ were serious, but her mother needed the best treatment she could get for her. And that meant getting AJ reinstated and building him a research center.

They stepped into an elevator and the attendant greeted him.

"Good morning, Mr. Rosenfeld. What floor?"

"My suite, Jimmy."

She could feel him watching her as he chatted with Jimmy. The feeling was familiar and comforting. He respected her professionally, but there was an underlying sense she got that he felt the need to protect her from the sharks that infested the water she dared to swim in. In the several years she'd known Daniel, he'd come to treat her like his little sister. She didn't have any siblings and the loneliness of being an only child to a single mother after her father had left, made her strong. But when Daniel was around she felt like she had an older brother she could lean on.

The elevator doors opened into a foyer and Daniel swiped his card to open the door to his suite. He led her across the threshold and the sheer lavishness of the room left her speechless.

"Have a seat, Sam, and I'll get you something to drink."

"Nothing for me, please. It's a little too early for that."

He smiled. "It's never too early for a well-aged

scotch."

She smiled and shook her head. She walked to the living room and tried to take it all in. She had never seen so much marble, gold, and glass in a hotel room. But then again, this didn't look like any hotel room she'd ever been in.

"So this is how the other half lives," she said.

"It's not all it's cracked up to be. This room can feel rather cold sometimes."

He didn't have to elaborate. Samantha knew all too well how cold nights could get when you were alone. She picked up the throw pillow on the couch and walked to the floor to ceiling window at the far end. She looked out at the city skyline and hugged the pillow against her stomach. Somehow it made her feel better to hold on to something soft and warm. Well, it would be warm soon enough from the heat of her own body.

She watched his reflection in the glass as he sat on the ornate davenport.

"Okay Sam, now I want you to tell me what this is really all about."

"It's about my mother, Daniel." She sighed and concentrated on the view. "Dr. Carrington is working on a new therapy for TBI patients with Dementia. My mother is declining faster and her bad days are getting more frequent." She turned and looked at him. "I need him to find a cure, or at least a treatment that will slow down the Dementia."

He rubbed his jaw. "I'm sorry to hear your mom is getting worse, Sam, but you know as well as I do, it's not that simple."

"You can make it that simple, Daniel. It was

your money that was embezzled. You could make this whole situation very ugly for Central Valley if you wanted to, and they know that. They'll give you whatever you want to keep your lawyers out of their hair."

"That's my trump card, Sam." He raised his eyebrows. "I'm supposed to save that for when I really need it."

"Daniel, please. AJ... Dr. Carrington has worked so hard, and he's so close to finding an answer. He has to keep looking. He's going to find a treatment to help her. I just know it."

"I take it you've been following his research."

"Of course. As soon as my mother was diagnosed I started researching everything I could about her condition. That's how I found A—Dr. Carrington's findings. Every specialist I found directed me right back to AJ. He's never given up on anything. He keeps searching until all hope has been exhausted."

"How long have you been following his research?"

"Years, I guess...I'm not really sure how long. I moved from Mercy Hospital to Central Valley so that I could see firsthand what he was discovering."

"I see." He leaned back in a relaxed slouch. "I must admit I don't really understand the nitty gritty of it all. I'm more concerned with the results and just how much they're going to cost."

Samantha stepped to the opposite end of the davenport. "Daniel, his work is so amazing. He has such a talent for understanding the mind and how it works. He's made incredible discoveries,

discoveries that have helped so many people. That's how I know he's going to find something to help my mother. And his work is so important to him. It's what he lives for. He…"

"Sam, who are you really doing this for?"

"I told you. I'm trying to save my mother's life."

"Yes. I guess you did mention that." He blew out a sigh and scratched his chin. "You know how these things work. If he got back to work tomorrow that doesn't mean he's going to find anything useful this week, this year, or even in the next ten years."

She propped the pillow against the arm of the davenport and crossed her arms.

"You're right. I understand… I have to pack." She headed for the door.

"Now, just a minute, Sam." He got up and stepped between her and the door. "I didn't say I couldn't help you, I just want to know exactly what's going on here."

"I'm doing this for my mother, Daniel."

He smiled. "I'll see what I can do. In the meantime, be nice to your friend, AJ, and don't push him too hard. I'm sure this isn't easy for him."

"Thank you."

Samantha squeezed past him and hurried out the door. She knew Daniel would take care of everything. All she had to do was pack. Once they got back to Lincoln she would make sure AJ got everything he needed to finish his research. Then it was only a matter of time and AJ would finally make things right.

Nine

AJ sat on the loveseat in his hotel room staring out at the Las Vegas skyline. His bags were packed and waiting behind him for the bellhop. The glass of bourbon in his hand was nearly empty when the sudden sharp pain of a muscle cramp shot through his wrist and jolted him from his thoughts. He looked at his hand and saw the stark white knuckles manacled around the etched crystal.

He set his drink on the table next to him and took a deep cleansing breath. He flexed his fingers to ease the ache and tried again to find a silver lining in this mess. Instead, he felt a muscle in his jaw twitch and rage began to penetrate his thoughts once more. Douglas could very well destroy everything AJ had worked so hard to create, and for what, envy?

A knock on the door drew his attention and he

groaned in disgust. He rose slowly and paced to the door. He was in no mood to talk to anyone, even the bellhop. When he opened the door Samantha rapped him firmly on his chest as she looked at her phone.

"Oh!" She giggled. "I'm sorry. I didn't think you heard me knocking."

AJ smiled in spite of his mood.

"Would you like to come in? I'm being evicted but I thought I would have one more drink before I go."

"Yes, actually, I was hoping to talk to you before our chaperone arrives."

He stepped back and opened the door for her to pass.

"Would you care for a drink? I still have this bar for another..." He looked at his watch. "Twenty minutes."

"Why not?"

AJ walked to the bar and dropped ice into a glass while Samantha spoke from behind him.

"Dr. Carrington, I am truly sorry for what has happened. I should have seen this coming."

He turned his head and looked at her.

"How could you have known what Douglas was up to?" AJ poured her drink and refreshed his. When she took the glass he sat across from her. "Unless *you* forged those documents and took the money."

She smiled when he winked at her.

"If I took *six point two five* million I wouldn't be in this hotel." She gulped her drink. "I'd be in a nicer one in the Caribbean."

AJ sat in silence for a moment then said,

"Samantha, I am the one who should be sorry. Douglas has been trying to discredit me for the last two years. I should have seen something like this coming. But I was too afraid how I would be viewed by others if I confronted the problem." He sighed. "Now you are caught up in this ridiculous war he has waged against me, and Central Valley's reputation is in jeopardy all because I was too busy protecting my own."

He looked down at the amber liquid. He hated the fact that he allowed another person to be hurt because he didn't do enough to stop a deranged man from wielding his power recklessly.

"I hate to admit it," she said, "but I underestimated that bastard too. I let him mold my reputation with the administrators and the board members because I convinced myself I didn't care what they thought."

AJ hated the fact that he was one of those men who believed Douglas' lies. How arrogant he had been to think Douglas wouldn't lie about her when he had been fabricating false claims against his work for the past two years.

She swallowed the last of her drink and jiggled the ice in her empty glass.

"I think I'll have another one." She looked at him and smiled devilishly. "I'm sure Ms. Mercedes Smith wouldn't be caught dead in anything other than the poshest of transportation so I doubt very much I'll be driving anytime soon."

AJ stood and took her glass. "Allow me. But I must warn you, getting drunk with me will get you nowhere. After all, my employment is in question not to mention my clout in the world of medical research. I might have to resort to selling my body just to pay for my dinner."

He watched her smile and felt a bit of the tension wash away. She seemed to be taking their situation better than he was. Maybe she felt vindicated to know others knew she wasn't the brainless bimbo Douglas had made her out to be.

AJ handed her another drink and they both sat in silence for a long while. Samantha seemed to understand his need to analyze what had happened. For the first time in his life he truly didn't know what to do next. His work was his life and now it was being ripped away.

"Dr. Carrington," Samantha said, "I spoke to Mr. Rosenfeld. I asked him to push for you to be allowed to continue your research. Your work is too important to a lot of people."

"I appreciate that, Samantha, but I do not think there is much hope they will concede on that point. They are money people. The human element gets easily lost in the counting of coins."

"We'll see." She smiled. "Mr. Rosenfeld usually gets what he wants one way or another. So, let's have a toast."

AJ raised an eyebrow. "A toast? To what?"

"To clearer vision. May we always see the enemy as he approaches."

He smiled and reached his hand across the coffee table to hers. "Cheers."

A knock on the door drowned out the clink of the crystal. He swallowed the last of his drink and opened the door for the bellhop.

He and Samantha followed their luggage to the lobby and, as she had predicted, they were led to a stretch Rolls Royce waiting at the front of the hotel. Mercedes was on her phone when they slid in across from her.

AJ sighed as he settled into the posh leather seat. At least he was going home in style.

Ten

AJ stepped into his condo, dropped his bags at the door and headed into the den for a drink. He didn't know how many he'd had since the board suspended him this morning, and quite frankly, he didn't care. He had lost count sometime around dinner. Since then his thoughts had become fuzzy and the anger had burned a hole so deep in his skull the alcohol wasn't enough to fill it. AJ slammed ice into a glass and a voice spoke from behind him.

"I think you've probably had enough for today, Golden Boy."

He kept his back to Warren. "How did you get in here?"

"Your brother let me in."

"I thought Matthew was camping on some God forsaken rock. It was nice of him to call his only brother and tell him he was back."

"You were supposed to be in Vegas courting investors, and he wasn't supposed to be back until Friday." He paused. "But in light of what's happened he cut his trip short."

AJ hesitated. "You had no right to tell him."

"I needed his help."

"Well I do not." AJ opened the decanter and filled his glass. "I don't mean to be rude, Warren, but I am not in the mood for company."

"Well, that's too bad. I had some paperwork to deliver." Warren cleared his throat. "Mr. Anderson sent a security guard to my office this afternoon and requested that I accompany him to search your office for anything that might help in the investigation."

AJ turned around with a full glass of bourbon and emptied half the contents in one swallow. "What the hell does that mean?"

"It means that's what Anderson told the other board members. He asked me to help them remove anything you may be working on." Warren gestured to several boxes in the corner of the room. "I don't know if we got everything but we had to move fast. Douglas' henchmen were trying to get past Anderson's roadblocks to supervise our collection of evidence."

AJ looked at the boxes and recognized a few of the books on the top of the pile. He took a few steps toward them and realized he was staggering. He stopped and looked at the glass in his hand, still half full of bourbon. He put the drink on the bar and dropped into the chair across from Warren. Drinking himself into oblivion wasn't the answer.

"Anderson told me there were files missing from my office," AJ said.

"Yeah, there were. Several drawers were empty and we could tell the locks had been tampered with."

"There were no empty drawers in my office when I left for the airport yesterday."

"Do you think Suzanne has anything to do with this?"

AJ rubbed his temples. "She's dumber than dog shit, Warren. I'm not sure she even knows what a file is."

"That's what I thought too, but Tracy told me Suzanne stayed late last night."

"And how would your secretary know that?"

"Tracy's sister had her baby yesterday and she stopped in to see her. She had bought her a gift and left it in her desk. When she went to get it Suzanne was in your office. She told Tracy she was working on a project you wanted finished before she went home last night."

"The only project I gave her to do was to update her résumé."

"Tracy also told me she caught her shredding a stack of files when she got back from lunch today. Suzanne told her they were duplicate files and that you had told her to shred them before you got back."

"That's a truckload of horse shit. I would never tell that twit to shred anything without direct supervision. For God's sake she needs to be micromanaged just to put paper in the damn copy machine."

"Maybe Jameson got to her. He could have given her those documents to shred and instructed her to keep his name out of it. Tracy has told me Jameson has intimidated quite a few of the secretaries, and Suzanne would be an easy target for his bullying tactics."

AJ hesitated. "Call Anderson… No, call Mercedes and tell her what Tracy told you. She is handling things here. Anderson is with Rosenfeld and Wisenthall following the money trail to God knows where."

"What else can I do?"

AJ looked at the boxes again and his tension eased a bit. Warren had gotten most of what he was working on and whatever was still in his office he could probably recreate if he had to.

"Just keep your ears open. I have to help them clear Samantha. It's my fault she is caught up in this mess."

"Yeah, I didn't see that one coming," Warren said.

"I wish I had. But now that I look back, it was a masterful plan. She is actually quite intelligent and Jameson was able to brand her as a gold digging floozy who pulled a fast one on him."

"Your support of her will go a long way," Warren said.

"I find that hard to believe when I'm being investigated as the mastermind of this grand theft."

"Douglas is very unpopular at Central Valley and you have more friends than I think you realize."

"Anderson said something to that effect."

"It's true, AJ."

"I just don't see it."

"You might have a reputation as a son of a bitch, but you earned the right to be. People respect you for your work and they understand your need to be cold and hard sometimes."

"Maybe." AJ closed his eyes and dropped his head to the back of the chair.

"Get some sleep, Golden Boy," Warren said. "Things will look better tomorrow."

AJ opened his eyes and watched Warren walk out the door. When he heard the front door close he forced his muscles to move. Waking up in his bed was going to feel a lot better than waking up in this chair with a kink in his neck.

****

AJ looked across Warren's backyard. The festive Halloween decorations hung from the trees and swayed lazily in the fall breeze. Each party guest wore a mask and mingled in a game of Guess Who.

He descended the steps of the deck and scanned the crowd. He studied their mannerisms and smiled in triumph as he identified each guest before they unmasked. He turned to his right and Samantha smiled at him from across the yard. Despite the red satin mask decked out in jewels and feathers his heart recognized her and leapt in excitement.

They met in the middle of the yard and she wrapped her arms around his neck.

"I've been waiting for you to recognize me."

He removed her mask and tucked a strand of hair behind her ear.

"I just got here," he said.

She leaned against him and opened her mouth on a sigh.

He cradled her face and kissed her passionately.

Samantha pushed him backwards and *he landed on a soft comforter. She straddled his chest with her gloriously naked body and knelt on the bed. Her beautiful breasts invited him to touch them.*

He reached up and caressed her flesh and she leaned forward to whisper into his ear.

'Make love to me, AJ...please.'

He kissed her once and guided her hips to his mouth. He extended his tongue and drew in her sweetness. A long forgotten hunger rushed through him and he devoured her arousal.

He thrust his tongue into her and a flash of lightning split the sky. He flinched and she was gone.

The sky was black and rain pelted his face. He stood and looked for Samantha.

'Where are you?'

'I'm right here, AJ.'

He spun toward her voice and Jackie looked back at him, pain branded into her features.

'How could you let him do this to us?' she said.

He looked beyond her into the yard and the decorations were gone. A shadow of a man stood a foot away and reached for Jackie.

'No!'

AJ wrapped his arms around her and she dissolved in his grasp.

'Jackie! Jackie, where are you?'

He heard leaves rustle behind him and he spun around. The rustle got louder but all he could see was darkness. He turned again.

'Jackie!'

'Don't let him hurt me, AJ. He's coming for me.'

He turned once more and Jackie stood in the moonlight under the oak tree. The red satin of her dress hugged her generous curves. The leaves swirled around her feet and her long silky hair danced in the breeze.

'Come to me, Jackie.' he said. 'I will keep you safe. Trust me.'

'But how can I trust you? I saw you making love to her.'

'I thought you were gone forever. I didn't mean to hurt you.'

The shadow reappeared and a flash of lightning danced along the blade in his hand. The Greek letters of AJ's fraternity glowed red on his chest. The man raised his head and AJ recognized his face.

'Jesse?'

The shadow raised the knife and turned toward Jackie.

'No!'

AJ lunged for the knife. He crashed into Jackie and pushed her against the oak tree.

'Tell her you love me,' she whispered.

AJ felt heat spread along his chest and looked down. The knife had impaled her heart and her blood stained his chest and hands.

He looked up and she was gone. The bark of the oak tree dug into his flesh as he leaned against it.

'Jackie,' he whispered.

The tree disappeared and AJ felt the earth give

way…

AJ woke in a cold sweat. His breathing was rapid and his heart raced. He sat up and ransacked his nightstand. He pulled out his journal and a pen and began scribbling everything he could remember.

The details were fading fast and he struggled to recall what she had said. Something about another woman he loved. But there was no other woman, there never was. And then there was Jesse's face on the shadow that was trying to take her away. Where the hell did that come from?

His head was splitting open and he knew it had little to do with his dream or his efforts to remember the details. He looked at the clock on his nightstand. The bright green numbers pierced his vision and set off another wave of pain through his head. Two thirty in the morning was a bit early to get up, even for him. He put the journal away and stumbled to the bathroom. He swallowed two aspirin then studied his reflection in the mirror.

Why was she haunting him again? There wasn't anything he could do to change what had happened. Jackie was the one who chose to walk away. She's the one who wanted out, and he's the one who never stopped wanting her back.

And these dreams, why the hell couldn't they be like the last ones, filled with erotic love making that left him wanting more? His mind seemed set on torturing him for a past sin he couldn't remember, a betrayal he couldn't believe he would ever commit.

He walked back to his bed in darkness and cracked his shin on the frame.

"Son of a…"

He lost his balance and let his body fall to the mattress. He crawled to his pillows and pulled one over his head. Hopefully Jackie would stay out of his mind long enough for him to recover from the hangover he knew was brewing.

Eleven

AJ slouched in the leather chair behind his desk. He could hear the rain softly pelt the window behind him. Somehow the sound soothed his aching head. A glass of water that had washed down another dose of aspirin sat next to the inventory list he was compiling.

The boxes Warren had delivered to his home last night were empty and the contents littered his office. Much to his dismay there were no flash drives, CDs, or any other handy devices that could be plugged in, connected, or otherwise downloaded onto his hard drive that would organize these documents for him. He was going to have to do this the old fashioned way. He groaned. He hated filing.

The doorbell rang and he looked for a path to get out of his office. When he realized he'd boxed himself in he said, "It's open!"

He heard the door swing open and shut, then the flutter of a coat being shaken.

"Dr. Carrington?"

"Samantha?" he whispered.

AJ rubbed his cheek. He hadn't bothered to shave this morning. He looked down and was relieved to see he had at least bothered to put on a pair of jeans and a sweatshirt.

"Samantha, you will have to come to me! I am not trying to be inhospitable but I seem to have barricaded myself in for the moment!"

He heard her laugh and smiled at the sound.

"Okay! Can you give me directions?"

"Straight ahead to the end of the hall! I'm in the last room on the left!"

He could hear the hardwood floor creak as she got closer. She appeared at the door with a small envelope in her hand. Her smile melted some of the tension that lingered from the events of yesterday. She too was wearing jeans and a sweatshirt and her long blonde hair was pulled back in a plain pink band.

"Did your file cabinet explode?"

He laughed. "Not exactly. These are files Warren brought from my office. I am attempting to organize them but I am afraid I am not very good at the basic clerical task called filing."

"What are all these files?"

"My research." He sighed. "I am afraid this is all I have to work with. He was not kind enough to include anything remotely resembling a CD or a flash drive."

"You mean like this?" She pulled three flash

drives from the envelope in her hand.

AJ's jaw dropped. If she had been close enough, he would have kissed her.

"Where did you get those?"

"I'd tell you but then I'd have to kill you."

He smiled and said, "If they have the information I need I wouldn't care if you stole them from the Vatican."

"Dr. Jameson is out today so I decided to take the afternoon off. I managed to ditch my chaperone by promising I would go straight to the garage. I just failed to mention I planned to take the scenic route past the mental health wing. I thought since Suzanne has been reassigned, and Dr. Jackson and his secretary are out all day that I should drop by to make sure everything was secure." She winked, dropped the drives back into the padded envelope and said, "Catch."

AJ caught the package and watched Samantha as she surveyed the sea of paper.

"I am surprised Anderson is not having my office watched," he said.

"He is. One of Mercedes' henchmen was there. He detained me while he called her then seemed disappointed when she told him Daniel had cleared me to be there." She looked up at him with a smile. "I told you Daniel would come through."

"Yes. You did."

She sat Indian style at the door and sighed. "You get started on those computer files and I'll get started on this." She looked up at him. "Where do you want me to put all this information?"

He pointed to a file cabinet next to his desk.

"This one would work the best." He stood. "I should show you what order—"

"You. Sit." She pointed to his chair.

He suppressed his smile at her stern expression and did as he was ordered.

"From the looks of this mess you haven't got the slightest idea on how to organize hard copies. You let me handle this and just worry about your work."

AJ sat back down and realized the last of his headache had gone. He pulled out the flash drives and copied the information to his hard drive. Warren was right, things were looking better today.

****

Douglas slid the gold box with the engraved pen into the breast pocket of his suit jacket. A slimy smile adorned his features as he exited the elevator and stepped into the mental health wing.

The last step to his plan would be easy. When he had noticed the imperfection left by the roller ball in the pen, he had decided to use it to forge the authorizations. Once he put the pen in Dr. Carrington's office, the forged documents could no longer be traced back to him and, in fact, would tie them directly to AJ.

All he had to do was slip in and out without being seen. The new software for the security cameras was being updated today so they were offline. He was officially "out" for the day and the mental health wing was deserted. Perfect!

Douglas walked to the suite and felt his heart race with excitement. He unlocked the door and stepped inside. When the master key slid into the lock on Dr. Carrington's door he nearly squealed with glee. This was almost too easy.

The waiting he had endured for each step to unfold had been grueling, but he had forced himself to be patient and he had completed each step with the perfection of a master. He closed his eyes and moaned. Watching the mighty Dr. Anthony Joseph Carrington fall was going to be orgasmic.

He stepped into the office and shut the door behind him. Despite the large windows, the office was dim. The overcast day abetted him in his plan to destroy Dr. Carrington. The lightly tinted windows would hide his presence from anyone in the courtyard below.

He paced to the desk and looked at the leather chair AJ sat in. It screamed power. The mahogany desk mocked him when he thought of his own bland desk made of walnut.

He fought the urge to touch it, to mar the flawless finish, but eventually the authorities would be involved and he couldn't afford the complications of explaining his fingerprints in this office. He had wiped the pen clean but left his prints on the box. Since the board had given it to him to deliver, his prints would be expected to be found there. His brilliant mind analyzed each detail. His plan was perfect.

A vision of AJ begging for mercy from the court after his sentence was read, made him laugh out loud.

"Find something amusing?"

Douglas dropped his keys and spun around. He saw Mercedes sitting in the large, leather, winged back chair in front of Dr. Carrington's desk, and his heart leapt into his throat.

"What the hell are you doing in here?"

She crossed her legs and twirled her foot carelessly.

"I could ask you the same thing," she said. "Your office is quite a bit out of the way from here."

"I am the hospital administrator. It is my job to make sure things are running as they should be."

"I suppose that's true, and perhaps it slipped your mind that there is nothing happening in this particular office at the moment." She leveled him with a glare. "But somehow I think even your cronies would have a hard time believing you forgot that little piece of information considering it was you who closed it down."

He crossed his arms and leaned back against the desk. "And what about you Mercedes? How exactly do you plan to explain your presence here when I tell the investigators I was checking the office because I heard a noise and found you lurking around in the dark?"

"I'm an interested board member, Douglas. I want to get to the truth. I'm sure it's no surprise to you that Dr. Carrington is claiming the documents you produced are forgeries. I am simply setting a trap for the real thief to return to the scene of the crime." She laced her fingers together across her waist. "And it appears he has."

"Bitch! How dare you speak to me that way. My highest priority has always been to protect Central Valley from any threat, especially when that threat is coming from an untouchable."

"Dr. Carrington is not an untouchable...and neither are you."

He sneered. "You're pretty brave without your keeper tagging along."

She laughed. "Your arrogance is based on ignorance, Douglas, and it will be your downfall. Not every woman needs a champion to fight her battles."

"Women like you operate under the delusion that you actually earned your way up in a vertical position." He looked at her long legs and pictured them wrapped around his hips. "Fortunately for you, I believe in providing a healthy dose of reality to misguided sluts like yourself." He gazed at her cleavage and licked his lips. "Your tits got you this far, Mercedes, not your brain. No one gives a shit what comes out of your mouth, unless it's their dick."

"Those are rather dangerous words for someone who is under suspicion. It would serve you better to remember your place."

"You're the one who needs to learn her place." He lunged for her and manacled his hands around her upper arms, but a sharp pain in his groin froze every muscle in his body.

Mercedes gently twisted the heel of her stiletto she had pressed against his scrotum.

"Care to rethink your position on that, Douglas?"

He loosened his grip and backed away from her slowly. A bead of sweat ran down the side of his face. He swallowed hard and tried to steady his breathing. The image of what she could have done to him played in his mind and his hands shook with fear.

"That's a good little boy," she said. "Now why don't you run along? I will make sure nothing is disturbed in this office."

Rage burned through his veins. She was nothing more than another power hungry whore who happened to wrap her legs around the right dick. She got lucky this time. Fate stepped in to keep him focused on what he needed to do. Otherwise, she'd be spreading those legs for him too, not just old man Anderson.

He straightened his jacket and tie, and left her in the dark office. He slammed each door as he made his way to the elevator. He may have lost this battle, but he wasn't about to lose the war. There was more than one way to get this pen into Carrington's hands.

****

AJ was watching Samantha when she closed the top drawer of the file cabinet and leaned against it. He smiled when she looked at him.

"I want to thank you for all your help today," he said. "It means a great deal to me."

"You're welcome." She smiled back.

He was silent for a minute then realized he was staring at her. He looked at his watch as a distraction, 7:00 p.m.

"Damn, I didn't realize it was so late. I should make something to eat."

Samantha's smile faded. "I'm sorry. I should be going." She reached for her purse.

"Are you going to let me eat alone?"

She stopped and gave him a surprised look. "But I thought... I mean I didn't stay because I expected you to make dinner for me."

"You think I would let you do all that work for me and not even feed you?" He frowned. "How bad is my reputation?"

"Um..." She bit her lip. "It's just that it isn't necessary, Dr. Carrington, I was glad to help."

"Wow. It is that bad, isn't it?" he whispered then said, "Well, I happen to think it is necessary and please, call me AJ. We are in my home, not the office."

She smiled and blushed. "I think I can handle that."

He stood and walked toward her. "So, what do you like? I have quite a variety in this house."

"I'm a meat and potatoes kind of girl." She opened the door to the hall and waited.

He rubbed his hands together and wiggled his eyebrows.

"The only thing I do better than my job is make a delicious steak." He hurried past her and headed to the kitchen. "After tonight you will be begging to help me again just so you can have another one of my steaks."

AJ couldn't remember the last time he felt this energized. It was the smallest of things, but somehow making dinner for Samantha was euphoric. He refrained from dancing around the island while he mixed the spices. At least he had the good sense not to make a complete fool of himself.

"What can I do to help?" she said.

"You, madam, can make the salad." He pointed to the cabinet above the coffee maker. "The serving bowls are up there, the utensils are in that drawer there, and you probably know where to find everything else."

"I'm sure I do."

AJ headed outside. He lit the grill on his deck and looked up at the overcast sky. The rain had stopped hours ago and the air had a bite to it, but it was invigorating. He took a deep breath and walked back inside.

He pulled the steaks from the refrigerator and watched Samantha from the corner of his eye as she gathered the vegetables. She chopped the carrots and celery like she executed every other task he'd seen her do, with confidence and tenacity. There was no hesitation. She knew exactly what she wanted to do and she did it with vigor and purpose.

A vision flashed in his mind.

Jackie stood at the kitchen counter in the fraternity house cutting up carrots and celery for their Super Bowl party. The precision of her movements made her look like a professional chef. He wrapped his arms around her and she laid her head back against his shoulder.

He cupped her breasts and bit her neck.

'They're a bunch of animals, Jackie. They won't appreciate the effort you're making.' He pinched her nipples. 'Let me lock you up in my room and ravish your beautiful body.'

A roar of cheers burst from the living room and she wiggled from his embrace.

'They know I promised to help with the party,' she said. *'I don't need to give them another reason not to like me.'*

He sighed. 'Jackie, I've told you a hundred times they do like you. Why won't you believe me?'

'Because they don't talk to me like they do to Stacey. They laugh and joke with her and when I walk into the room you can hear a pin drop. It's like the wicked old witch just flew in on her broomstick or something.'

He wrapped his arms around her waist and laid his chin on her shoulder.

'They flirt with Stacey because Tony lets them get away with it.' He pulled her hair back and kissed her neck. 'And they don't flirt with you because it pisses me off. You deserve to be treated better. You shouldn't have to tolerate catcalls and sleazy innuendos.'

'Well maybe it would be nice to know they think I'm as pretty or as sexy as Stacey.'

He sighed. 'I don't get it, Jackie. Why do you care what they think?'

She looked down at the vegetables and severed a fistful of carrots in one chop. She struggled to remove the knife from the wood.

'I just want your friends to like me.'

"Dr. Carrington… are you okay?"

AJ blinked and saw Samantha standing at the end of the island. She had almost finished mixing the salad.

"Yes. I'm sorry. I was just lost in thought for a moment." He rubbed the mixture of spices into the meat, then managed a weak smile and said, "I will be right back."

He stepped onto the deck and dropped the steaks carelessly onto the hot grate. He listened to the sizzle and flexed his fingers to keep them from forming fists. He realized he was grinding his teeth and opened his mouth wide to stretch the muscles of his jaw.

"Why the hell can't you stop thinking about her?" he whispered to himself. "She left you, let her go."

He turned and looked through the window. Samantha pulled dinner plates and glasses from his cabinets and set them on the island. Next she folded two cloth napkins and placed them next to the plates under the silverware. She moved around his kitchen like it was hers. She seemed to know where everything was.

A twinge of sadness settled in his chest. If only things had been different he could be looking at Jackie, as his wife, through this window. She could be setting dinner for the two of them, and maybe their children.

"Stop it."

He spun back around and concentrated on making sure the steaks turned out just right. He flipped the meat to sear the other side. The door behind him slid open and he kept his stare on the flames licking the edges of the filets.

"Dr. Carrington—"

"Please, Samantha, call me AJ. I don't feel much like Dr. Carrington right now."

"I'm sorry." She paused. "AJ, did I do something

to upset you?"

He spun around. "No." He exhaled. "I'm just a little tired. I didn't get much sleep last night."

"I know how you feel. I didn't sleep at all last night." She sat on the bench along the house. "I'm surprised I'm still awake, actually."

He leaned back against the railing next to the grill.

"A lot has changed in the last thirty-six hours, hasn't it?" He looked down to avoid her gaze. The guilt he felt was strong. "I imagine it was difficult for you today. I am truly sorry that I have gotten you caught up in this mess."

"AJ, if anyone should have seen this coming it was me. I'm the one who worked with Dr. Jameson every day." She sighed. "He's such a pig."

AJ couldn't stop the smile and kept his gaze on the wooden planks under his feet. Samantha was always so proper that her blunt and graphic description of Douglas was amusing.

She continued, "Mercedes was right. I should have filed a complaint a long time ago. I could have prevented this. I certainly had enough violations to report. He would have been forced out even with all his cronies sitting on the board."

He stood once again in front of the grill and poked the steaks.

"I guess neither one of us really thought he would go this far." He decided they were done and put them on a clean platter then turned to head back into the house. "Dinner is served."

He opened a bottle of red wine and poured them each a glass. He served the steaks while Samantha divided the small salad she had made. He could feel her watching him through most of the meal and he hated the fact that he was unable to hold a conversation with her. Thoughts of Jackie infected his brain and he struggled to get out the one word answers he managed to utter.

He almost threw the dishes into the sink before he decided he couldn't take it anymore. He had to get Jackie out of his head and there was only one way he could think of to do it.

Samantha reached around him to put her glass in the sink and he pinned her against the counter. She gasped and he swallowed the sound in a crushing kiss.

She moaned and melted against him. He twirled her around and swept the island clear. He ignored the clatter of cutlery bouncing off the ceramic tile and pressed her to the granite surface.

He combed his fingers into her hair and struggled not to hurt her. Jackie's face began to blur as he forced his mind to picture Samantha. He kissed her harder and she broke away to catch her breath.

"AJ," she whispered.

He opened his eyes and saw her watery gaze. He jumped back and braced himself against the counter.

"I'm sorry, Samantha. I shouldn't have done that." He shook his head. "I'm so sorry."

She sat up slowly, her breathing still labored. "It's... You just... I wasn't expecting you to do that."

"I know. I'm sorry. You deserve to be treated

with more respect than that. I should never have done that."

"It's alright…"

"No. It's not alright. That wasn't fair. I…"

She smiled and moved close to him. "Maybe we could try again."

This wasn't right. He knew it deep in his heart somewhere, but he couldn't stop himself. He cradled her face in his hands and kissed her softly. She opened for him and he pulled her against his chest.

She wrapped her arms around his neck and pressed their bodies even tighter together. Her kiss was intense and she seemed desperate for his. When he grabbed her hair at her nape she growled softly and pulled him with her as she leaned back against the island.

He couldn't keep Jackie from his thoughts despite how real and soft and exciting Samantha's body felt next to his. He lost himself in her kiss and forfeited the fight. Jackie's face was branded in his mind. He could hate himself later.

Samantha broke the kiss again and hugged him tight against her. She whispered, "I've missed this."

He nibbled her earlobe. "Missed what?"

She gasped and pushed him up then stepped away from his embrace.

"Nothing. I mean…"

AJ swore internally. "Samantha, I didn't mean it like that. I'm sorry. I know the rumors—"

"No. It's alright." She straightened her clothing. "I should be going."

"Samantha."

She turned around at the door to the hall and looked at him.

AJ swallowed. "Will I see you tomorrow?"

"I'll be here."

She smiled, then turned and walked out the door.

When he heard the front door close he exhaled. That was a mistake he couldn't repeat. Samantha deserved better than that. He'd have to find another way to destroy Jackie's memory.

****

AJ opened his eyes to near pitch black space around him. His heart raced and a shiver of fear crept up his spine. He'd lost sight of Jackie. He sat up and rubbed his eyes. She had disappeared into the darkness again. He could feel a chill where her body had been pressed against his just a second ago. She couldn't have gone far.

He took a deep breath and looked around. His sight was adjusting to the night. Dim light from the moon peaked in above the drapes at his bedroom window. His robe hung over the back of the chair next to his closet. He was home... which meant he was alone. Jackie wasn't here. It had only been a dream.

The bed sheet was tangled around his feet. He removed his restraints and swung his legs over the side. A shiver traveled up his limbs into his torso when his feet hit the cold hardwood floor. He rubbed his hands together and put on his slippers.

He grabbed his journal from his nightstand and recorded everything he could remember from the dream. Jackie wanted him to tell her it was a mistake, that he didn't mean for it to happen. He combed his fingers through his hair. He didn't mean for what to happen? What the hell was she talking about? He needed to talk to Warren.

AJ closed his journal and placed the call then looked at the clock. It was almost midnight.

"Shit," he whispered. Hopefully he hadn't just woke up the X-man.

"AJ, everything okay?" Warren said.

"Yes. Look, I'm sorry. I didn't realize what time it was. I'll talk to you tomorrow."

"Talk to me now while I'm awake. I can't guarantee you I will be coherent later. The X-man had an extra-long nap this afternoon so he's been up twice already playing in his crib. Loudly, I might add." He yawned. *"It was my turn to get up. So now everyone is asleep except me. Tell me about the dream."*

"How did you know I had another dream?"

"Seriously? AJ, when was the last time you called me at midnight to bullshit?"

AJ laughed. "Probably never."

"Exactly. So make it worth my time and tell me you had hot sex with at least one of them."

"Sorry," he said. "I'm too tired to come up with something believable."

"That's too bad. What did you get to do?"

"Not much." AJ paused. "What happened to me that night? I mean... you've always said I was really sick, but what exactly was wrong with me?"

"It was the worst hangover I've ever seen. And it was straight from the textbook. You had every symptom ever recorded."

"I think I remembered some of that. This time when she walked away from me I got a stabbing pain in my head that blurred my vision. The pain was so bad I felt like I was going to throw up. Then she said, 'they took you away from me.' What the hell does that mean?"

"Maybe it has something to do with Jesse. You said he was in the last dream you had and that he was holding a knife to her throat." He paused. *"It could be symbolic of what happened. Jesse produced the knife, but you're the one who stabbed her in the heart."*

AJ closed his eyes. "I just can't believe I would do that to her. I just…"

"Look." Warren took a deep breath. *"We both know Jackie didn't like Jesse. He was a dick to her. Maybe her leaving had something to do with him. Obviously something happened that neither one of us knows about."*

"But why wouldn't she talk to me about it? Why would she just walk away?"

"I don't know. Honestly, I would have expected her to fight for you. If there really was another woman, I thought Jackie would have taken her down. She loved you, Golden Boy. I know that better than I know my own name." Warren sighed. *"But you know, a lot of weird shit happened that night. Like Mike and Jesse falling down the stairs and the fact that Tony never brought Stacey to the house again after the party. No one ever talked about that night either. No stories about drunken escapades, no stories about who scored and who didn't. It was like the night never happened."*

"So what do I do? How do I make these dreams stop?"

"You figure out the mystery." He yawned. *"Be patient. We'll get it this time. Get some sleep and I'll talk to you tomorrow."*

AJ blew out a heavy sigh. "Yeah, I'll try. Thanks."

"No problem. Later."

AJ set his phone on the nightstand next to his journal and exhaled.

"Jackie, why can't I forget about you?" he whispered.

He laid back and pulled the blankets up to his waist. Thoughts of her filled his mind and he tried to focus on the memory of how good it felt to hold her in his arms. Despite the hole she had left in his heart, her memory eased the pain. Now all he needed was to get some sleep. If he didn't, he was going to lose his mind.

Twelve

AJ sat at his desk and reviewed the latest study on drug therapies versus cognitive therapies, and their effectiveness in treating Traumatic Brain Injuries. He preferred traditional cognitive therapies, but to ignore the benefits of medications would be irresponsible.

Sarah had responded better to cognitive therapies but she still needed her medications to maintain her daily level of functioning, and in fact, that was his biggest challenge with her case. He had yet to find a drug that produced consistent results for her. The one she was on now seemed to be increasing her rate of decline instead of slowing it.

He thought about her and sighed. Helping her was important. It soothed his soul when life got too hectic and threatened to overwhelm him completely. Plus there was the small hope that if he could help restore her memory maybe he could find out how to restore his own.

He looked up at the empty room and wished he wasn't so isolated. He missed having colleagues to discuss his work with. Talking with someone always helped the mind explore different avenues it hadn't considered before. Even Samantha could talk it out with him. She may not understand the science of it but she was certainly intelligent enough to discuss his theories. She seemed to know his research better than anyone outside of his peers.

But she had cancelled on him. She told him she had a personal matter come up that couldn't wait, yet he couldn't help but feel he had crossed the line yesterday. His intent, to use her to simply erase the memory of another woman, was unforgiveable. But when she had kissed him back, he felt a spark of desire he hadn't felt in a very long time. Then his intent changed and the need to take her, make her his own, was born.

His phone vibrated against the polished wood of his desk and he looked at the caller ID. He didn't recognize the number but this time he welcomed the interruption. Looking at the study results for too long made them meaningless.

"Dr. Carrington."

"AJ, how the hell are ya?" Daniel Rosenfeld's voice brought a grin to AJ's face.

"Fine, Daniel. And you?"

"Pretty good today. Charles, David, and I found something we'd like to talk to you about. I was hoping you could shed some light on it for us."

AJ looked at his watch. He'd been studying this

particular research for more than two hours. It was time to walk away from it to clear his mind for another look later.

"I have time now. Where would you like me to meet you?"

"You stay put. We'll come to you. Twenty minutes sound good?"

"That works for me."

"Have a scotch ready for me. I really need one after all this damn ghost hunting."

AJ smiled. "I am sure I can scrounge up some of that rotgut for you."

"And don't try to hand me any of that sissy bourbon shit you Yankees call booze."

AJ laughed. "I will see you in twenty minutes."

****

"Thank you, Edna. I appreciate the update on Sarah." AJ scribbled some notes in the private chart he kept for her case.

"Just don't forget. You didn't hear this from me," Edna said.

"My lips are sealed. Let me know if you are able to persuade Dr. Hanson to simply lower her dosage and wean her off the medication. Terminating her drug therapy too quickly could do more harm than good."

"I will. I hope this mess gets cleared up soon. I'm too old for this spy stuff."

AJ smiled. "I will keep you informed of the situation. Thank you again."

"I gotta go. The nosy little CNA is on her way back."

He laughed when he heard the dial tone and dropped his phone onto his desk. Edna took his request to keep him informed very seriously, despite his current sabbatical, as the board had labeled it. She was from the old school and still believed bending the rules in the best interest of the patient was okay, as long as you didn't get caught. And she had treated his request like a secret agent mission.

The doorbell rang and AJ headed down the hall. He opened the door and greeted the three men who held his future in the balance, Charles Anderson, Daniel Rosenfeld, and David Wisenthall.

A brisk October wind rushed past the men and Daniel hurried across the threshold.

"Good God, this is why I don't leave Texas unless I have to. What the hell's the temperature out there?"

Charles sighed and followed him in. "I believe it is the same as it was ten minutes ago." He brushed something from his lapel. "Stop whining."

AJ hid his smile. He guessed it was about forty degrees Fahrenheit. David and Charles exchanged a look that told AJ this wasn't the first time Daniel had complained about the weather.

AJ closed the door and led them to his office.

"I did manage to find some Glenmorangie." He turned at the end of the hall and indicated for them to precede him into his office.

"Not a bad choice for a bourbon drinker." Daniel made himself at home and poured his first drink before the other men were settled.

AJ looked at Charles and David. "Can I get you gentlemen something to drink?"

"I've had enough, thank you," Charles said.

"Bourbon for me," David said. "I'm not particular. Any brand will do."

AJ dropped ice into a glass and removed the stopper to the decanter. Charles spoke from behind him.

"Dr. Carrington, we have several questions for you." He waited for AJ to hand David his drink and get settled behind his desk before he continued. "We managed to track the funds to a Swiss bank account and that's where we ran into a dead end. Without proof of serious criminal activity or formal charges being filed, we won't be able to access the account holder's identity."

Daniel finished his drink and poured himself another.

"The private numbered account was opened eighteen months ago," Daniel said. "Prior to that, the money had been deposited into a Swiss account that had been opened online. According to the computer backup tapes at Central Valley, that account was opened from your office terminal. Security tapes show no one was in the department at the time, which means, whoever opened the account logged into your terminal from somewhere else." He took a drink. "I'm guessing you're too smart to remote into your own computer to steal millions."

AJ scratched his jaw. "I can honestly say I have not given the matter much thought, but I would like to think I am a bit smarter than that."

"The most recent wire transfer was made this past Saturday just after 6:00 a.m. our time. It came from a mobile terminal," David said.

AJ crinkled his eyebrows. "A mobile terminal?"

"That refers to a computer that belongs to the IT department," Charles said. "It is used to temporarily replace one that is no longer useable until a permanent replacement can be installed. They are not used very often because the goal is to replace a computer before it needs to be, but occasionally unforeseen events occur."

David continued, "Mercedes has someone looking at the hospital's security logs. I'm sure it doesn't surprise you the terminal that was used was not logged out for use. They are checking badge records to see who was in the building during that time. Since it was so early on a Saturday we're hoping it won't take long to locate the culprit."

AJ closed his eyes and slumped back into his chair.

Daniel took a swig. "Something wrong with that?"

"I was there." AJ got up to fix himself a drink. "When I met with Douglas on Friday he told me he was backing out of the Las Vegas presentation. I went in early Saturday morning to work on the proposal I had put together. I assumed his absence would be interpreted as a red flag that the deal was bad. I wanted to make sure the presentation was flawless."

"6:00 a.m. seems mighty early for a Saturday," Daniel said. "Was Jameson in his office?"

AJ felt a lump form in his gut. "No... but Samantha was."

Daniel looked at AJ. "You sure about that?"

"She called me from her office and I met with

her ten minutes later."

Charles cleared his throat. "That's going to make things rather difficult for us to explain away since Douglas claims you two are working together."

AJ leaned back against his desk. "But he should be able to remote into his office from anywhere. I have access... had access to my files and worked from here many nights. He could have easily made the last transfer from a Central Valley computer when Samantha and I were the only ones there."

Charles rubbed his temple. "The accounting files are only accessible from an on-site workstation. You cannot remote into the system from outside of the hospital campus."

"Could he have scheduled the transaction?" AJ said.

"Possibly." Daniel refreshed his drink. "But he would've had to know exactly when the two of you would be there alone and when the bank would process the transfer then coordinate it all. Personally, I think the bastard just got lucky on this one."

"Douglas has done a hell of a job with this," David said. "I don't know Samantha very well but from what Daniel has said about her she's too smart to embezzle the money and put herself at the scene of the crime."

Charles looked at David. "Douglas has done a great job of painting her as a useless bimbo who can be manipulated. He has already hinted at the theory that Dr. Carrington is using her to cover his tracks."

David leaned forward and rested his elbows on his knees. "Alright, let's concentrate on who opened this account. The rest of this could be circumstantial if we can prove Jameson opened the Swiss account." He looked at each of them and said, "Does anyone know if Jameson was in Switzerland or even had the opportunity to open the private numbered account. That at least, has to be done in person."

Charles shook his head. "Mercedes has already determined Jameson hasn't left the country in the past five years. There are companies who can act as a middleman and open an account for you, although, the intelligence we have discovered indicates it was opened in Switzerland. Additionally, I think Jameson would want as few people involved in this as possible. Therefore, if Jameson is the one we're looking for, I believe the account was most likely opened in Switzerland by him or someone he felt he could trust."

David looked at AJ. "What about you? Could you possibly have been in a position to open the account?"

"No. The last time I was in Europe was six years ago. I wasn't planning to return until next month for the conference in London."

"What about Samantha?" Daniel took another swig of his scotch.

Charles shook his head again. "Mercedes looked at all three of them, Jameson, Carrington, and Samantha. None of them were in a position to open that account that we can determine." He looked at AJ. "That's one of the questions I have for you. Can you think of anyone who is even remotely involved with Jameson or Central Valley who could have been in a position to open that account?"

AJ laughed. "The only one I know of who was in Europe and is tied to Central Valley is my…was my useless assistant, Suzanne Chadwick. She spoke incessantly to Dr. Jackson's secretary about her seven day tour of Europe."

Charles raised an eyebrow. "When was she in Europe?"

"I don't know exactly. She has only worked for me for the last six weeks and it was prior to her start date."

Charles pulled his phone from his pocket. "Excuse me." He stood and paced to the far corner of the room.

AJ shook his head. "She is not smart enough to pull off something like this. It has to be a coincidence."

Daniel smiled. "The most successful con artists are the best actors on the world's stage."

"But that's just another connection to me." AJ ran his hands through his hair. "Christ! This could put the final nail in my coffin."

Daniel rubbed his chin and watched Charles as he spoke on his phone at the other end of the room. "Maybe, unless we can find a connection between Suzanne and Jameson."

AJ tossed his drink to the back of his throat. "I need another drink."

Susan M Baer

Thirteen

AJ stood in front of the mirror above the vanity and carefully dragged the straight blade under his chin. He should have used the electric razor, it was faster, but the blade gave him a closer shave. One more swipe down his sideburn removed the last of the shaving cream. He rinsed the blade and splashed cool water on his face then quickly pat dried his skin with the soft towel he had draped around his neck. He finger combed his still damp hair before he peaked around the door jamb and looked at the clock on his nightstand. Shit! He was running out of time.

Samantha had called twenty minutes ago to say she was on her way and had roused him from a deep sleep. He hadn't set his alarm last night with the hope that he would get an extra hour or two of rest. He never imagined he would have gotten three, and if she hadn't called him, he'd probably still be sleeping.

He shook his head. On any other day he would have completed a dozen tasks by now, but today he'd be lucky if he was fully dressed by the time Samantha arrived. He hadn't slept in this long since he was a kid, and it had been just as long since he'd felt this rested, so apparently it was exactly what he needed. To his immense relief he had also slept straight through the night, because it was the first night in nearly a week that he hadn't dreamt about Jackie.

He sat on the end of his bed and pulled on his socks as thoughts of both women drifted through his mind. Samantha's face filled his vision and he remembered how she had kissed him the other day. She was certainly not shy when she wanted something, and she had definitely wanted to kiss him. At least until he had insulted her.

AJ propped his elbows on his knees and sighed. His desire for her was strong and considering how much he missed her yesterday, he was sure it had nothing to do with using her to forget Jackie. Jackie would become a faded memory soon enough, he just had to be careful not to insult Samantha again. More importantly, he had to take it slow, and the best way he knew how to accomplish that was to let her come to him. He smiled. He just had to find the patience to wait for her to make her first move.

He heard the clock in his den strike half past nine and the doorbell rang. He hurried to fasten the buttons of his shirt and stepped into his leather shoes. The buttonholes on his cuffs were tight and giving him a problem. He cursed his frustration and pulled the shirt over his head. He tossed it to the floor of his closet and yanked another one off a hanger. He wrapped the second one around his torso and made quick work of the closures. When he got to the sleeves he found the right cuff was missing a button.

"Son of a bitch!"

The doorbell rang again and he scanned the row of shirts for another one to wear. He checked the cuffs of one and stopped suddenly when he realized what he was doing.

"For God's sake, old man, it's just a button." He closed the closet door and turned to leave the room. "Apparently, getting up late turns you into a pansy."

He folded the cuffs twice to hide the imperfection and walked into the hallway. This was definitely going to be the last time he let himself sleep in. He headed for the stairs and tucked the tails of his shirt in as he hurried down the steps. A tingling of fear danced in his stomach at the thought that she might have gotten tired of waiting for him and left, but he didn't think it would be appropriate if he answered the door only half dressed.

He could have easily thrown on a pair of jeans and a sweatshirt instead of the khakis and light blue, cotton, button down shirt he was donning, but he wanted to look good for her. It was silly, he knew, but after she had cancelled on him yesterday he thought she was avoiding him, and that bothered him more than he thought it would.

He blew out a heavy breath and opened the door.

"Samantha…"

Her name was all he got out before the air rushed from his lungs. The morning sun was at her back and cast a breathtaking glow around her. She looked like an angel. She wore her hair down again and a few wispy strands played along her chin. She smiled.

"Hi. May I come in?"

"Oh, uh, yes. Of course."

She stepped past him and hung her jacket on the oak coat rack in the corner as he closed the door. He turned to face her and they stood in an awkward silence before he cleared his throat.

"I guess we should get to work."

She looked down the hall toward his office. "Yes, I guess we should."

He started down the hall and he could feel her following behind him. Every step was grueling as he suppressed the urge to turn around, back her to the wall, and kiss her senseless. He stepped across the threshold of his office and stopped in the middle of the room. He wasn't sure he could do this. How was he going to concentrate on anything when all he wanted to do was ravish her? His fingers even twitched with the need to touch her.

"AJ, I..."

He spun around to face her and took a half a step back. She was too close. He couldn't trust himself not to take her in his arms.

"Is everything okay?" she said.

"Yes," he said and hesitated. "As crass as it may sound, I am finding it quite difficult not to touch you."

She blushed. "Would that really be so bad?"

He shook his head. "I won't hurt you, Samantha. I refuse to treat you like the others have. I won't use you like that."

"You're not like those men, AJ."

"I would like to think I'm not, but what I did the other day, the way I attacked you in my kitchen was completely disrespectful, and right now…well, I just want to do it again."

"Then maybe we should talk about what happened and make sure we understand each other."

His heart leapt into his throat. Maybe he had been too blunt. She obviously didn't realize his reasons today were different. She didn't realize that today he wanted her because he found her overwhelmingly desirable. All she knew was that two days ago he had tried to use her, just like Douglas had, and now she was going to call him on it.

He thought about what he'd done. She had spent the whole day with him, looking beautiful and sexy, especially when she chewed on her lip as she figured out a solution to whatever she was working on, so of course, he had wanted to kiss her. But more than that he had been desperate to eradicate Jackie from his mind and he had made a conscious decision to use Samantha to do it.

It didn't matter that he felt differently today. He knew he deserved whatever harsh words she was about to speak because what he had done was unforgiveable. He needed to pay for his sin.

"I want to apologize for the other day," she said. "I know I was sending you mixed messages and I'm sorry."

"What?" He almost flinched at her unexpected apology. "No. You definitely weren't the problem. I was completely out of line when I kissed you. I was arrogant and thoughtless when I assumed I could just take what I wanted."

AJ stuck his hands into his pockets and curled his fingers into fists. The image of throwing her over his shoulder and carrying her up to his bed filled his mind and he glanced at the door to judge how long it would take him to make it upstairs.

She stepped close to him and he could feel the frosty morning chill that still radiated from her cheeks. She held his gaze for another breathless minute before she spoke.

"No. I think I was the problem, so I thought maybe I should clear things up."

She kissed him on the cheek then held her face to his. She whispered into his ear, "Was that okay?"

AJ slowly pulled his hands from his pockets and cradled her face. He touched her lips to his and exhaled a shaky breath.

"Oh yes," he said and looked at her mouth. "That was definitely okay."

He tilted his head and kissed her gently. He licked the seam of her lips and dipped into the spicy warmth of her mouth when she opened for him.

She wrapped her arms around his chest and dug her fingers into his back to pull him closer to her.

A familiar aroma filled his senses and his limbs vibrated with arousal. He broke the kiss and panted into her ear.

"Is that a new perfume?"

"Kind of. I haven't worn it in a while. Do you

like it?"

"Yes," he whispered. He held her tight to him and tried to control the quivering of his body. "Samantha, are you sure about this? You don't owe me anything. Whatever you think you did or said. It…it doesn't matter. You weren't teasing me. I swear—"

She grabbed his head and swallowed his words in a crushing kiss. She wrapped her leg around his and rubbed her pelvis against his thigh. She took a quick breath and spoke into his mouth.

"Make love to me, AJ."

He took her to the floor and straddled her body with his, then pulled his shirt over his head to avoid the extra effort of unbuttoning it. He undid the closures on his khakis and stood to remove them. When she pulled her sweater over her head he held his breath and froze.

His last dream flashed in his mind and hope warred with fear as he waited to see which woman would emerge from the petal soft wool. Samantha's face appeared and a soft sigh escaped her lips.

He knelt beside her and pulled the pant legs of her jeans from her body, as well as her silk and lace panties, then waited while she removed the beautiful satin that encased her breasts. He gently ran his hands along her soft flesh and felt his cock twitch when her nipples hardened.

Samantha closed her eyes and arched her back to push her breasts firmer into his touch. She whispered, "Please."

AJ leaned over her and kissed her tenderly on her temple.

"I want you," he whispered.

She moaned and whispered again, "Please make love to me."

He took her mouth again and covered her body with his. The warmth of his skin fled to her body and a tremor of excitement raced up his spine. She wrapped her arms around him and a small shiver sprang from her touch as more doubt abandoned his mind. She wanted him too, he could feel it.

She encircled his thighs with hers and rocked her hips forward against his heavy erection. The moist heat escaping her body spread along his cock and he nearly lost his control.

He pressed his arousal against her mound and growled as he nibbled his way down her neck. He raised his head and looked at her beautiful breasts. God, he wanted her. He closed his eyes and whispered, "Is this right?"

He opened his eyes and locked his gaze with hers. "Tell me this is what you want."

"This is what I want," she said.

He dragged his parted lips over her collarbone and circled her nipple with his tongue before he sucked her breast into his mouth. He supported his weight with his left hand as his right explored her mound. He slid his fingers into her slit and began a synchronized dance as his middle finger teased her clit and his tongue played with her nipple.

"I need you," she whispered.

Her voice was so soft he thought perhaps she hadn't intended for him to hear her. Her declaration of her vulnerability strengthened his desire to take her, to protect her, to care for her. The need was strong in him too and he loosened the reins on his control to show her he felt the same.

He heard her moan softly and increased his movements. When she pressed her hips into his hand he drove two fingers into her passage.

"Yes!" She dug her nails into the carpet beneath her and he smiled to see her reaction to his touch. "Oh God, AJ, don't stop."

He abandoned her breast and nibbled a path to her clit. When he sucked the delicate nub into his mouth her legs began to vibrate. He flicked it with his tongue and reveled in her loss of control.

"Yes!" She wrapped her legs around his shoulders and dug her heels into his back.

Her taste was intoxicating. He couldn't get enough. It was just like... He pushed his thoughts aside and sucked harder. When her whole body began to convulse he held her pussy tight to his mouth and rode out her orgasm.

He gently lapped at the sweet arousal that poured from her and kissed the juncture of her legs before he sat back to roll on a condom. Before her limbs had settled completely he slowly pressed himself into her.

Her body molded to his when he rocked twice and sheathed himself fully into her. The feel of her softness as she drew him inside her made his heart quiver. It had been so long since he felt this kind of acceptance, this kind of true connection with a woman.

He began a slow rhythm and watched her breasts move as he grazed her nipples with his chest. The feel of her beneath him was euphoric because for this moment in time she belonged to him.

"Take me," he whispered. "Take all that I have to give."

She wrapped her arms around his shoulders and dug her nails into his flesh. She closed her eyes and opened her mouth with a soft sigh. Her lips moved without a sound but her message was clear.

'I need you. I've missed this so much.'

Was she thinking of another man? Perhaps the one she had loved so much, the one who had hurt her so deeply. The need to protect her rose fiercely in AJ's heart and he increased the speed of his thrusts. She would know that he cared for her. He would show her he would never betray her heart.

Her body tightened around him and his climax drew closer. The need to possess her became as necessary as his next breath. His soul was demanding the possession of her heart.

"Take me!"

Samantha matched his rhythm and he watched her breasts move with their frantic thrusts. He was close. He reached between them and pinched her clit. Her body tightened further around his flesh and tremors rippled through his spine.

"Take me, Jackie! Take me!" He thrust hard again and exploded. His body jerked with the aftershocks of his release.

He collapsed on top of her and pulled her with him as he rolled to his back. His breathing was labored as she curled against him and laid her head on his shoulder. He felt a hot tear touch his skin and his words echoed in his mind.

'Take me, Jackie! Take me!'

His blood ran cold and self-loathing engulfed him. Words escaped him. What could he say to make it right?

Samantha lay quietly against him and held him tight to her. She had to have heard him. She couldn't have missed it. But she wasn't pulling away.

Another hot tear dropped to his chest and pain seared him. She had heard him, and she chose to ignore it. Maybe he could too. It was just a slip of the tongue. The heat of passion fogged his mind and he had said Jackie's name because she had been dominating his dreams. It meant nothing. It would never happen again.

****

AJ sat behind his desk and leaned on his forearms while he tried to make sense of the data in front of him, but the guilt clawing at his conscience had consumed his thoughts. After he'd made love to Samantha he'd carried her to the couch where they had lain in each other's arms for nearly an hour. Neither of them had spoken and he'd taken the opportunity to memorize the feel of her skin next to his.

He kept telling himself he'd made love to her for the right reasons, that it had nothing to do with Jackie's memory. Samantha was beautiful and smart. What sane man wouldn't want to make love to her? And she had kissed him first. He rolled his eyes. He sounded like his five year old self declaring to his mother that he hadn't started the fight between him and his brother.

Eventually he had summoned enough courage to speak and asked her if she needed anything. The awkwardness of his question made him wince. He had sounded like a butler asking her if she needed him to do anything else for her. She had politely shaken her head and dressed in silence.

'Good God, old man, you're an idiot. You just fucked her brains out while you called her Jackie then ask her if she needed anything else. What the hell did you expect her to say?'

He looked up at Samantha. She was sitting at the far end on the leather davenport typing up another summary of one of the many studies she'd found on Dementia. Her knowledge and clinical understanding of the condition was impressive.

The first time she'd done it he had smiled and accepted her help to avoid offending her. But after he had read both the study and her summary he was impressed by how much she had actually understood. The details she had pulled from the article and highlighted in her summary were what he would have chosen as the key elements to focus on.

She looked up at him and smiled.

"Do you need my help with something?" she said.

"No." AJ sat back in his chair. "I was thinking I should tell you about my meeting yesterday with Daniel, Charles, and David," he lied.

"Did they find anything?" Samantha put her laptop on the cushion beside her and moved to the winged back chair next to his desk.

"Yes. But… I don't want you to worry about it."

He spun his chair to face her squarely. "What they found could be used in our favor, or it could be used against us."

She folded her arms under her breasts and he suppressed a moan.

"AJ, I've run with the big dogs. I need to know what's going on. My career is in just as much jeopardy as yours."

"You're right." He hesitated and when she raised an eyebrow he continued. "The money has been deposited into a Swiss account and the last transfer was made from a computer in Central Valley's system."

"That's not so terrible. Central Valley is a huge system and Douglas could have made those wire transfers as well as either of us. In fact, he would've had easier access than you."

"Yes. But you had access to him. You could have used his computer, maybe discovered his passwords. Any number of theories can be crafted to explain how you did this at my direction."

"The transactions would have date and time stamps. There's bound to be at least one of them that was made when neither one of us was in the office."

"Actually, that's where the problem comes in."

"What do you mean?"

"The last transaction was made just after 6:00 a.m. on the Saturday before we left for Las Vegas. The same Saturday when you and I were meeting in my office."

"Well, maybe Douglas was there. Did they check the security logs? He could have come in after I left for your office. I didn't go back to my office when I left yours. I went straight home."

He rubbed his temples. A slight headache was forming beneath his fingertips.

"They checked," he said.

He watched her shoulders slump.

"He wasn't there was he?" she said.

"No."

She sighed. "Then someone else is taking the money."

"It would appear that way but Douglas is pointing his influential fingers at us. And so far half of the board is leaning toward him. He only needs one more vote to tip the scales and force them to press charges with the authorities."

He watched her swallow hard and almost regretted telling her. But she needed to know and he needed her intellect on his side.

She lifted her chin and narrowed her gaze. "I've let him get away with too much already. He's going to make a mistake sooner or later. Men like him always do. And when he does I'll be waiting with the hammer. I can't wait to nail that bastard to the wall."

Fourteen

AJ stood outside Sarah's door and looked over the last note Dr. Hanson had made in her chart. Hanson was resisting every recommendation AJ was making via Edna, and that was frustrating the hell out of him.

He had met Dr. Hanson several years ago at one of the presentations he'd done on his research for Central Valley, and the man had come across as a shallow windbag. He was the type of doctor AJ hated to explain his findings to, because if they couldn't follow what he said the first time, they argued that his logic was wrong instead of simply asking him to clarify it. On the other hand, AJ rather enjoyed proving them wrong in front of the rest of their colleagues. He figured he must have done that to Hanson at some point, since he seemed determined to take Sarah's care in a completely different direction.

Edna poked him in the ribs and whispered, "Here comes the snitch. Get in there, quick."

He rapped his knuckles on the door and slipped inside. He closed the door quietly behind him and left Edna in the hallway. Sarah's soft humming drew his attention and he saw her sitting in her rocking chair by the window. He smiled to see the peaceful look on her face, even though he was pretty sure she wasn't in the here and now.

The door nudged him and he stepped out of the way as Edna slipped in and closed the door without a sound.

"The snitch has moved on. I told her I was going over Sarah's meds and that I'd be a while. But we don't have much time. Dr. Hanson should be here soon."

AJ looked at her and smiled.

"Thank you," he said. He turned back and looked at Sarah. "How has she been today?"

"Well, that depends on your point of view. She's been very happy and content but she's living in her memories of about twenty-five years ago."

"Maybe she needed the break. Peace can help heal her mind too."

"Wherever she is today it sounds beautiful. There's an old oak tree in the backyard and the leaves have fallen. She talked about raking the leaves so her little girl could jump in them but the wind keeps blowing them around the yard." Edna grunted. "She seems to be delighted to rake them again but I'd be damn annoyed and tell my daughter to go play with her dolls."

A memory of Jackie flashed in AJ's mind. They were sitting up against the oak tree in her mother's backyard. It was a cool fall day and he held her on his lap under a fleece blanket. Piles of leaves littered the yard and a rake sat on the ground next to them. They had just taken a break from cleaning up the yard for her mother.

He remembered the high he got from holding her so close. The need to do it again suddenly surfaced and he barely stopped the moan that was about to escape him.

"Oh well, at least she's not ornery today," Edna said.

Her voice jolted him back to reality and he watched her gather Sarah's medications to fill her organizer. She left him standing in the middle of the room and sat down at the far end to complete her task.

AJ walked quietly toward Sarah. He watched her smile broaden as she looked at him and spoke.

"I'm so glad you aren't working late again, Bill. Your little girl has missed you so much."

AJ sat next to her and took a minute to think. Bill was Sarah's ex-husband who left her many years ago. She had obviously regressed to a time before things had gone wrong in their marriage. AJ decided to play along so that he could evaluate her current state. If he upset her, she would most likely become combative and this visit would be a lost opportunity.

"I have missed her as well, Sarah. I will try to spend more time with her."

She reached over and squeezed his hand.

"You've said that before, my dear, but this is the first time you've made it home before ten in months. I think I'll have to speak to that secretary of yours and tell her to make sure you leave the office on time more often."

"That might be a good idea."

AJ squeezed her hand back and thought about how to approach his questions. He remembered a conversation he'd had with Sarah several years ago when he first took on her case. She had told him about how difficult her divorce had been on her daughter. She regretted not shielding her more, but when Sarah had discovered Bill's infidelity that had gone on for years with his secretary, she had let her pain and anger consume her. Sarah hadn't thought about what it was doing to her daughter as she had stood by and watched her parents fight bitterly.

Sarah looked out the window again. "She just loves jumping in those leaves. They'll need raked again soon."

"I can do that for her, Sarah. But first I want to see how your day is going."

She kept her gaze out the window. "My day has been fine. Although, I'm a little behind on the laundry. I just know if I hang the sheets out there that little spitfire will have them a dirty mess in no time." She sighed. "She loves to run through those too."

"Yes, she is her mother's daughter."

"No, no. She is just like her father, bullheaded and full of determination."

AJ crossed his legs. "So what else have you done today?"

Her smiled faded. "Most everything else I wanted to do, I think. But I've been kind of tired today and I get the feeling I'm forgetting something. So, I thought if I sat for a while it might come to me."

AJ uncrossed his legs and reached for her hand. "Are you not feeling well, Sarah? Is there something I can get for you?"

She squeezed his hand again. "No, dear, I just need to rest. I'll be fine."

AJ tried to do some quick math in his head. If she was remembering feeling tired on such an otherwise happy day it may have some significance. Perhaps she was remembering early symptoms of dementia, some that might have been present before her brain injury. If he could determine a more accurate onset of her disease he might be able to tailor her treatment more effectively.

AJ felt a hand on his shoulder. He turned to see Edna standing behind him.

She whispered, "I'm sorry to bother you, Dr. Carrington, but we need to cut this short. Dr. Hanson will be here any minute. I have to get you out of here before he sees you."

AJ nodded his agreement and turned to Sarah. "I think it is a good time for me to rake those leaves. You stay here and rest. I will see you later."

Sarah kissed the back of his hand. "Thank you, dear. I'm going to close my eyes for a while."

AJ watched her lay her head back against the high back chair and close her eyes. The peaceful look she had when he walked in was still on her face. Despite her current state of mind he felt good to be leaving her in a peaceful mood. At least for now she was happy.

****

AJ waited for Samantha to return from the ladies room as he sat at the table for two in a secluded corner of the Red Door. The five star restaurant was Lincoln's premier private dinner club. Central Valley purchased annual memberships for all the department heads, but AJ only used his when he was asked to court investors, otherwise he usually ate at home alone.

The restaurant was divided into two sections as you came in the front doors. If you went through the archway to the left you entered the area the hospital used for business meetings and conferences. The décor was elegant but platonic. Bright lights and large tables were arranged to accommodate crowds of six or more, and a well-stocked bar ran the full length of the wall on the far side of the room. AJ was familiar with that side. He had seen more than a dozen contracts negotiated for the hospital at one of those tables.

The dining room to the right was for smaller, more intimate gatherings. Most of the tables accommodated only two, so AJ had never been in this half of the Red Door before. It wasn't that he had an aversion to fine dining, he just didn't care for the way the atmosphere emphasized the fact that he was alone in this world.

The tables were generously spaced apart from one another and soft violin music muffled the occasional voice that carried. Each table had a small candelabrum and discreet recessed lighting above to provide just enough light to read the menu comfortably.

AJ watched an elderly couple as they were led to a table near the entrance. The man smiled when the maître d seated his wife then kissed the back of her hand. The affection he had for his wife was evident in his expression. He loved her.

A subtle feeling of envy surfaced and he looked away. The scene was remarkably similar to the vision he had embraced when Jackie was the center of his life. He had let himself believe they were going to grow old together. But that wasn't his destiny, at least not with her, and hopefully one day his mind would actually accept it.

Maybe tonight he could start a new chapter in his life, one with Samantha at his side. He knew he was falling for her, almost as hard as he fell for Jackie. But with Samantha the bond could be stronger. She could understand his past, the pain he suffered with Jackie's betrayal. He smiled and looked at the elderly couple again. Maybe he could have that dream after all, and if he played his cards right, it could start tonight.

Samantha had worked late at the hospital and agreed to meet him here. Today had been a cold and dreary day and he had felt a bit tired before he left home, but when he saw her walk in the restaurant excitement rushed through his limbs. It felt good to treat her like she was special. His smile broadened and he tapped his fingers on the table. Yes. His happily ever after was going to start tonight.

AJ had ordered a bottle of wine and an appetizer

with several varieties of shrimp. They were being delivered to the table when Samantha returned.

"Oh, you read my mind. Shrimp cocktail is my favorite." She sat down and let the waiter push her chair in for her.

"I was hoping you did. Their seafood is hard to beat." He smiled at her and waited while she asked the waiter for recommendations.

A small flash of light caught his attention and he looked to see a couple being seated two tables behind her. The woman's diamond bracelet sparkled as she walked through a gentle beam of light. When the man turned to sit AJ recognized him. He couldn't remember his name but he knew the man was one of the administrators at Central Valley. The young woman he was with was familiar too, and AJ was pretty sure it wasn't his wife.

He sighed. The amount of infidelity that occurred at the top of the food chain in that hospital was sickening. Not only was it condoned, but it was encouraged, especially by Douglas.

AJ looked at Samantha as she chewed her bottom lip and perused the menu. Everyone thought she was one of the players in that despicable game. Even he had believed it at one point. Now he knew better. She was a victim of the gossip fueled by Jameson's twisted plot to frame her as his accomplice.

She had been mistreated by so many at the top. Her reputation had been forged out of lies perpetrated by Douglas and his cronies. She was misjudged because of her beauty and it continued because of her good nature to try and move past it.

He thought back to the other day when he had made love to her. He had called her Jackie. He'd convinced himself he wasn't like the others, that he hadn't used her to forget the past. He told himself that he had wanted to make love to her. But did she know that? They hadn't talked about what he'd said. He couldn't find the right words, and since she hadn't brought it up he had hoped to forget about it.

He groaned internally. He really wasn't very good at relationships, but if he wanted to make a fresh start with Samantha tonight, he needed to start with a clean slate. He waited while the waiter took her order then spoke when they were alone again.

"Samantha, I need to apologize to you. I have been putting it off, hoping that I could just forget about it, but…"

She smiled. "What could you possibly have to apologize for?"

"The other morning I said something I shouldn't have. I made a terrible mistake."

He watched some of the color drain from her cheeks.

"AJ, I think I know what you're going to say, and it's really not necessary."

He stared at the empty plate in front of him. It was painful to look her in the eye and admit he'd hurt her, but he needed to do this right. He took a deep breath and locked his gaze with hers.

"I don't want you to think I wasn't sincere when we… I wasn't trying to use you. I just…"

"AJ, please, we don't have to talk about this."

"Yes we do… I do. I need you to know I wasn't trying to… I mean I wasn't thinking about… I don't know why I said Jackie's name."

He watched her swallow and he hated the uncomfortable look in her eyes. Now he knew he had to explain to her what had happened. He reached across the table and held her hand gently.

"I need you to understand who Jackie is, or rather who she was. I don't want you to think—"

"You don't owe me any explanations. I'm a big girl, AJ, I wasn't expecting a commitment."

"I'm not talking about a commitment. I'm talking about making sure you know I wasn't using you, Samantha. I hate the thought that I hurt you like other men have."

Samantha maintained her eye contact with him but said nothing, so he continued.

"Jackie was a big part of my life. We were together for a little more than three years. She was my girlfriend while I was completing my undergraduate degree." He huffed out a nervous laugh. "Actually, Jackie was more than just my girlfriend, she was my world. When I fell for her, I fell hard. I had never felt that way about anyone. I thought we were going to be together forever." AJ glanced at the elderly couple.

Samantha cleared her throat and spoke softly. "So, what happened?"

"Honestly… I don't know." He let go of her hand and sat back. A heavy weight settled in his chest. He wasn't sure who this conversation was going to be harder on, him or Samantha. Either way, he couldn't let Jackie stand between them.

"Did you love her?" Samantha's voice was soft, almost a whisper.

AJ hesitated. He had gotten used to talking about Jackie with Warren, but Warren knew what he had gone through. He wasn't sure how much he wanted Samantha to know. He looked down at his salad fork as he ran his finger over the ornate pattern in the silver.

"I loved her more than life itself. I thought she felt the same about me, but it didn't work out that way." He cleared his throat. "One day she just walked away."

"Well, something must have happened. Maybe you did something that hurt her, something that meant more to her than it meant to you."

He shook his head. "I did everything for her, Samantha. If Jackie even thought she wanted something, it was hers. I moved heaven and earth to make her happy."

Samantha looked past him toward the door and sighed. "A lot of men think they're making an effort when they're really not."

"You don't know what you're talking about." AJ stopped and took a deep breath. He lowered his voice and said, "Look, Samantha, I don't want to argue about this, I'm just trying to be honest with you. I don't want you to think there's some big, deep, dark secret I'm keeping from you, or that I'm taking our relationship casually while I sleep around with other women."

"I understand." She crossed her arms and looked down at the table.

"Do you?" he said.

She looked up at him.

"I've moved on, Samantha. Jackie isn't a part of

my life anymore… For God's sake, I'm just trying to say I'm sorry…" He leaned his elbows on the table and rested his head in his hands. He took a deep breath and sat back again. "I'm really screwing this up. I wanted this evening to be fun and relaxing, and I'm making a mess of it."

"I told you we didn't have to talk about it."

"You're right. I should have listened to you. I should have just let it go."

She huffed out a sigh. "I understand what you're trying to do and I appreciate that you want to make things right, but surely you realize how illogical you sound. I mean seriously, a woman doesn't just walk away from the man she loves because of something trivial."

AJ looked at Samantha. She didn't believe him, and she probably never would. Yet she wanted to move on like nothing immoral had happened. He wondered how many men had betrayed her to make her lower her expectations to the point where being called another woman's name at the pinnacle of sex was okay.

Had any man treated her like the beautiful and incredible woman she was? He doubted it because she obviously didn't trust men to love her without betraying her at some point. Or maybe the one who had left the scar had succeeded in completely destroying her self-worth.

His heart ached and his hope of starting fresh with her was fading. It was obvious this conversation was bringing up bad memories for both of them. But he needed to see it through to the end. He needed her to know he hadn't betrayed

Jackie and that he wouldn't betray her either.

"The night she walked away from me, Samantha, something happened, or so I've been told. There was a formal event for my fraternity and a big party at the house afterwards." He shook his head. "But I have no memory of that night. In fact the whole day is a blur. I've remembered bits and pieces over the past thirteen years but nothing about what must have happened, except…"

"Except what?" Samantha's voice was softer.

"I don't know if they are memories or not but I have these dreams about Jackie. She keeps telling me that I betrayed her, but I don't know what she's talking about. I was never unfaithful to her…and then I have to watch her walk away all over again."

AJ saw his hand tremble and he placed both of them on his thighs to hide it from Samantha. Maybe he wasn't ready to tell her about this.

Samantha crossed her arms over her midsection and looked away. "Maybe you regret what you did and you can't bring yourself to accept it."

"I suppose you're right." He combed his fingers through his hair. "I shouldn't have brought this up. I wanted tonight to be a fresh start, not a painful trip down memory lane." He sighed. "I just wanted you to know I didn't mean to hurt you." He looked her in the eyes. "I want to make things right between us."

"We don't need to talk about this to make things right between us. We can move forward by letting go of the past."

"The past? Samantha, I'm talking about making right what I did two days ago."

"I'm just saying it doesn't matter to me. I know you care about me. I don't feel threatened by the memory of an old girlfriend you let walk away. You obviously didn't love her enough to go after her, so why should I feel threatened by her memory?"

"I didn't just let her walk away from me!" AJ took a quick breath. "I spent months looking for her. I talked to her friends every day, asking where I could find her. I even went to see her mother and begged her to tell me where I could find Jackie… But you want to know something? Jackie had mysteriously vanished." He snapped his fingers. "Just like that. And as amazing as it sounds, no one knew what had happened to her."

AJ could feel the pain of the past spreading through his chest. Maybe he wasn't over Jackie. He closed his eyes and lowered his head. Would he ever be able to let go of his love for her? He opened his eyes and kept his gaze lowered.

"The day I finally realized I needed to let her go was the day her mother refused to file a missing person report." He smiled sadly. "That was the day I realized what a fool I'd been. Everyone knew where she was… Everyone except me. That was the day I realized she wasn't coming back to me."

"I'm sorry," she whispered.

"Don't be," he said.

He couldn't look at her. This night was a disaster and it was all his doing. He had wanted to treat Samantha to a wonderful evening. She had helped him so much since his life had been turned upside down and he wanted to show her how much he appreciated her. Then he was foolish enough to think this night could mark the beginning of a lifelong love affair. But instead, he started an argument about an old girlfriend he just couldn't seem to let go of no matter how much he wanted to. And on top of that he reminded Samantha of her own painful past. God, he was still such a fool. He cleared his throat and continued.

"I'm the one who ruined this evening and I think it would be best if I just called it a night."

He pulled out his wallet.

"No, AJ, don't go. I'm sorry about what I said. I didn't mean it." She reached across the table and grasped his hand. "Please stay."

The warmth of her soft skin penetrated his body and he wanted to wrap himself around her, but she deserved better than a man who couldn't let go of the past. Samantha was right. He needed to let go of the past before they could move forward. He swallowed hard.

"I'm sorry, Samantha, this just isn't going to work. You deserve a better man."

AJ dropped several large bills on the table and walked away. When he stepped into the cold November night the wind stung his cheeks. He turned his collar up and walked briskly to his car. He needed to get home before he changed his mind. If he gave in to his desire for Samantha he was just going to keep hurting her, and he would be damned if he was going to join the ranks of men who had used her.

****

AJ walked down the middle of the trail that led

from the campus to the fraternity house. The leaves had fallen and blown into small piles that littered the path. He watched the colorful pieces scatter as he gently kicked them out of his way. The cool air from the breeze that rushed toward him swirled a kaleidoscope of foliage around him as it drifted down from the tree tops. He looked up at the clear blue sky and took a deep breath. The cool fall air filled his lungs and he smiled. It was his favorite time of year. He dropped his head to see his way forward and Samantha stood in the path in front of him.

"AJ, why did you leave me?"

Her beauty robbed him of speech. The subtle changes were breathtaking. Her cheeks were fuller, brighter, and her eyes sparkled with the most striking color of blue. Her face was more stunning than ever. The sun streamed through the tops of the trees and glistened in her hair where streaks of auburn mingled with her usual blonde color.

He reached up to caress her cheek and she leaned her face into his hand. Her soft skin was warm against his touch. He stepped closer to her.

"I hurt you, Samantha."

"No. He hurt us, AJ." She locked her gaze with his and the blue of her eyes swirled with a deep emerald green. "Tell me you love me and I will believe you."

"I do love you. But I love Jackie too."

"That's why we can be together. Don't you see? Love is all we need to make things right."

Samantha combed her fingers into his hair and kissed him. She pressed her body against his and her warmth enveloped him.

He wrapped his arms around her and returned every kiss with the same intensity. God, he wanted her. She was pure ecstasy. He knew he shouldn't let this happen, but he wanted her too much to stop it.

He broke the kiss to catch his breath and pushed her head to his shoulder. He caressed her hair and spoke softly.

"Don't let me do this, Samantha. I don't want to hurt you."

The leaves rustled behind him and he turned around.

Jackie stood in the path. Her long auburn hair danced in the gentle breeze, streaks of blonde flashed in the rays of sunlight.

'Love is all we need, AJ.'

Samantha was gone and the whole world contracted to him and Jackie. His heart nearly burst from his chest and he took a step toward her.

'Yes, Jackie. Our love will get us through this.'

He wrapped his arms around her before she could vanish. He kissed her as he spoke. He couldn't wait another second to do either.

'She knows how much I love you. I told her last night.' He leaned his forehead against hers. 'Don't leave me this time. I can't watch you walk away again. Please.'

He dug his fingers into her hair and held on for dear life. He kissed her harder with an urgency he couldn't deny. She had to stay this time, she just had to.

'Our love is too strong to deny.' Samantha's voice came from behind him.

'No,' he whispered. He cradled Jackie's face in his hands. 'I love you, Jackie. Stay with me. We can get through this. We can work things out together.'

'You walked away from me, AJ,' Samantha said. 'I need you to come back.'

He hugged Jackie again and took a deep breath, but her red satin dress fell limp in his arms. She had vanished from his embrace.

'NO!'

He spun around and looked at Samantha. The pain in his chest was suffocating. 'What am I doing wrong? Why won't Jackie stay with me?'

'They tore us apart.' A tear ran down her cheek. 'So much has changed. We're so different now, but our love is just as strong. We need you to bring us back together. Your love can do that.'

'No. I need Jackie. Please, tell me how to make her stay.'

'She saw you making love to her,' Samantha said. 'He told her you didn't love us anymore. Tell me you love us and everything will be just like it used to be.'

He grabbed Samantha by the shoulders. 'That's a lie! I never betrayed her!'

Pain rushed through his head and he screamed in agony as he let go of her and dropped to his knees. A gust of wind blew between them and he looked up at her. Her hair tangled in the rush of cold air. The red satin material of her dress quivered wildly around her legs.

Lightning flashed across the sky and Jesse appeared next to Samantha. He wrapped his arms around her and laid a knife against her chest as he *pulled her away.*

*'Don't touch her!' AJ stood and ran toward her,
but pain gripped his body and he fell again to his
knees. Lightning flashed and he was alone. Thunder
rolled across the sky and darkness surrounded him.
In an instant the earth fell away and pulled him into
nothingness.*

AJ woke suddenly as he sat up. His breathing
was labored and he struggled to free himself from
his trusses. The top sheet was wrapped around his
legs and he kicked wildly until he was free. He
scrambled to his feet and scanned the dark room for
Jackie. The sound of his heartbeat thundered in his
ears and the pain in his chest was nearly impossible
to bear. He could still feel her in his arms, the
warmth of her body next to his. She had to be here.

He rubbed his eyes with the heels of his hands
and looked again. His sight was adjusting to the
dark and he realized he was in his bedroom...
Jackie wasn't here. He hadn't held her against him,
and he hadn't kissed her.

He leaned his head against the wall behind him
and swallowed the pain welling up in his throat. It
wasn't real. It was just a dream. He absently rubbed
the tightness in his chest. How many times could he
lose Jackie before it killed him?

He slowly paced the length of his bedroom until
his heart rate began to drop. A shiver ran up his
spine and he noticed a fine sheen of sweat had
gathered on his skin. He ran his hands through his
damp hair then sat down beside his nightstand.

His dream was still fresh in his mind. He should

be writing it down, but he couldn't get himself to care. It was useless. He was never going to figure this out.

He looked at the clock, 3:03 a.m. Fatigue weighed heavy on his limbs and he dropped back onto the bed. He didn't want to sleep. He didn't want to see her again. It was too painful.

He forced his body to move and peeled off his damp shirt and boxers on his way to the shower. When he stepped under the hot spray he leaned his forehead against the cool tile and let the water beat down on his shoulders.

He didn't know how long he had stood there but when the water started to cool off he quickly lathered his hair and body and got out before it gave him a chill.

There was still no light coming in from behind his drapes when he walked back into his bedroom and the clock proudly displayed the time, 3:55 a.m. He pulled on sweatpants and a T-shirt, grabbed his phone, and headed to the kitchen.

Two hours later he had consumed nearly three pots of coffee and every fruit and vegetable in his refrigerator had been cut, bagged and packed into the freezer. His pantry had been restacked and every inch of the room had been cleaned spotless.

He checked his watch, 6:02 a.m. Warren was probably up by now, but even if he wasn't, AJ couldn't wait any longer. He was about to lose his mind.

He pulled out his phone and dialed.

"You're damn lucky the X-man is an early riser or I'd have to skin you alive for calling at this

hour."

"Sorry." AJ hesitated. "I can't do this anymore, Warren. I have to find someone who can tell me what happened. I think that's the only way to stop them."

"How bad was this one?"

"Bad." He swallowed hard. "They're starting to merge into one woman. Nothing is making sense anymore. This time Jesse took Samantha...I think."

"You're connecting Samantha to Jesse? Are you afraid that whatever you did to Jackie you're going to do to Samantha?"

"How the fuck should I know? I don't remember what happened."

"I know that, AJ. But you're remembering new pieces to the puzzle with each dream."

"They're not memories. They're twisted pieces of shit my mind is using to drive me insane."

"I don't think so. Your subconscious is giving you clues. We just have to figure this out."

"I can't wait that long. Give me some names and numbers. I don't care who it is. I'll talk to anyone who might know something."

"I'll give you a copy of the list I'm using." Warren sighed. *"How long have you been up?"*

"Since about three."

"Christ, AJ, why didn't you call me?"

"Why? Because I think Marie might've had an issue with that."

"She's worried about you too. She would've understood." He paused. *"Look, I marked the list to show which brothers I've already spoken to, but they all swear they don't know anything. I have two*

more I'm waiting to hear back from. One of them is Mike Hollister. I think he's our best chance of finding out anything so I'm hoping he'll call me today. Why don't you spend the day with Samantha? You need a distraction."

AJ scrunched his face and rubbed his temples. That was the last thing he needed. "I don't think that's such a good idea. I ruined dinner last night and honestly... I think seeing her is making the dreams worse."

"What do you mean?"

"The dreams seem to get worse every time I see her. I care about her, Warren. I think I might love her, but... Jackie's memory is getting in the way. I can't do that to Samantha."

"Hang in there, Golden Boy. I'll stop over tonight and let you know what I find out today."

"Thanks."

AJ ended the call and dropped his phone to the counter. Hopefully he had enough cleanser, if not he'd probably start painting his condo to keep from falling asleep.

Fifteen

Douglas looked at the schedule Dr. Jackson had submitted to the ER for the month of November. Warren was finally at full staff which meant he would be in his office instead of the ER covering the gaps. Which also meant it was going to be harder for Douglas to get that damn pen in AJ's office.

Mercedes had made sure someone was camped out in Carrington's office day and night. Bitch! She needed to mind her own damn business and learn her place. Since no one else seemed willing to do something about that it was time he did.

Douglas paced to the window behind his desk and looked at the people hurrying across the courtyard. The wind had picked up and the winter temperatures were settling in.

Two young ladies rushed from one building to

the next holding their thin sweaters tight around them. He smiled at their discomfort. Their nipples would be rock hard and most definitely showing through the thin layers of clothing they were wearing.

He reached inside his pocket and shifted his cock when it twitched. They could use a good, hard fuck too. That's all women were good for anyway. They'd spread their legs for any dick as long as he whispered in their ear what they wanted to hear.

The blonde turned around and he recognized Samantha. He scowled. The stupid bitch should've been barred from the hospital campus. How many times did he have to discredit the brazen whore before they realized she was worthless? He watched her guide a wisp of hair from her face that had blown across her mouth and he sneered. She obviously sucked a few more dicks on the board for them to vote to keep her on staff. It was time to take matters into his own hands.

His phone hummed as it vibrated against the polished walnut of his desk. He answered the call without taking his eyes from the two young women.

"Jameson."

"It's time for another installment."

Douglas smiled. "It's the little messenger boy. Tell Vasquez I've got it ready but I want negotiate a change in the contract."

"The time for negotiations has passed. The arrangements have already been made."

"Tell him I'll make it worth his while. I have another obstacle I want eliminated."

"That would require a new agreement, my good

doctor. Vasquez does not negotiate commenced contracts."

"Just tell him I want the Assistant Administrator out of my way before the end of the week. He can worry about Carrington later."

Douglas got no response and he looked at his phone to check the connection. The call was still live.

"Did you hear me? I want Sam—"

"I heard you, good doctor. Bring the payment with another twenty percent to the exchange location in thirty minutes. Don't be late."

Douglas grinned in triumph as he heard the line go dead. He'd pay any price Vasquez wanted, especially if he got to watch the bitch die.

****

AJ stared blindly at the report in front of him. The data swam in nauseating patterns as he struggled to stay awake. He had nodded off once but the brief slumber was restless. He got up and started pacing the room.

His phone vibrated against his thigh and he answered the call on the first ring. He didn't care who it was, talking would keep him awake.

"Carrington."

"AJ, it's Daniel. Mercedes' people traced a withdrawal from the Swiss account about ten minutes ago. The transaction originated from the computer in your office."

"I thought she was having my office watched. How did someone get in there?"

"That's the six million dollar question, now isn't

it? She's having the security tapes reviewed. But her goon claims no one got past him today."

"Well, at least they know it wasn't me. I haven't been near my office in almost three weeks."

"Neither has Jameson. But Mercedes has had a big smile on her face all day today, and you know how much she's gunning for the money whore. She is up to something and I'm just glad she's on our side. I would not want to piss that woman off."

AJ smiled for the first time since he woke up at three o'clock this morning. Daniel Rosenfeld wasn't afraid of anything, least of all women. But if AJ wasn't so damned tired he would swear there was a bit of genuine fear in Daniel's voice.

"Let me know if I can do anything to help."

"You just stay put and let Mercedes do her thing. You do not want to get caught in her crossfire. Besides, I think you might need a bit of rest you sound exhausted."

AJ's smile faded. "I'll see what I can do."

"Make it happen, AJ. One of us will call you later."

AJ listened to the line disconnect and he dropped his phone onto his desk. If it was only that simple, he'd be sleeping right now. He scratched the stubble on his cheek and headed for the stairs. Maybe a cold shower would wake him up.

****

AJ's house was clean from top to bottom, including himself. The cold shower had helped keep him awake, but daylight was fading, and with it so was his strength. Warren had called and said he was on his way. AJ rubbed his temples and sent a prayer heavenward that Warren had something useful to tell him.

He heard Warren come through the front door and waited. He looked out the window and kept his gaze on the dismally brown fall colors adorning his backyard. When he heard Warren's footsteps halt at the threshold he spoke.

"Please tell me you know something… anything."

"I'm sorry, AJ, either no one wants to talk about it or they honestly don't know what happened."

"What about Mike? Did he get back to you?"

"Yeah. He swears he doesn't know anything. I don't know if I believe him but it doesn't matter. If he does, he's not talking."

"Did you talk to Jesse? He and Mike were best friends. If Mike knows something then you know damn well Jesse does, and if Mike isn't talking, maybe Jesse will."

"Jesse was MIA until I talked to Mike. He told me Jesse is serving time in prison for drug trafficking."

"Somehow that doesn't surprise me."

AJ sighed and closed his eyes. The familiar burn from lack of sleep was therapeutic. Sometimes you had to feel pain before you could feel better. He turned around and faced Warren.

"Jesus, AJ, you look like shit."

"Thanks for reaffirming that for me. I appreciate it." AJ dropped back into the leather chair at his desk and threw a swallow of bourbon to the back of his throat.

"You have to let me find Jackie," Warren said. "We need to hear her side of the story. It's the only solution we haven't tried yet."

"No."

Warren walked to his desk and grabbed the edge. He leaned toward AJ. "Why are you being so stubborn about this? These dreams have to stop. Have you looked in a mirror lately? This is killing you, AJ. You want me to help you but I can't do that until I find out what she knows... Let me talk to her."

"No." He carelessly dropped his glass onto his desk and shook his head. "I can't believe I lost a whole fucking day of my life and Jackie is the only one who knows what happened."

"AJ, I'm out of options. She's the only one I haven't talked to."

AJ saw the frustration on Warren's face. He had given him a nearly impossible task.

"I can't do it, Warren. I can't watch her walk away from me again."

"You don't have to watch anything. I don't need you to be there when I talk to her."

AJ huffed out a sarcastic laugh. "And you seriously think I won't be following you just to get a glimpse of her?"

"So what are you going to do? Watch her walk away every night in your dreams instead? Or do you plan on finding a way to live without sleep?"

"I'll find another way to deal with this."

"There is no other way, AJ," Warren yelled. "You think you're the only one who's had his heart cut out by a woman? It happens every day. Suck it up!"

AJ jumped to his feet and matched Warren's challenge. "I love her—loved her! I gave her everything. All she had to do was ask and it was hers... For three years I devoted my life to her and because of one night that I can't even remember she threw it all back in my face!"

Warren relaxed his posture. "I know that, AJ, I lived in that house for the same three years. I saw how you were with her. I know what she meant to you. But you have to admit something had to have happened. Jackie would never have walked away from you without a damn good reason because she loved you just as much."

"Obviously not."

"She loved you, AJ, and you know it. She took a lot of shit from the guys because they couldn't have her."

"What are you talking about?"

"She was an untouchable because she belonged to you, but that didn't stop them from wanting her. And because they couldn't have her, they cut her out of everything. Didn't you ever notice how the room fell silent every time she walked in?"

AJ dropped his head. He had, and it used to drive him crazy. They talked to all the other girlfriends, but they treated Jackie like she had leprosy. The only way he could think to deal with it was to keep her away from the other guys as much as he could.

Warren continued, "I imagine she thought they hated her since the only one who did talk to her was Jesse, and all he did was make sleazy come-ons. You honestly think that was easy for her?"

"Jackie was a strong woman. She could handle Jesse... and the rest of them."

"And you think that made it okay, that somehow that made it easy for her? AJ, her self-esteem was battered every time she walked into that house. But she did it anyway, because she did it for you."

AJ looked at him. Warren was right. Jackie had tolerated a lot for him. He had tried so hard to shield her from it all but she wasn't stupid, she knew they treated her differently. AJ had always wondered what was worse for her, the silent treatment or the way Jesse had treated her.

The day AJ had walked into the great room and caught Jesse stroking his dick as he stared at her from across the room, AJ had nearly come unglued. All it took was a look and Jesse knew he was going to pay for tormenting her, but the damage was done. Jackie knew he was taunting her.

Jackie never complained about it, but he knew deep down it had bothered her. She did so much to try and fit in, to make the guys want to include her, but it never worked. They did it because she was his, and as long as she stayed his it never changed.

But thirteen years had passed since she had walked away. Maybe she had moved past it all and she would be willing to talk to him, tell him what he couldn't remember. He could tolerate a little more pain to give Jackie a chance to explain.

"Fine. If you can find Jackie... talk to her. But leave her mother out of this. She's not well and I don't want her dragged into the middle."

Warren sighed. "Okay. I'll see what I can do."

AJ watched Warren walk out of his den and

listened for the front door to close. He closed his eyes and prayed for a peaceful rest. He didn't have the strength to stay awake any longer and he didn't think he could survive another nightmare.

Sixteen

Warren sat at his breakfast table and looked out at the tree-lined backyard. The leaves had gathered near the back corner of the hedges that framed his property. The howling wind from the night before had died down, but every now and then a gust would kick up the telltale symbols of the season and churn them like a tornado. He studied each little storm with analytical eyes and tried to decode the meaning of the swirling leaves in AJ's dreams.

He spooned a bite of mashed peas, or strained carrots, or some such mush that his son seemed to love, and watched as the wind picked up another pile of foliage. The leaves flew higher and higher until a sudden halt to the gust released the fragile bits and they floated gracefully back to earth.

He sighed. The rain in AJ's dreams was another element that had stumped him, as well as the dress getting soaked by the storm. The only parts of the dreams that he could identify as real were the red dress and the oak tree.

The night of the formal had been unseasonably warm, which was the reason Warren had been three hours late for the party. He had spent the time in vain on a pretty brunette's back porch trying to convince her to be his date for the party. By the time he had arrived at the house alone, AJ was already desperately trying to find Jackie.

AJ had looked pale, almost grey, and had occasionally mumbled something incoherent, and that had freaked Warren out. He'd never seen AJ like that but had managed to calm him down by promising to help him search for Jackie. When they finally found her she was in the backyard of her mother's house sitting on a swing under a big oak tree. There had been no wind or rain, and she had changed out of the red dress AJ had bought her for the party.

Before Jackie had left AJ standing in her mother's backyard, Warren had watched her fire questions at him that he didn't seem to have answers to. Warren couldn't hear their voices clearly from where he stood and AJ hadn't made any sense when Warren had tried to talk to him about it later that night. So whatever Jackie had seen or heard that had made her run was a complete mystery.

AJ had shaken visibly when he had walked back to Warren's car that night, and by the time they got back to the house AJ had started vomiting. His sleep was restless and he woke nearly every hour. Warren had sat up the whole night afraid to go to sleep because he wasn't sure AJ wouldn't do something stupid if he woke up alone.

In the morning AJ had awakened with no memory of what had happened that day, even his conversation with Jackie in her mother's backyard was as if it had never happened. When Warren told him what he knew, AJ refused to believe it and spent the whole day looking for a woman who had seemingly vanished from the planet. Each new day AJ started his search over and Warren was forced to watch his best friend slide deeper and deeper into an abyss.

After about a week of searching, AJ had been summoned to Jackie's mother's house to collect items she had said were his. Jackie's apartment had been cleaned out and, according to her mother, no one had seen her since the night of the formal.

Warren had watched him go through the box labeled "AJ's Shit" and when he found the dress crumpled into a ball at the bottom of the box, Warren had expected AJ to lose it. Instead, he had hung it on the back of his closet door where he could see it every day. The day AJ had given up hope of getting Jackie back, the dress had disappeared.

Warren hated Jackie for walking out of AJ's life the way she had. He had deserved better than that, especially from her. AJ was always so serious and "business first" that he never made time for a personal life, that was until Jackie had come along. With her, he had jumped in headfirst and she turned his life upside down without even trying. His focus completely changed from planning his life around his career to planning his life around her. The change in him was so obvious he was forced to endure a fair amount of ribbing from their fraternity brothers.

AJ and Jackie did everything together and he rarely saw one without the other. So it was no surprise AJ had been devastated when she disappeared. Warren had never seen him so lost. It was like watching an empty body with no soul wandering the house and because of it the whole atmosphere had changed. AJ had always been the strong one, the rock that had kept them all grounded, and when Jackie had torn his heart out, they had all felt it.

Warren spooned another portion of mush for the X-man. A squeal and a jerk on the spoon caught his attention. He looked at his son just in time to catch a splotch of baby mash above his eyebrow.

The door opened and he turned to greet Marie as she came in from the garage carrying a small bag from the new outlet store she had planned to check out.

"Hey baby, how'd the shopping go?" he said.

She smiled. "I think I had more fun than you're having."

He looked back at Xavier and sighed when he saw the pattern of mush on the tray that very much resembled a Rorschach ink blot.

"Sorry. I wasn't paying much attention to what he was doing," he said. "Apparently he was trying to tell me he'd had enough."

Marie handed him a warm washcloth and moved

in to take charge of her son's masterpiece.

"What's got you so preoccupied?" she said.

"AJ's nightmares. What else?" He wiped the baby food from his forehead and put the small bowl and spoon in the dishwasher then sat back down at the table.

Marie had their son and his artwork cleaned up so fast it still amazed him. She handed Xavier a Sippy cup and poured herself a drink. She sat across the table from Warren and sighed.

"You know," she said. "I've been thinking about his dreams too. I don't have any ideas about why Samantha is in them but the part with Jackie I think has something to do with change."

"Well, Samantha does change into Jackie." Warren leaned back in his chair.

"Yeah, but, the part that represents change comes with Jackie. The swirling leaves, the wind, the rain. That all represents change doesn't it?"

He shrugged his shoulders. "I guess it could."

"I know I'm not the expert here but I wrote a paper on dreams for my freshman psych class. The element I was assigned to write about was storms. According to the research I found most people who fear storms fear change, because storms represent change. You said Jackie changed his whole life when he fell in love with her. Maybe he's afraid the same thing is going to happen with Samantha and he's using the storm to represent the changes he's afraid of."

"Maybe. But why would Jackie appear with the elements of change instead of Samantha if she's the one he's afraid will change his life?"

Marie smiled. "He's probably trying to make things as obvious as possible to his conscience. You men can be pretty thick sometimes."

He wiggled his eyebrows. "That's because you like me when I'm thick."

Her cheeks turned bright red and he smiled when she tried to hide it.

"I'm trying to be serious, Warren." She crossed her arms. "Maybe what's happening between him and Samantha is too similar to what happened between him and Jackie, or maybe something about Samantha reminds him of Jackie."

"I suppose that's possible. She looked familiar when I first met her but I just couldn't place her. I still feel like I should know her but..." He looked at Marie. "Get your iPad, babe, I want to check something."

He stood and headed for his office. Several boxes littered the floor that were full of memorabilia from college. He had been using it to track down some of their fraternity brothers he hadn't kept in touch with. The yearbook he had used to find Mike Hollister was still sitting on his desk. He grabbed it and headed back into the kitchen.

Marie was browsing through items on her favorite site when he dropped the book on the table.

"You're friends with Samantha on Facebook, right?" He didn't look up and thumbed through the yearbook.

"Yes," she said.

"Good. Bring up her picture, a good one. Preferably a headshot but a full body shot will do too."

"Why?"

"We're going to compare something."

Warren found the picture he was looking for. He studied it a moment and looked up at Marie.

She tapped the surface and a picture of Samantha filled the screen. "Here ya go."

Warren took the iPad and the picture from the yearbook. He placed them side by side and felt his heart pound, just like it did when he finally broke through the wall a trauma patient puts up to protect themselves from the event they are trying to forget.

"Marie, look at this."

Warren slid his chair back and pulled her onto his lap. He hugged her around her waist and waited for her reaction.

She studied the pictures for a minute then said, "Oh, my, God."

Warren buried his face into her hair.

"How am I going to tell him?"

Marie twisted on his lap and kissed the top of his head. "You're not going to tell him." She turned back to the pictures. "She is."

Susan M Baer

Seventeen

"Thank you."

Samantha smiled at the waitress when she put her glass of iced tea on the table. She squeezed the lemon and stirred in the juice absentmindedly while she waited for Marie. They had been friends since Marie's first day as AJ's Executive Assistant. Marie had handled AJ with perfection, and Samantha couldn't help but enjoy watching her get the best of him. A month later, Samantha had run into her in the coffee shop. They laughed lightheartedly together, at AJ's and the other administrator's expense, and had decided to meet once a week to vent. Even though Marie no longer worked at Central Valley they still met weekly for lunch. But now they discussed more pleasant matters rather than the arrogant bastards at CV.

AJ was still a topic they discussed frequently and

Marie knew how Samantha felt about him. Marie also knew how close they were getting. So, hopefully she could help Samantha figure out where to go from here.

Samantha thought about everything AJ had said to her the other night at dinner. When he had talked about Jackie, Samantha could see the pain he felt over losing her. She hadn't expected that. He was so strong she didn't think anything could affect him so deeply, but then she had seen his hands trembling before he'd hid them under the table.

Knowing how much he had loved Jackie, and still loved her, made Samantha want him even more. But first she had to help him forget about Jackie, and to do that she had to help him let go of the past.

He said he couldn't remember his betrayal, but was he telling the truth or did he just not want to admit what he'd done to the woman he loved? AJ loved Jackie, and now he loved Samantha too, she could feel it. But if he could betray Jackie, what would stop him from betraying Samantha?

She sighed. She never thought she'd be in such a bizarre love triangle. She needed to figure out how to fix this mess she'd gotten herself into.

"Hi, Samantha."

She looked up as Marie sat in the chair across from her. Marie's somber expression made her worry.

"Is everything okay?"

"Not really."

"What's wrong?"

Marie looked down and straightened the fork

lying on the table in front of her, then looked back up at Samantha.

"I have two good friends caught up in a Shakespearean drama and there's nothing I can do to help them." Marie sat back and laced her fingers together before she rested her hands on the edge of the table.

Samantha smiled. "Thanks."

"For what?"

"For worrying about me and AJ." She removed the spoon from her tea and took a sip. "That means a lot to me, but there's really not a lot any of us can do except wait."

"No. There's not a lot the rest of us can do. You, however, can fix this by talking to AJ."

"Marie, we've talked this out a million times." Samantha frowned. "Dr. Jameson was excellent at hiding his tracks."

"That's not what I'm talking about. AJ doesn't know what's going on. And quite honestly I see no reason why you haven't been honest with him."

"I have been honest with him. He knows everything I know."

"Really?" Marie crossed her arms and cocked her eyebrows.

"Yes. He does." Samantha set her glass down hard onto the table.

"Hmm. It seems odd then that he wouldn't tell his best friend about the return of an old girlfriend that cut his heart out thirteen years ago." She paused. "It has been thirteen years since you walked away from him, hasn't it, *Jackie*?"

Samantha flinched. She hadn't expected the pain

to be so strong to hear someone call her Jackie. She had locked away the agony of her past when she started using her middle name...Samantha.

She could feel tears burning in the back of her eyes. She needed to hold it together.

"How did you...?"

"Does it really matter?" Marie said.

"Yes." Jackie sucked in a deep breath. "Does AJ know?"

"No. But if you don't tell him I will."

A tear dropped to Jackie's cheek and numbness engulfed her. An ache constricted her throat and she could feel the pain rise to her temples. Time reversed and the world around her vanished. The torment of having half of her soul ripped away flooded back and rippled through her body. She closed her eyes to hide from the ugly memories. But instead of finding sanctuary, the hellish image of AJ's betrayal filled her vision.

She slowly opened her eyes and saw the look of disappointment on Marie's face. Marie didn't understand. AJ had fooled her just like he had fooled everyone else. No one would ever believe he could do something so horrible, so deliberate, and Jackie couldn't blame them. If she hadn't seen it with her own eyes she would never have believed the man she had given her heart to, her soul to, would have ever thrown it away so callously.

Heat rose from her feet and she could feel the fires of hell surround her. Her whole world was burning to the ground and she felt helpless to stop it. And the last friend she had in this world, Marie, had been the one to light the match.

"Please don't," Jackie said. "I swear I'll tell him. I just need some time to…"

"Think up another lie?"

"No!" Jackie wiped the tear from her cheek. "You don't understand," she whispered.

"Then help me understand. Why are you doing this to him?"

"I didn't plan this. I'm not trying to hurt him." Jackie took a deep breath. "I love him, Marie. I never stopped loving him. Even after he…" She swallowed past the pain. "I never expected to get this close to him. But then Dr. Jameson pulled out of the Las Vegas conference and ordered me to go in his place." She paused. "I didn't want to go. I was afraid everything would…"

"Blow up in your face?" Marie frowned.

Jackie crossed her arms. "That's one way to put it."

"Then why did you go?"

"Because my mother needs AJ's research."

Marie rolled her eyes. "His research would have continued with or without the new wing."

Jackie looked at Marie and bit her lip just hard enough to stop the quivering. "I missed him."

"He's been right here for years, Samantha. You've had plenty of opportunities to say hello."

"It's not that simple. I didn't want to fight with him. I just… I wanted to be close to him just one more time." She exhaled. "And the conference was the perfect excuse." Another tear escaped. "Even if he didn't know it was me. I wanted to be a part of his life again, just for a little while."

"Just tell him who you are. For God's sake he

loves you."

Jackie shook her head slowly. "He'll never forgive me. I'll lose him again."

"What do you mean you'll lose him again? You left him."

"No. It wasn't like that."

"Warren told me you disappeared without a trace and that AJ doesn't remember what happened that night."

"It wasn't just one night. He just doesn't remember the night I caught them."

"Tell me what happened," Marie said.

"I can't," Jackie whispered. She couldn't speak the words. The image was still too vivid. Seeing him wrapped around her best friend was a vision she had never been able to erase. She made fists and dug her nails into her palms to keep from sobbing uncontrollably then took a deep breath.

"He loves me again," she continued, "but I'm not Jackie anymore. I'm not the overweight brunette all his friends couldn't stomach long enough to have a conversation with. I know that's why AJ wanted her. She was a petite, blonde, little cheerleader." She raised her chin. "But now I'm Samantha. I'm thinner, I'm blonde, and that's who he loves now." She swallowed hard. "If I tell him I'm Jackie. I'll lose him all over again."

"That doesn't make sense. Warren told me you left AJ. He didn't leave you. And according to him, there was no other woman. Warren said AJ's life revolved around you and he was completely blind to every other woman."

Jackie looked at Marie. "Except her. He didn't

bother to leave me before he started sleeping with her because if her boyfriend had caught them it would've all been over." She squared her shoulders. "It was just like Mike said. They'd been sleeping together for months."

"Samantha, you're not making any sense. AJ is the most honest, straight forward man I know. He would never do that to a woman, especially a woman he loves."

Jackie closed her eyes. "I saw him, Marie. Mike told me he had been messing around with her right under my nose. He said every time I left the house they would run up to AJ's room and... The night of the formal I arrived early. My last class had been cancelled and I wanted to surprise AJ." She glared. "But they surprised me instead."

"Who? What are you talking about?"

"My best friend, Marie." Jackie opened her eyes. "He was..."

"Samantha you have to talk to him. That doesn't sound like AJ."

"So you think I'm lying? I saw him, Marie. I saw the two of them in his bed."

Marie shook her head. "No. There has to be some other explanation. I just can't believe AJ would—"

"Well he did. And the part that makes me really want to hate him is that... I can't hate him." She swallowed her tears. "No matter how much I try, I just can't make myself hate him."

"You can't keep up this charade forever, Samantha. He's bound to figure it out eventually. You have to tell him the truth."

Jackie wiped the tears from her cheeks and took a deep breath. "I wanted to tell him so many times, but I didn't know how. I don't know how to fix this without losing him."

"The longer you wait the worse it's going to be. Tell him now. Maybe the two of you can still work things out. If you wait too long neither one of you will be able to overcome the hurt."

"I don't know how."

"Talk to him. Please. Don't lie to him anymore."

Jackie took a deep breath. She knew Marie was right. If AJ was hurting half as much as she was it was no wonder he had walked away from her the other night. Losing him now wouldn't hurt anymore than being with him and knowing he was in love with a lie. She had to tell him the truth and maybe by some miracle of Fate, he could find it in his heart to forgive her.

Eighteen

AJ was reviewing the notes Edna had sent him from Dr. Hanson. The requests AJ was making via Edna, and the other nurses, were still being ignored. Apparently his replacement didn't feel nurses were qualified to make medically intelligent recommendations. He grunted. He had to find a way to get around Dr. Pompous Ass and get Sarah better care. He pulled his phone from his pocket and called Edna.

"Greenhill Estates, how may I direct your call?"

"The Acres nurses' station east please."

"One moment."

AJ listened to the music play and rubbed his temples. He had asked a lot of Edna since he'd been suspended and she'd been willing to help him in every way she could. Hopefully she would be willing to do one more favor for him. He blew out a heavy sigh and prepared himself to put his personal feelings aside and do what needed to be done for Sarah's sake.

"Acres east, this is Edna."

"Edna, this is Dr. Carrington. I have been reviewing the files you sent to me on Sarah and I have a few concerns."

"So do I, Dr. Carrington. Sarah is struggling and her nurses are frustrated. Something has to change or we're going to have big problems on our hands."

"Yes. I can see that. Dr. Hanson is ignoring a few things he should not be and that brings me to the reason I called." He paused. "I know I have asked a lot of you and I truly appreciate everything you have done for Sarah but I need one last favor."

"I'd dance naked in the streets of Lincoln if it would help." She laughed. *"But hopefully for the sake of the general public it won't come to that."*

AJ smiled. "You are a trooper, my dear. But I am not that desperate yet. What I need you to do is see if you can locate Sarah's daughter and tell her what is going on. If you could persuade her to request that I be reinstated as Sarah's chief physician, I think Central Valley would allow it. Besides, I think it is time we look at appointing her as Sarah's guardian."

"Well, for crying out loud, Dr. Carrington, we could have done that from the beginning. Dr. Hanson signed the guardianship paperwork the first day he took over Sarah's case."

"Really?"

"Well, yes. I thought she would've told you

seeing as how you've been Sarah's doctor for so long."

AJ sighed. Jackie has been this close and still hiding from him. A flicker of pain raced through his veins and he smothered it with a heavy breath.

"I am sorry to say that does not surprise me. There is a bit of history between us, Edna, a bit of bad history. That is why I am asking you to speak to her. I doubt she would listen to me. She would probably reject my recommendations simply because they are mine. I want what is best for her mother so I must be very careful how I approach this matter with her."

"I don't know anything about this history you're talking about but I'm betting she won't hesitate for a second to make that request."

"I would like to believe that, but I would rather play it safe. I think it would be best if you told her your concerns about Sarah's rate of decline."

"Well now I'm not trying to be difficult, but I think it would be better if I told her you were concerned. After all, she's the one who requested we contact you in the first place. She was rather upset when you were removed from Sarah's treatment team."

He hesitated. "Are you sure about that?"

"As sure as my name is Edna Townson. From the very beginning she insisted we do everything we could to persuade you to take Sarah as a patient. She even suggested that we present it as an opportunity for you to further your research since you don't see patients anymore."

A spark of hope ignited in his chest. Jackie

requested him as her mother's doctor. Maybe that was a good sign. Maybe she had forgiven him for the past. She probably didn't ask him herself because she wasn't sure how he would react to her after all these years. Maybe she realized she was wrong and was afraid he wouldn't be able to forgive her. Excitement sprang to life. He could finally make things right. He could talk to her about Sarah and then...

"Tell her Sarah's doctor is requesting to speak to her and let her assume Dr. Hanson is the one making the request. If she knows it is me who wants to speak to her she might not agree to the meeting."

"That won't be a problem. But I'll play along anyway, Dr. Carrington, just in case. Sarah misses you and we all know how much you have done for her. She needs you back at the helm."

"Thank you Edna. But I am only doing what I feel is best for Sarah." He looked at his calendar. "See if she can meet me there in an hour."

"I think that will work. She usually comes in to see her about that time each day. I'll call her and make sure she's coming."

"Thank you, Edna. I owe you one."

"You don't owe me anything except getting your butt back on her case before I strangle Dr. Hanson."

AJ laughed. "I will do my best. I will see you in an hour."

"Thank you, Dr. Carrington. We'll be ready."

He disconnected the call and slid the papers back into the envelope they had been delivered in. Now all he had to do was convince himself he could talk to Jackie without falling apart. Sarah needed him to make this work.

****

AJ looked out the window of Sarah's room. The view was so serene. The gentle rolling hills and fields of wild grasses were perfect for her bad days. The scene would calm even the most agitated of minds. It was even helping him stay calm as he waited for Jackie to arrive.

Edna had taken Sarah to the community room to enjoy the old time band that was playing for the residents. Despite his hope that Jackie was ready to talk to him, he wasn't about to take the chance that she wouldn't be able to keep their conversation civil, and the last thing Sarah needed right now was more mental stress.

The door opened behind him and before he could turn around he heard Samantha speaking.

"Dr. Hanson, I'm sorry I'm late. I needed to pick up a few things but the market was so busy I ran out of time. I still have another errand to run but I didn't want to keep you waiting."

AJ turned around. She was emptying a bag of toiletries and putting them in the closet.

"Samantha? What are you doing here?"

She turned around and froze. When she started to tremble he went to her and took her hand in his. God, her skin felt good. He wanted to wrap his arms around her and soak in her warmth.

"Samantha, are you alright?"

She swallowed hard. "Yes, I'm fine. I... I wasn't expecting you to be here."

He smiled. "And I was not expecting to see you here. I didn't know you knew Mrs. Dean."

"AJ," she whispered. She pulled her hand out of his grasp. "I'm not ready to talk to you. I mean…"

He frowned. "I realize I made things difficult between us, and I am truly sorry about that." He stuffed his hands into his pants pockets. "If I had had any idea you were going to be here I would have scheduled this meeting for another time. As you know, I am not technically supposed to be here, but I am waiting for…" He crinkled his eyebrows. "How long have you known Mrs. Dean?"

"I…" She closed her eyes for a minute then looked at him. "AJ, there's something I need to tell you. I…" She pulled in a deep breath. "I just, don't know how to say this."

He thought about dinner the other night and their conversation that didn't end well. He had told Samantha about how losing Jackie had devastated him, and Samantha had defended her. Now she was here in her mother's room helping her take care of Sarah. He sighed.

"I guess I can assume then you know Jackie." He inhaled softly. "Now it all makes sense. You two are obviously close."

"No, AJ, you don't understand."

"Actually, I think I do." He rubbed his temple when a small stab of pain hit him. "Samantha, I am waiting for Jackie. I need to speak to her concerning her mother and she does not know I am here. She was led to believe Dr. Hanson is the one who wants to speak to her. All things considered, I do not believe she will react well to seeing me. Therefore,

I think it would be best if I met with her alone."

"No one else is coming, AJ."

He hesitated. "I see," he said. "Edna must have told her I was going to be here. After all, she feels Jackie would be happy to meet with me. But I was afraid this would happen." He inhaled a deep breath. "I had hoped that enough time had passed that she could at least speak to me."

"AJ, I need to tell you the truth." Samantha pulled a small case from her purse and removed her contact lenses. When the contacts were secure in their protective case she slid it back into her purse and lifted her head to look into his eyes. "I don't want to pretend anymore."

Despite her watery gaze, the most beautiful cobalt blue eyes he had ever seen took his breath away. But then again, they always had.

"Jackie," he whispered.

The earth tilted violently and he took a step back to steady himself. The dreams raced through his mind. Samantha's face dissolved into Jackie's and then back again. The wind, the rain, and the lightning all replayed in his head and he flinched as though it was real.

He grabbed the back of the chair next to him and held on as his world stilled itself again. Heat rose in his neck and spread to his temples. Humiliation consumed him. The dreams played again as he stared at her beautiful face and a single tear rolled softly down her cheek.

The pain in his chest was excruciating. She had been this close, yet she was still a lifetime away. He had touched her, kissed her, made love to her, and each moment they were together his mind rejected the truth his heart couldn't deny. He swallowed hard and realized he'd known all along Samantha was Jackie. His heart was trying to show him through his dreams, but he was simply unable to accept the truth.

Samantha's familiar perfume filled his senses and halted his breath. How could he have forgotten? It was Jackie's favorite.

"AJ," she whispered.

She reached for him and time stood still. Jackie, his life, the other half of his soul, was back. She came back to him. He should take her in his arms, he should kiss her. He should tell her how sorry he was that he didn't... recognize... her...

He hadn't recognized her and she knew it. She didn't tell him who she was and she let him believe she was someone else, someone he had never met. Anger ignited in his gut.

"No! Don't," he said.

He took a step back. How could she do this to him? How could she despise him enough to torture him like this? My God, what had he done that was so horrible?

He wanted to look away but he couldn't. The pain felt good. Somehow it soothed the guilt he never understood; the guilt for hurting her, the guilt for not remembering what he'd done, the guilt for giving up his search to find her, and now... the guilt for not recognizing her when she was right here in front of him.

He studied her eyes hoping to feel again the old familiar warmth, but without her love he felt cold and empty. Yet, the pale freckles that speckled her cheeks, the gentle slope of her nose, and the soft curve of her earlobes as they met the edge of her face, all made him smile in spite of the ever growing pain in his heart.

"AJ, please let me explain."

"There's no need. You have made your point quite clear. I will assume my request to be reinstated as your mother's physician has been denied."

He turned to leave and Jackie stepped between him and the door.

"Wait," she said. "What do you mean? Can you do that?"

"No. You can. I had hoped that despite my leave of absence from Central Valley I could convince you to request my reinstatement."

"Yes. Yes, of course. I can do that. Oh, AJ, that's wonderful."

"That would not have been my first choice of adjectives, but then again I am not enjoying your little game of Guess Who. So, considering the circumstances I do not think it would be in your mother's best interest to make such a request."

"But, AJ, you're the best. She needs you."

"I am afraid I will no longer be able to maintain my objectivity."

"Nothing has to change. We can still..."

"We can still what? Pretend you aren't Jackie? Pretend you aren't the one who walked out of my life and took my soul with you?"

"No. We can work things out."

He took a step toward her. "You can't be

serious! You actually think I would be gullible enough to believe anything that came out of your mouth?" He looked at her eyes and fought his desire for her. He had to hold on to the anger. It was the only way he was going to survive. "I may have been a colossal fool to think you actually loved me, but I am definitely not a masochist. I think I have been punished enough."

"I'm not trying to punish you!"

"Yes, of course, how could I forget? This is all fun and games to you."

"This isn't a game!"

"The hell it isn't!" He turned his back and stepped toward the door. He couldn't look at her. He closed his eyes and lowered his voice. "I have told you a thousand times how much I love you and that I never wanted to hurt you." He opened his eyes and looked at his hand as he gripped the doorknob. "And I know you've never believed me, but it's the only truth I know... I have never stopped loving you."

"AJ, don't go," she whispered. "We can talk this out."

She wrapped her hand around his bicep and electricity shot through his body. He froze every muscle and erected a wall around his heart.

"I would prefer it if you did not touch me, Ms. Dean." He yanked his arm from her grip. "And from this point forward you will refer to me as Dr. Carrington. Our personal relationship has come to an end."

He stepped through the door and walked briskly toward the exit. He needed to be alone. And he really needed a drink. If he didn't get out of this place now he was going to lose his composure.

A blast of cold air slapped his face when the automatic doors slid open. The sting was almost therapeutic and he clenched his jaw against the discomfort. He got into his car to start the engine and his cell phone vibrated against his chest. He pulled it out and took the call without checking the caller ID.

"Dr. Carrington."

"Dr. Carrington, Mercedes has found something we would like to talk to you about," said Charles Anderson.

"Is this something that can wait?"

"No."

AJ rubbed his throbbing temples. Of course it couldn't wait. "And I suppose you want to discuss this with me in person."

"That would be preferable."

AJ shook his head. He really wanted to be alone right now. But, if Charles Anderson felt it was urgent then he could damn well trust that this wasn't something he could put off for a later time.

"Where should I meet you?"

"We are at my office."

"I will be there in ten minutes."

"Use my private entrance and come alone."

AJ's heart skipped a beat. "I am on my way."

He ended the call and pulled into the lane. Anger burned at the edge of his conscience. Charles was referring to Samantha, or rather Jackie. Whatever he wanted to discuss was a problem with her. Great! Just what he needed, more proof that his taste in women sucked.

Nineteen

AJ pulled into the back parking lot of the Parker C. Anderson corporate office complex. The building was stunning but not overstated. The silo shaped twelve story structure was covered with aged charcoal slate that framed ebony tinted glass. Four foot Bird's Nest pines were smothered in white lights and circled the structure. The lighted wreaths that he knew would soon adorn the rustic looking tower were stacked near the service building at the far end of the parking lot.

Thanksgiving was next week and by the evening of Black Friday the entire town of Lincoln would be visible from space. He groaned at the thought. Celebrating was the last thing he felt like doing.

Other than a few flurries, snow had not yet come to Lincoln. Wind swirled the aged and dismal colored leaves around the parking lot, and despite the loss of greenery on the lush foliage that surrounded the lot, it still provided a natural camouflage for the expensive vehicles tucked away neatly in their reserved spaces.

AJ followed the serpentine path from the parking lot to the discreetly placed back entrance and typed the code Charles had given him into the keypad. A low hum followed a click and he pulled open the slate embellished door. He followed the hall to the end and met a young woman waiting for him.

"Dr. Carrington?"

"Yes."

"Follow me please."

She swiped a card through the reader to her right and pressed her thumb against the tiny screen next to it. Another click and a hum hailed the opening of the panel that revealed the private elevator to Charles Anderson's office. AJ would have missed it if he hadn't been through this door before. He envied the absolute solitude the entrance provided.

He followed her into the small space and enjoyed the silence as they waited for the elevator to reach its destination. He had managed to push the pain of Jackie's betrayal to the back of his mind but the strain was showing through in the shaking of his hands. If his fears were true and she was behind Jameson's accusations against him, she could destroy the only thing he had left in this world, his work. Prison would be a welcomed destiny.

The door opened and the young woman motioned for him to precede her into the office. AJ scanned the room. Charles and Mercedes sat near the window at the far end of the table, Daniel

Rosenfeld and David Wisenthall sat adjacent to them, and Jake Winston sat alone across from Daniel.

AJ felt a chill run up his spine. If Jake Winston was the something they wanted to talk to him about he knew it wasn't going to be pleasant for him. He, Warren, and Jake grew up together. AJ and Warren never got along with Jake as children and it had carried into their adult lives. AJ had assumed there was an unspoken agreement that they just avoid each other, but maybe he was wrong. If Jake felt the slightest inclination to do so, he certainly had enough money and influence to bury AJ alive in an airtight sarcophagus.

Charles looked at the young woman from the elevator.

"Pour Dr. Carrington a drink from the bar and secure the door on your way out. He'll take the bourbon on the right."

AJ walked to the table and sat at the only unoccupied side. He wanted to be able to see everyone's face. Four of the five seated in the room had been working to prove his innocence, but now that Jake was involved that may no longer be the case.

The young woman placed the drink in front of him and exited the door to the outer office. The silence was deafening as he waited for someone to speak. AJ took the opportunity to take his first swig before the interrogation began.

Mercedes tapped the fingernail of her index finger on the polished mahogany.

"Dr. Carrington, how well do you know

Samantha?" she said.

AJ tightened his grip on the glass and felt his head throb as the blood shot through his veins. "Apparently, not as well as I thought I did."

"Did you know she was in Switzerland the week the account we traced was opened?" she said.

He closed his eyes briefly.

"No. I did not."

He looked at the amber liquid in the glass in his hand. He knew he should be studying the faces of the others but he found he didn't have the strength to lift his gaze. The knife Jackie had thrust into his heart less than an hour ago was being dragged downward. He closed his eyes and wished for death to come quickly.

Mercedes continued. "I missed that bit of information the first time I looked because she was traveling as Jacqueline Dean. As it turns out, Samantha is her middle name. She started using Samantha officially several years ago when she began omitting her first name on legal documents. She never filed the necessary court papers to make the change permanent so I was still able to trace it."

AJ downed the rest of his drink in one swallow and leaned back in his chair.

"It does not matter," he said. "You would have been able to trace her eventually when I told you about her deception." He looked at Mercedes. "I recently discovered her charade. Not even an hour ago, to be precise. I suppose she is the one who opened the account."

"We haven't been able to confirm that as of yet," Charles said. "But the intelligence we have acquired indicates it was a woman."

"I'm not convinced it was Sam," Daniel said. "I always suspected there was something to the fact that she never used her last name, but I've worked with her too many years. My gut is telling me she has nothing to do with this. I believe she's as much a target as Carrington."

AJ wanted to believe that, but the lengths Jackie had gone to to hide her identity were too incriminating to ignore.

"Ms. Dean has been purposely trying to deceive me by changing her appearance." AJ stood and paced to the windows. He couldn't look at them when he admitted what a fool he'd been. "She has lost weight and dyed her hair." He looked at the bare trees devoid of their lush green leaves. "She even changed the color of her eyes."

"You knew her before?" Jake said.

"Yes."

"How well?" Charles said.

AJ took a deep breath. "Well enough that I should have recognized her."

"Intimacy is an age-old weapon women have used against better men than you, Carrington," Jake stated matter-of-factly.

AJ hated giving Jake any reason to gloat. Could this day get any worse? He turned toward the group still seated at the table and leaned back against the window sill.

"So, what brings you here, Jake?" AJ said. "Looking for some entertainment? It pleases me to know I can make you feel better about yourself."

Charles cleared his throat. "Mr. Winston is here

because he owns the controlling interest in Central Valley. He has been kept informed of the situation from the start, and as a silent partner, his identity is generally kept confidential. But he has requested to take a more active role in our investigation."

The air left AJ's lungs. His day just got worse.

"My sole concern in this matter is to protect my investment, Carrington. Whether or not you're getting any is of no interest to me." Jake turned to Mercedes. "Is anyone following this Jacqueline Dean, or Samantha Dean, or whatever the hell her name is?"

"Yes, Mr. Winston. My men have been following her for the past eighteen hours."

Daniel sighed. "I feel better about her being tailed for her own protection, but my money's still on Jameson. That son-of-a-bitch is slipperier than a greased armadillo."

AJ rubbed the knot forming in the back of his neck and looked at Mercedes.

"What about the withdrawal that was completed from my office yesterday? You said someone had logged into my computer from a remote location. Did you find out who that was?"

Mercedes exchanged a look with Charles then said, "We're still working on that."

AJ looked at Charles. His expression gave no clue as to what he had silently communicated with Mercedes. What weren't they telling him? Did they suspect he had done it from his home?

He looked at David Wisenthall. David hadn't spoken a word since AJ had walked in the room. His expression was vague and AJ couldn't help the feeling of dread that crept over him. The last time he had spoken to David he had expressed his belief in AJ's innocence. Did he still feel the same?

"Dr. Carrington," Mercedes said. "We feel it would be in your best interest to avoid all contact with Ms. Dean until this investigation is complete."

"That will not be a problem. I have made it clear to her that I have no interest in any further contact with her."

Charles held up a business card and gestured for AJ to take it. "I want you to give this gentleman a call. He has done some work for me in the past. I think it would be best if you secured legal counsel."

"I have an attorney."

"I know your attorney." He waited for AJ to take the card from his hand. "Your chances of an acquittal are better with mine."

AJ slid the card into his pocket. The trembling in his hands was spreading to his limbs. His life was falling apart and all he could do was watch.

AJ looked at Charles. "I will call him in the morning."

"He is expecting your call tonight." Charles pressed the intercom in front of him. "Dr. Carrington is ready to leave. Please escort him down the back entrance."

AJ scanned their faces one last time. The only one who made direct eye contact with him was Jake, and his expression was unexpected. Jake looked battle-ready, but his focus seemed to be beyond AJ.

The young woman stepped into the room and looked at AJ.

"Dr. Carrington? This way please."

AJ followed her into the small elevator and listened for any encouraging words from the group he had just left. But only silence carried into the box before the doors sealed them in, and for just a moment AJ felt like his coffin had been closed.

****

AJ sat in the last pew of St. Mary's Catholic Church. The finish had worn dull on the hardwood bench and it creaked when he shifted his weight to sit up straighter. The marble tiled floor had lost its sheen and gained friction from the many generations of parishioners traversing the centuries old cathedral.

He slid his right foot forward to stretch the muscles in his leg and the soft grinding sound was absorbed by the heavy drapery hanging behind the statue of St. Anthony of Padua in the alcove to his right, the same saint for which he was named. Today he couldn't feel farther removed from the patron saint of finding lost people if he tried. He had never felt more lost in his life.

AJ looked up at the tangle of colors that draped the granite altar as the late afternoon sun shone through the stained glass windows. Despite the beauty of the divine masterpiece that reminded him of the wonders of God, his soul felt lonely and isolated.

The place where he sat alone was quiet and dark, and tinged with a slight chill. A few candles were lit in the opposite corner under the statue of the Blessed Virgin, but other than the colored rays of sunlight, the church was dim.

A few people had come and gone while he'd sat there nearly invisible in the dark corner. They would kneel or sit in silence for a short time, then go. He supposed they were looking for the same thing he was, guidance.

He couldn't remember the drive from Charles Anderson's office, or for that matter, most of the conversation he had participated in. All he could think about was Jackie.

He was on administrative leave that would most likely lead to his termination. His credibility would be destroyed once the charges became public. The research he had done for the past seven years would be labeled as unreliable, or at the very least ignored. His career was virtually over and he was very possibly facing time in prison. Yet, none of that seemed to matter.

The pain of Jackie's deception was even greater than the pain she'd caused him when she had walked away thirteen years ago. He was still no closer to understanding what went wrong, and at this point it was moot. She hated him enough to go to great lengths to make a fool of him. There was no hope of a future with her. She had made her message clear.

AJ closed his eyes and whispered once more, "So where do I go from here, Lord?"

Silence met his question and he smiled sadly. "I guess I have to figure that out for myself."

He heard footsteps on the tile floor to his right and turned to see Henry Jensen genuflect before he sat in the pew next to him.

"I like to come here at this time of the day," Jensen said. "It's quiet and I can think… It helps me put things into perspective."

AJ looked at him and smiled. Jensen was the butler for Jake Winston's family and Jake's caretaker when he was young. In fact, AJ had thought Jensen was Jake's father, until the first time he and Warren had gone to the Winston mansion for a birthday party.

After meeting Sir Winston, AJ had felt sorry for Jake. It was obvious to him, even as a child, that Jensen cared more for Jake than his own father. Actually, Jensen had seemed to care a great deal about Jake's friends as well.

"I cannot imagine you would need to change your perspective," AJ said. "You have always been so logical and fair minded."

"Logic and fairness are important, but perspective can be altered when trust is absent." He turned and looked at AJ. "Trust is an elusive commodity. Even when you possess it, it can be difficult to hold on to."

"That is something I have never had much of, I am sorry to say. It has always been difficult for me to rely on someone else to do what must be done."

Jensen leaned back and folded his hands in his lap. "That is because you were always the strong one. You knew how to keep the peace when the other two boys lost their heads."

"Hmm. Well I believe I have come to the end of my strength and I am out of answers."

"Perhaps the answer must come from someone else this time."

AJ lowered his gaze. He wasn't sure he knew how to function without knowing exactly what to do next.

Jensen sighed. "You remind me so much of myself as a young man, Anthony. Trust wasn't always easy for me either, yet it was in those times that I learned to accept that the most fitting solution was not always mine."

"I guess it is my turn to learn that lesson. I find myself at the mercy of others and there is little I can do to help myself." He looked at Jensen and frowned. "I do not like feeling this way."

"Many of life's lessons are unpleasant."

"Yes, they are." AJ looked down at his lap. "I just wish I knew what I was supposed to learn this time."

"Trust, Anthony. Trust that God has a plan for you."

AJ looked up at him. "I do. I just do not trust that I will know what to do when the time comes for me to act."

"Have faith in yourself. You will know when the time is right." Jensen smiled and looked toward the altar. "There is a common belief that if you want to know what really goes on in the household you speak to the servants." He hesitated. "I am well aware of Master Jacob's business affairs, and one thing he truly excels at is separating his personal life from business." He smiled gently. "I believe you may have less to worry about than you realize."

"I wish I could believe that."

Jensen stood and genuflected before turning to face AJ. "Trust, Anthony. You must learn to trust."

AJ watched him walk to the corner and disappear through the heavy oak door. What other choice did he have? He paid his own respects to God and passed through the same door to the parking lot. When he started his car he pulled the business card of the attorney Charles had recommended from his pocket. If he couldn't trust an attorney to help him at this point, who could he trust?

Twenty

Jake Winston stood behind his desk in his high rise office and looked out the large windows at the city of Lincoln. The sun was setting over the tree covered mountains in the west and it cast a shimmering glow across the underside of the clouds. It had dropped below the moisture laden billows that had hung over the city most of the day, threatening to drop the rain and snow mixture that had been predicted. A fitting view for the end of his day filled with golden opportunities.

He swirled the ice in his glass of bourbon and smiled. It had been a good day for business, well at least for him anyway. His competition? Not so much. Everything had gone Jake's way. Hopefully, his good fortune would hold out for a few more hours.

He sipped his bourbon and his cellphone

vibrated against his thigh. He checked the caller ID and took the call.

"Winston."

"He stopped at the Starlight Lounge. He looks like he's planning to stay for a while."

Jake sighed. The Starlight Lounge was part of the country club, and he hated the country club. It reminded him too much of his parents.

"How long has he been there?"

"About twenty minutes."

"I'll be there in an hour. Let me know if he leaves."

"Don't wait too long. Vasquez wants the information tonight."

"Jameson has to be inebriated enough to talk. I'll get the information and call Vasquez personally."

Jake ended the call and finished his drink. He studied the skyline and thought about what he needed to do. Despite the fact the updates he'd been hearing from Charles Anderson were virtually the same, they did serve to convince Jake that Douglas was behind the embezzlement.

Jameson had made a deal with the devil and taken out a contract on AJ. Then the arrogant bastard had upped the ante and included Miss Dean as well. Apparently, he didn't want any loose ends that could challenge his incrimination of AJ and Samantha once he took off with the millions he had stolen.

Jake suspected he had an accomplice. Something told him it wasn't Miss Dean but that's what he needed to find out. Jameson's hands were too clean and he was too far separated from the whole thing to be realistic. He was the hospital administrator, for God's sake, he had to be in close proximity of at least one of the transactions. Otherwise the real embezzler was trying hard to make Jameson look innocent.

Mercedes' people had hit dead ends on the leads they had followed and couldn't find anything strong enough to use as a motive, even after a little digging into Jameson's closet had revealed a skeleton, one that Jake felt was quite interesting. Yet for some unknown reason they refused to take it seriously. That's when Jake decided to take a more active role in the investigation.

He finished up what he'd been working on and headed home to change into something more casual than his silk suit and tie. The drive gave him time to plan his questions. They had to be vague enough that Jameson wouldn't suspect he was being interrogated, but specific enough to garner useful information.

He changed his clothes and sat on the end of his bed. He took out his phone and checked for any missed calls. Nothing. He rubbed the ache that was growing in the back of his neck and sighed. He was hoping Jameson had moved on to another bar. Jake really hated the country club.

In the twenty minutes it took Jake to drive to the Starlight Lounge he had been able to convince himself he really wasn't at the country club. The Starlight was the only part of the club that was open to the public and therefore the only part of the club his parents, or any of their uptight friends, wouldn't be caught dead in.

He stepped inside and saw Jameson sitting at the bar. Jake took a table in the back corner and waited. He smiled when he saw Sophia pouring drinks. She was the little spitfire that tended bar at Parillo's. He liked her style. She didn't take shit from anyone, even him, and she enjoyed watching people mess with each other. Jake could count on her to let him play a little with the good doctor.

Jake was still nursing his first glass of bourbon forty-five minutes later and Jameson hadn't moved from his stool. Sophia had just served him another drink and he was beginning to sway, so Jake decided it was time to make his acquaintance.

Jake sat on the stool next to Jameson and winked at Sophia when she glanced his way. He ignored Douglas and waited for Sophia to make her way to him.

Jameson slammed his glass onto the bar.

"You're getting slow there, Toots. I need another one." He looked at Jake and smiled. "And so does this young pup."

Jake smiled back at Jameson and turned to look at Sophia when she stopped in front of the two men.

"I think you've had enough, Dr. Jameson." She cocked her hip and folded her arms under her breasts. "And as for this *young pup*—"

Jake put his finger to his lips and Sophia smiled devilishly. She uncrossed her arms and batted her eyes.

"I do apologize for my manners, Dr. Jameson. Would you like another… *whiskey*?"

"A double." He jammed two fingers into the polished wood of the bar.

Sophia looked at Jake. "And for the young pup?"

"Double Glen, please."

"Rocks?"

"Always." Jake winked at her and watched her ass as she walked to the other end of the bar.

Jake felt a heavy hand drop onto his shoulder and he looked to see Jameson leaning toward him.

"Don't waste your time on that little hussy. She's got a hell of an attitude." He pushed hard on Jake's body to straighten himself up.

Jake straightened his shirt at his shoulder and tried not to smell the stench of stale whiskey that was emanating from Jameson. It was bearable until he spoke, and then Jake had to fight back the nausea.

"Thank you for the bit of advice," Jake said. "I'll keep that in mind."

He winked again at Sophia as she placed the drinks in front of them. He knew she had heard Jameson. Anyone sitting within twenty feet of them had heard him. He lifted his glass and turned to Jameson.

"So, what are we celebrating?"

"Success!"

Jameson clinked his glass against Jake's and tipped his head back. Most of the whiskey made it into his mouth with the exception of a small drop that ran from the corner of his lips to his chin. Jameson wiped his sleeve along his cheek and swayed a bit.

"And what success is that?" Jake set his glass down without tasting the contents.

Jameson looked left and right then smirked. He

leaned close to Jake and whispered loudly, "I finally evened the score. The bastard stole my woman..." He swayed and grabbed the edge of the bar. "So I'm taking away his favorite son."

"You kidnapped a man's child?"

"Of course not, you moron, his son is thir— thirty... something." He tipped his drink back and let the last drop of whiskey fall to his tongue then slammed the glass onto the bar. "The arrogant prick is going to prison."

"Prison? Wow. What did he do?"

"Not a damn thing. That's the beauty of it. I found a way to rid the world of his pomp— pompous ass."

Jake hid his smile. He was about to hit the jackpot. The skeleton they'd found in Jameson's closet was a long forgotten arrest record for simple assault. The charges had been filed by Edmund Carrington, AJ's father, and later dropped after he'd spent a few nights in jail. The day Jameson was released a restraining order had been filed against him by Olivia DeMarcus, who married Edmund Carrington six months later. Another six months after that, she gave birth to her first child, Anthony Joseph Carrington.

"If he didn't do anything, what is he going to prison for?"

"Embezzlement," Jameson whispered then smirked.

Jameson fumbled for something in his pocket. He pulled out a few bills and tossed them onto the bar. When he slid off the stool he nearly dropped to his knees but grabbed onto the bar and held on.

"Whoa there!" Jake jumped to his feet and caught him before he lost his grip on the polished wood. He didn't want him passing out just yet.

"Maybe we need to get a cup of coffee in you," Jake said.

Jameson mumbled something Jake couldn't understand but he managed to sit back down onto the stool.

"Soph, can we have two coffees down here?"

Jake waited for the coffee to be delivered and for Jameson to take his first sip. He leaned his elbow on the bar and rested his head in his hand.

"So, tell me. Who did this guy steal money from?"

"What?" Jameson looked genuinely confused.

Jake smiled in spite of himself. "This arrogant prick you were telling me about who's going to prison for embezzlement."

Jameson's smile returned and his eyes sparkled. "Central Valley."

Jake whistled. "That's a big hospital. He must be pretty smart to steal money from a place like that."

"He's not smart." Jameson shoved his thumb into his own chest. "I did it. He's just going to take the fall for it." His smile faded a bit. "And so is his stupid slut girlfriend. The fucking whore will spread her legs for every man but me." He turned forward and stared into his coffee. "But she'll fuck him." He took a long swallow of his drink. "He's just like his father."

"Sorry to hear that."

"Why would you feel sorry for him?" Jameson swayed.

"No, no. I'm sorry about the no one wanting to fuck you part. That must really suck."

Jake watched as Jameson tried to decide whether or not he'd been insulted. To keep from laughing he spoke again.

"Let's call you a cab, shall we?"

Jameson tried to straighten his shoulders and puff out his chest but he lost his balance and Jake had to catch him before he fell off the stool again.

"I'm not riding in a damn cab," Jameson said. "They stink. I'll call my daughter. She'll come get me."

Jake looked at his watch, 9:50 p.m. "Really? So is this how you keep the bad boys away from your daughter?"

"What?" Jameson swayed a bit.

"You're keeping the bad boys away from your daughter by getting so intoxicated you need to call her for a ride. If she's waiting for you to call surely she isn't planning on getting laid tonight." Jake raised his eyebrows. "It's quite ingenious, actually. You should teach parenting classes."

Jameson scrunched his eyebrows and hesitated then said, "I didn't raise the little hussy, her mother did. But I paid enough money for that slut she'll do as I say or I'll send her ass UP the river." He shot his index finger into the air and nearly slid off the stool.

"She mustn't be very smart if you've convinced her she can go to jail for forcing you to ride in a smelly cab."

"I can't send her to jail for that, you moron! I'll send her to jail for doing all the dirty work."

"Hmm. She must really love her daddy if she is willing to risk jail time."

Jameson frowned. "The stupid slut doesn't love me. She couldn't resist earning a piece of the action."

"Gee, that's too bad. Is there anyone who loves you?"

Jameson mumbled something that sounded a lot like, "fucking bastard," and pulled out his cellphone. Jake watched him blink his eyes several times as he tried to focus on the screen. After the fourth unsuccessful try Jake reached out his hand toward him.

"I'll find it for you. What's her name?"

Jameson slapped the phone into Jake's palm and said, "Suzanne Chadwick."

And just like that, the piece of information Vasquez wanted most. Jake found her name in the address book and touched dial. He handed Jameson his phone and walked to the end of the bar where Sophia had been watching the conversation. He handed her several large bills and kissed the back of her hand.

"Thank you, my dear. Your help was invaluable."

"My pleasure. That was quite a show."

"Do me a favor, Soph. Don't repeat anything you heard until it comes out in the papers. Promise?"

"Promise." She winked.

Jake headed for his car. He'd been at the Starlight long enough. He was just about ready to break out into hives.

Twenty-One

AJ sat at his desk and pulled out the latest reports from the lab at Central Valley. Warren had delivered the copies Jackie had printed for him to review. He hadn't spoken to her since he had discovered her deception. There was simply no reason to. He understood her push for him to continue his work. She was doing it for her mother, for Sarah... not for him.

Despite her obvious distaste for him, he decided Daniel was right about her role in the embezzlement. It just didn't make sense for her to frame the doctor who was trying to heal her mother. He felt confident her trip to Switzerland was simply a coincidence.

Still, the fact that she could be so cruel to him with her blatant game of 'Guess Who' cut a wound so deep he didn't think a civil conversation with her would be possible. He pushed aside the anger that tried to resurface and looked at the papers in his hand. His research was the only thing he had left and he was clinging to it with both fists.

The results of the testing so far were showing promise and he was close to proving his theory. Yet anything "Dr. Carrington" would discover may be worthless. Of course that didn't mean he couldn't let someone else take the credit. As long as the discoveries were made and patient's lives, like Sarah's, were improved his efforts would be worth it.

His cellphone hummed when it vibrated against the hardwood of his desk. He glanced at the screen, it was Charles Anderson. He answered the call and laid his head back against his leather chair to close his eyes.

"Carrington."

"We have concluded our investigation, Dr. Carrington. I would like you to come to my office. Would an hour be convenient?"

AJ opened his eyes. Shouldn't they send the authorities to pick him up? Considering the amount of money that had been stolen, he half expected a SWAT team to show up at his home.

"Yes, of course."

"Very good."

AJ heard the line disconnect and he dropped his phone to his desk. An hour was good. It gave him time to shower, shave, and dress in something that would at least make him look good when the news cameras taped his arrest.

****

AJ pulled into the front parking lot of the Parker C. Anderson corporate office complex and was surprised to see the news crews hadn't arrived yet. Maybe Charles wanted to make sure he made it into the building before he was arrested.

He stopped at the front desk and the young woman behind it smiled.

"How can I help you today?" she said.

"Dr. Carrington to see Charles Anderson. I believe he is expecting me."

"Yes, of course, Dr. Carrington. Please follow me." She jumped to her feet with more energy than he'd felt in a month. "They're waiting for you in the executive lounge."

AJ followed her down a long hall to the back of the building. She ran a card through the reader next to the frame. When the light flashed green she pushed the door open but remained standing in the hallway.

"They are just inside the next door Dr. Carrington. It should be unlocked, but if it is not, just press the call button. I am not authorized to go beyond this point." She smiled and pulled the door shut leaving him alone in the small foyer-like room.

He took a deep breath and turned the handle. It was unlocked and the door opened into a medium sized space that looked more like a den than a corporate lounge.

Daniel Rosenfeld slapped him on the shoulder and handed him a glass of bourbon.

"AJ, glad you could join the party. Make yourself comfortable."

AJ took the glass and scanned the room. Overstuffed leather chairs arranged in a half circle around a stone fireplace varied slightly in size and shape, but each was the same color of dark caramel. He walked cautiously to the only one left unoccupied. Unfortunately it was between Mercedes Smith and Jake Winston. The remaining chairs were taken by Daniel, David, and Charles.

Charles spoke first. "I won't leave you in suspense any longer, Dr. Carrington. You and Ms. Dean have been cleared of all the charges Dr. Jameson had leveled against you."

AJ exhaled the deep breath he hadn't realized he'd been holding and smiled. "I guess that explains why the authorities have not shown up at my door."

"They still may," Charles said. "But not with a warrant for your arrest. I expect they may want to question you."

Charles held up his glass and a young woman AJ hadn't noticed until now, walked silently to Charles, took his glass, and walked just as quietly back to the bar behind him. He continued.

"There are some aspects of this whole perversion we simply cannot find answers to. For instance, why would Douglas want to frame you in the first place? Considering the fact that your employment with Central Valley alone draws more benefactors and investors than all the other professionals combined."

AJ took a quick sip of his bourbon and said, "I wish I knew the answer to that one. If I did, I might have been able to see this coming." He paused. "May I ask what you found to clear me from suspicion?"

Charles nodded to Mercedes.

"We finally caught the slimy bastard," she said. "In fact, he incriminated himself because the damn fool drank too much and ran his mouth to a total stranger. That stranger just happened to be one of us."

Daniel laughed. "Not only did he admit to setting you up, but he named his accomplice."

"Accomplice?" AJ set his glass on the table at his elbow. "But I thought you said Jackie was cleared."

"Sam—hell, Jackie wasn't his accomplice." Daniel continued. "It was Suzanne Chadwick."

"But she's an idiot," AJ said.

"Actually, she's quite street smart," Jake said. "She's a hustler by trade."

"Then the documents she was shredding in my office while I was in Vegas were the copies of my financial authorization forms?"

"Among other things," Mercedes said. "She's also the one who opened the account in Switzerland. Ms. Dean was there by coincidence looking for a specialist for her mother."

"I am surprised Douglas trusted a street hustler not to double cross him. He must have had something on her."

"You could say that," Jake grinned. "She's his daughter."

"His daughter?" AJ cringed at the thought that Douglas had procreated.

"Douglas was finishing the last year of his residency when a Miss Darlene Chadwick gave birth to a daughter, Suzanne." Jake rubbed his finger along the rim of his glass. "Douglas denied the child was his until Suzanne's mother forced a paternity test. Unfortunately for her Douglas promised to support the child as long as she wasn't given his name. Suzanne's mother agreed and Douglas began grooming his daughter for a lifetime of swindling."

"How do you know all this?" AJ crinkled his eyebrows.

"As it would happen, Douglas makes a habit of getting shit-faced at the Starlight Lounge and running his mouth to the bartenders. One in particular is a... friend of mine."

"He coerced his own daughter to take part in his plan to steal millions?"

"She's a hustler, Carrington," Jake said. "I doubt he had to do much coercing. She was promised a cut. Hustlers don't work for free, family or not."

"So Suzanne opened the account in Switzerland for Douglas, and a year and a half later he arranged for HR to hire her as my Executive Assistant to help him on the inside." AJ looked at Mercedes. "Is she the one who has been making the transfers from my office?"

"The source of the money transfers is still under investigation," she said, "but I wouldn't doubt she had a hand in that as well."

AJ turned toward Jake. "I take it you are the stranger he bragged to about the set up."

Jake raised his glass in recognition and swallowed the last of its contents.

"Did he happen to mention why he did this?" AJ

said. He turned to Mercedes when she spoke.

"We suspected Jameson had been skimming money from projects about eight months ago so we placed a mole in his camp of supporters. Then about six months ago our mole came to us and reported that Douglas was looking for a hitman."

"What?"

"He took a contract out on your life, Dr. Carrington," she said.

"Excuse my bluntness, Ms. Smith, but why the hell didn't anyone tell me?"

Charles said, "Because you were never in any danger, Dr. Carrington, and we needed to limit the information to as few people as possible. Otherwise, our investigation would become too large and unmanageable." He set his glass on the end table at his elbow. "We arranged for Dr. Jameson to pay the world renown, Vasquez, for the hit. As we expected, he made the assumption Vasquez was a man and never questioned his existence since he was only contacted by a middleman."

"You said I was never in any danger yet it sounds as though this Vasquez is real."

"Precisely. Mercedes Vasquez Smith is a very important part of our team." Charles smiled. "She so enjoys a good masquerade."

"When Jameson brought the ledger to us that he had created to frame you with," Mercedes said, "we were able to use the entries to locate the account Jameson was using. Then we just waited for him to make another transaction. We were able to track the deposit he made the day you and Ms. Dean were together at your office because the trail hadn't been written over yet, but we couldn't tie it to him. So we waited, and eventually Douglas gave us the perfect opportunity. Our contact called him and told him Vasquez wanted the next installment. That was when Douglas requested another contract. Obviously, that was going to require a larger sum of cash so my men tailed him and notified us when he was about to make the withdrawal."

AJ looked at Charles. "Another contract? On who?"

Charles hesitated. "Ms. Dean."

"Jackie?" AJ whispered.

The room fell silent and AJ leaned forward to rest his head in his hands. He felt sick. Douglas wanted Jackie dead. What if he had made that contract with a real assassin? Jackie might have been...

His chest felt tight. He stood and paced to the far corner of the room. He pulled air into his lungs and his chest hurt from the expansion of the muscles. He fought the panic that threatened to overwhelm him.

"AJ, she's not in any danger," Daniel said. "You know I would never let anything happen to her."

AJ nodded his head to acknowledge Daniel's statement but he couldn't speak. Despite Jackie's games, despite her deception, he still loved her. That, he knew, would never change. Living in this world without her, even if she wasn't in his life, was something he knew he couldn't do.

He kept his back to the others and took another deep breath.

"Have they arrested Douglas yet?" he said.

"No," Charles said. "They are still arranging the

warrant. They did take Miss Chadwick into custody this afternoon on an old warrant. I expect they will charge her as an accessory before she can make bail. They expect to make an arrest on Jameson within the hour."

AJ spun around. "What are they waiting for? What if he goes after Jackie himself? If his daughter warns him somehow he could—"

"Whoa, AJ. She's safe." Daniel paced to AJ and put his hand on his shoulder. "We're watching both of them. So are the police. They've got an unmarked car tailing that damn snake and as soon as the warrant goes through, they'll take him in. They know he's a threat to Jackie and if he takes one step in her direction they'll take him down."

Daniel handed AJ his drink and he finished it in one swallow. His hands were shaking. He had to see for himself that she was okay. Even if he didn't speak to her, he had to know she was alright. "I have to go."

"Dr. Carrington," Charles said, "It would be best if you stayed out of their way. I cannot hold you here against your will, but I can guarantee no one can get to you here. Despite the security we have watching you this is the safest place for you until Jameson is taken in."

"And what about Jackie? Is she safe from that bastard?"

"Damn it, AJ," Daniel said. "You know I would never let her be put in danger. Between the Lincoln police department and the men Mercedes and I have watching her she's safer than the damn president."

AJ nodded again. They didn't understand. He

needed to see for himself she was safe. But he also knew the danger he could put her in if he got in the way. As much as he hated it, he knew it was best for him to stay. He needed to let them take care of Jackie. She wasn't a part of his life anymore. This time he needed to let go for good.

Daniel made his way to the bar and AJ watched as the others began discussing details of what they needed to do next. Mercedes took a call and headed for the door. Hopefully she was going to check on Jackie.

He dropped his gaze and stared at the intricate pattern in the marble tile on the floor. How the hell did his life get so out of control?

"Can I ask you something, Carrington?"

AJ looked up and Jake leaned against the wall next to him. He thought about Douglas bragging to Jake about the embezzlement and how ironic it was that Jake was the one instrumental in clearing his name. He smiled.

"Sure."

"Do you know why Jameson went to all this trouble to frame you?"

AJ shrugged. "Who the hell knows? Maybe I took his parking space." He looked sideways at Jake and smiled. "Or maybe he wants my office."

"Not quite."

"I do have the nicer office," AJ said.

Jake grinned. "He hates you by proxy."

"He told you that?"

"Not exactly. He just verified what I suspected." Jake sipped his drink. "Mercedes dug into Jameson's past and found a connection."

"To me?"

"Indirectly. Jameson was arrested for simple assault about a year before you were born but the charges were dropped. Those charges were filed by Edmund Carrington."

"My father."

"Yes, and the day Jameson was released Olivia DeMarcus filed a restraining order against him."

"My mother? How did you find all this?"

"It's public record, Carrington. Anyone can get this information if they know to look for it." He looked AJ in the eye. "Mercedes' people didn't think this connection was relevant because the charges had been dropped, and the conflict was over before you were born. I wasn't convinced so I had my people dig a little deeper." He pulled out a cigar and lit it then took a long draw before he continued. "Your mother was involved with Jameson for many years. In fact, she was with Douglas when Miss Chadwick popped out his daughter. My guess is your mother left him when she found out about the affair."

"And what else did you find?"

"Edmund and Olivia were married six months after the restraining order was filed and your birth certificate was registered six months after that."

Christ! They didn't waste any time. AJ looked around at the others in the room. None of them seemed to notice his conversation with Jake and somehow that was a relief. He never felt particularly close to his parents but the need to protect their privacy still existed. He looked back at Jake.

"What exactly does he blame me for? Did he say?"

"He blames your father for taking his woman. Evidently he feels his infidelity had nothing to do with your mother's departure from his life." Jake grinned. "His revenge was to take down Edmund's favorite son. He took the contract out on you and specified that it had to look like a suicide. That would give credibility to his accusations against you with the added benefit of eliminating your opportunity to prove your innocence." He sipped his drink. "Or maybe he just got tired of dealing with your popularity."

AJ laughed quietly. "Edmund's favorite son? My father speaks to me twice a year, once on my birthday and again on Christmas."

Jake shrugged his shoulders. "That's what he said."

"Why are you telling me this?" AJ looked at Jake.

"It will come out in court. If our attorneys don't bring it out Jameson's will." He looked away. "When your name is dragged through the mud because of something your parents have done, it's always easier to separate yourself from the backlash when you're expecting it."

"I suppose that is true. But why would you care about my name?"

"I've had a controlling interest in Central Valley long enough to know who the real assets are." He looked directly at AJ. "You've made me a lot of money, Carrington. I don't shit where I eat."

AJ smiled. "You know, I was worried when I

saw you at that last meeting. I thought you were there to nail my ass to the wall."

"I would have, if you had been the one stealing from me."

"I have no doubt you could have." He hesitated. "I want to thank you for your help."

Jake threw the last of his bourbon to the back of his throat. "I didn't do it for you, Carrington, I did it for me. That son-of-a-bitch crossed the line when he stole my money."

AJ watched Jake walk to the bar and pour himself another drink. He'd never seen this side of Jake before, the business man who swam in shark infested waters. Something told him Jake was one of the great whites not too many people crossed, and this time AJ was on the winning side.

He breathed a sigh of relief but the tightness in his chest hadn't gone away completely. His career was safe and that should have been enough, it had always been enough. But this time something was different, this time he needed more. This time he needed Jackie.

They had cleared her. He had been right, her trip to Europe was a coincidence. She hadn't been out to get him. He wished he could feel better about that, but she'd still lied to him. She'd lied about who she was, even after he had told Samantha how much Jackie had meant to him. Part of him wished he'd never seen her again, yet he knew he would never regret making love to her one last time. Even if he thought he was making love to Samantha, deep down he knew. Somehow he'd always known it was Jackie. He sighed. If only he could find a way to take back the past, maybe they could start again.

Twenty-Two

Douglas was pacing in his office. Charles Anderson had called and told him the board had concluded their investigation. He and Mercedes Smith were on their way to discuss their findings with him. Charles and Mercedes were the two most influential board members he hadn't been able to sway to his advantage yet. But that didn't matter anymore. Once Carrington was convicted they would have no choice but to trust his word. The pressure from the other members would be too great for them to fight any longer.

Samantha hadn't been in the office at all today and he suspected she had already been taken into custody. The thought brought a smile to his face. The bitch was finally going to pay for her arrogant rejection of his advances.

He imagined the impending conversation and

gloried in his victory. Charles Anderson would no doubt agree with the board's decision without having to admit he was wrong about Dr. Carrington. The thought annoyed him that the old bastard would never ask for forgiveness for doubting his word. Douglas would love to have the old man voted off the board, but unfortunately Charles was too well liked and too well respected by the other members to have him successfully ousted.

Mercedes, on the other hand, would now be vulnerable to him. She may be Charles' pet, but where his mistake would be forgotten, hers would not. He smiled. It was only a matter of time and he would have enough support to push her out.

She had been a hurricane from the start, completely uncontrollable and deadly if you weren't properly prepared. Memories of the first time he'd seen her materialized in his mind. She'd been wearing a jet black suit with red accents and matching stilettos. When she walked toward him he'd been mesmerized by the shape of her legs. He'd savored each line and curve as he slid his leer up her form. When he reached her face the heat that had been rushing through his veins instantly vanished. The icy daggers shooting from her eyes could have frozen the deepest caverns of hell despite the heat radiating from her dark crimson hair.

He sighed. Mercedes had been a thorn in his side since he had taken over as hospital administrator. She had been the first board member he had courted, assuming his charm was more than enough to woo her into submission. When that hadn't worked he took every opportunity to discredit her in the eyes of the other board members, trying to get her ousted. Somehow she was always prepared for his attack and had managed to neutralize him every time.

Douglas paced to the windows behind his desk and looked out at the hospital campus. He turned his head from left to right and focused on his reflection instead of the courtyard on the other side of the window.

"She must be one of those damn feminazis. No sane woman would've passed up the opportunity to be my mistress."

But she had. And he had seriously underestimated her keen business sense and insatiable appetite to put men in their place.

The memory of her spicy perfume wrapped around his senses and threatened to launch him into full-fledged arousal. He closed his eyes to force her into submission the only way he knew how...

He pulled her naked body to his chest and claimed her mouth with his, his hands like steel manacles around her upper arms.

'Wrap those long legs around me, bitch, and suck my cock with your pussy.'

She moaned with need and impaled her body on his when he picked her up and slammed her back against the wall. Her cries of lust filled his ears and she succumbed to his every demand.

He fucked her without mercy and reveled in the way he dominated her. The thought of controlling her response to him filled his soul and an evil smile spread across his face.

'I'm coming!' she screamed.

He tightened his hold on her and thrust forward in a hard fast stroke. He felt her muscles tighten and waited to feel her body push the juices from her pussy in a rush and bathe him in triumph.

Instead she shoved his shoulders violently, twisted his body around, and suddenly his back was against the wall. She wrenched free of his hold and grabbed his hair at his nape. She kissed him forcefully and pressed her rock hard nipples into his burning flesh. She broke the kiss and held him against the wall by his arms the way he had caged her.

'My turn,' she whispered.

She backed away from him and held him frozen with her gaze. The hazel in her eyes began to swirl and sparkle as she ran her palms over his shoulders and down his arms. The sweat of his body made his skin hypersensitive to the chill in the air. The color of her eyes began to change and he felt his heart beat faster with excitement. He lifted his hand to grab her again but she moved from his reach.

In a flash she thrust a jeweled dagger into his heart. Her wicked laugh echoing in his head as she slowly backed away from him, evil shining from her blood red eyes...

He opened his eyes with a sharp intake of breath and stepped back from the windows. He took a handkerchief from his pocket and wiped the sweat from his forehead. He couldn't even control her in his fantasies. She definitely needed to be taken out.

"Stupid bitch. She doesn't need a man to handle her she needs a guillotine to put her out of my misery." He rubbed his temples. "Maybe she'll fall down the elevator shaft."

Douglas tried to focus again on what he was going to say. He had to maintain his composure and not say too much. Until Carrington and his whore were securely behind bars he had to make sure any connection between him and the embezzlement still seemed farfetched. Especially with Mercedes, she would jump at any chance to take him down. As far as he knew, she was still Anderson's favorite pet and if she grabbed on to the right thread, everything would unravel before he had a chance to explain it away in front of Charles.

Having to be careful when dealing with a woman meant she had power over him, and the thought of any woman, least of all Mercedes, having power over him made his blood boil. He would give anything to wrap his hands around her neck and squeeze the life out of the devil's progeny.

He clenched his hands into fists. He could feel a bead of sweat run down his brow. He reached for his desk phone when the intercom buzzed and noticed his hand was shaking.

"Damn it," he whispered.

He hit the speaker button hard enough to move the phone several inches. "I told you not to disturb me until it was time for my meeting!"

"Yes, Dr. Jameson, but Ms. Smith is here already. Shall I send her in?"

'It figures the bitch would be early.' He took a quick deep breath. "Give me five minutes then send

her in."

He growled and picked up the receiver just so he could slam it. He hated temps and the one they sent him today was old, unshapely, and snotty as hell. The least they could have done was send him something pleasant to look at.

He walked to his private bathroom and ran the cold water. He held a cloth under the faucet and exhaled as the icy temperature penetrated his hands. His thoughts began to focus and his breathing returned to normal. He twisted the rag and drained the excess water before he held it to his face. A deep breath carried the chill to the rest of his body and he dropped the rag to the vanity.

He dried his hands and face then looked at his reflection. His color was good and he looked calm and confident. He smiled. This was the beginning of the end. With any luck he would never have to lay eyes on Carrington again.

He stepped back into his office and found Mercedes seated in his chair looking bored.

"Can I get you something to read while we wait for your keeper?" he said. "Perhaps a coloring book to amuse you?"

"I'm just here as a witness, Douglas. It's a privilege afforded to a team member involved in taking down the bad guy."

Douglas opened his mouth to speak and stopped when a man in a suit stepped up to him.

"Dr. Douglas Jameson?"

Douglas looked behind the man and saw two uniformed City of Lincoln police officers. He looked back at the man in the suit and said, "Yes, and you are?"

"I am Detective Jack Henson and I have a warrant for your arrest."

"That's ridiculous! I don't even have a parking ticket."

"You are under arrest for the embezzlement of funds from Central Valley Health and Wellness Center—"

"That's preposterous! I had nothing to do with that."

"You are also under arrest for conspiracy to commit murder in the cases of Dr. Anthony Joseph Carrington and Miss Jacqueline Samantha Dean."

"What!"

Mercedes crossed her legs and smiled casually. "You took out a contract on Dr. Carrington and Samantha Dean, Douglas."

"You have no proof."

"Oh, but we do. Maybe I should introduce myself. My name is Mercedes Vasquez Smith. Vasquez was my mother's maiden name and I only use it in certain circles."

"That's impossible! Vasquez is a man."

Douglas felt the blood drain from his face the instant the words were out of his mouth. She'd done it. Mercedes had set the trap and he had walked right in. The smile on her face was nauseating.

"You'll pay for this bitch. I promise."

"Keep talking, Douglas. The hole you're in is getting deeper with every word you utter."

"Douglas Jameson, you have the right to remain silent..."

Douglas looked at the detective when the ringing

in his ears became deafening. Henson's lips were still moving but the sound of his voice had dissipated. The uniformed officer to Douglas' right turned him toward his desk and twisted his arm around to his back. He could feel the cold metal against his wrist as the cuffs were locked into place.

Douglas turned his head toward Mercedes and his vision turned red. She blew him a kiss and the ringing in his head became painful. He tightened his jaw and glared at her before he closed his eyes and allowed the officers to lead him from his office.

That bitch would pay for this. One way or another he would see to it she suffered a painful death, even if he had to do it himself. It would be worth getting his hands dirty.

Twenty-Three

AJ opened his eyes on a sharp intake of breath. "Jackie!"

"AJ, wake up. You're dreaming." Warren was leaning over him and his hand was on AJ's shoulder. "You with me?"

"Where's Jackie?"

"She's not here, AJ. You're at my house."

AJ took a deep breath and focused on Warren. "What?"

"It was a dream." Warren stood up straight. "Are you awake yet, Golden Boy?"

AJ looked at the couch he was sitting on. A blue baby blanket was draped over the armrest at the far end of it.

"Maybe," he said and rubbed the kink in his neck. "You aren't going to tell me I should apologize to Jackie, are you?"

Warren stepped back and sat in the chair across from him. "Not unless you want me to."

"No thanks. I've heard that enough for today."

AJ combed his fingers through his hair. It was damp. He could feel his heart beating against his ribcage. He took a quick survey of his surroundings and swallowed to rehydrate his throat. They were in the den at Warren's house and the TV was on. The volume was low but he could still hear the commentators discussing the high points of the game.

He sat forward and rubbed his eyes with the heels of his hands. Now he remembered. He was there to watch the Thanksgiving NFL match ups. The last thing he remembered the Lions were playing the Eagles. He pushed out a heavy breath.

"You okay?" Warren said.

"Yeah..." AJ cleared his throat. "Yeah, I'm okay. How long was I asleep?"

"A couple hours. You looked exhausted when you got here, so when you dozed off we decided to let you sleep."

"We?"

Warren smiled. "Just me and Marie. The rest of the family was already gone."

AJ checked the room again. They were the only two there. "Where is she?"

"She's upstairs with the X-man. They went up about an hour ago for a nap. I was beginning to feel left out."

AJ ran his hands around his neck and squeezed the tight muscles at the back. "I wish I had been the one left out."

"You want to tell me about this one?"

AJ shook his head. "I don't know... I thought they would stop. I mean, I know Jackie's secret. What else is there to figure out?"

"Why she left you in the first place." Warren paused. "So, did she walk away from you this time?"

"No... I went to her mother's room to find her, but she was gone. Edna was there and told me Jackie left because I told her it was over. I didn't believe it, so I went looking for Jackie. When I found her she begged me to stay." He sighed. "I tried to, but I started sinking into the mud and no one would help me. They kept telling me to apologize."

"Who's they?" Warren said.

"Everybody. Edna, Jackie...even Daniel Rosenfeld was in my damn dream telling me I didn't know how to treat a woman properly."

Warren smiled. "Yeah, I can see him saying that." He drummed his fingers on the armrest. "So, are you going to apologize?"

"For what? I don't even know what happened."

"AJ." Warren scratched his chin. "Your subconscious has been using your dreams to tell you what your conscious can't see. Do you really think this last one was any different? It seems to me you're the one who believes you need to apologize."

AJ exhaled. "How do you apologize for nothing?"

"Didn't your dream give you any clues?"

AJ looked at the floor. "Daniel said it didn't

matter what I apologized for. He said if I apologized to Jackie I could stay with her."

Warren leaned forward and rested his elbows on his knees. He tapped his fingertips together and spoke.

"Okay," Warren said. "You want to know what I think?"

AJ covered his face with his hands then slid them down and laced his fingers in front of his mouth. He looked at his best friend. Warren would tell him the truth, no matter how awful it was. He just wasn't sure he wanted to hear it.

"Maybe," he said.

Warren sighed. "I think you feel like this is still unresolved with her. I know you said it's over, but I don't think you really believe that. You want to keep hope alive in case one day you find a way to work things out." He paused. "And I don't think the dreams are going to go away this time until you do that."

"So what am I supposed to do? How do I make this insanity stop?"

"You work things out with her. My guess is you already knew that, and you think apologizing for the past is going to make things right with her."

"Or maybe I think she should apologize to me." AJ plopped back against the soft cushions of the couch. "Look what she did to me."

"She hid from you in plain sight, so what?"

"She made of fool of me, Warren." He dropped his voice. "All because of a ridiculous delusion she has about a betrayal that never happened."

"How do you know you didn't betray her? You

can't remember anything about the whole day."

AJ got up and paced to the window. He stared at the dusting of snow that had gathered in the corners of the yard. His heart ached when he thought about all the things that could have happened that day. He knew he couldn't prove his fidelity, but he also knew he couldn't live with the truth if he had truly betrayed her. So holding tight to his declaration of innocence was easier.

"You know what she meant to me," AJ said. "I would have given my life for her." He turned around and faced Warren. "I would have sooner cut my heart out than even consider betraying her."

"Maybe that's why you can't remember it. You can't bring yourself to admit that you slipped, that maybe you had a moment of weakness."

"No!" AJ could feel his limbs trembling. "I would never have done that to her."

"Okay... but don't you think Jackie was too rational of a person to turn on you like that without a good reason?"

AJ kept silent as he considered what Warren was saying. Jackie had never been prone to irrational conclusions. She was smarter than that.

"Put your feelings aside and talk to her," Warren said. "I know it's going to be hard but I don't think you're going to get to the bottom of this any other way. Find out what she remembers. Maybe whatever she saw, or thought she saw, was enough to justify her deception."

AJ looked down at the floor. He knew Warren was right. He just didn't know where to start.

"What do I say to her?"

"Hi? You look great? I love you?" Warren hesitated. "I'm sorry?"

AJ felt the blood rush through his limbs as his heart hammered. Apologize? Was it really that simple? Could he offer her a sincere apology without knowing what he was sorry for? Jackie would see right through him if he didn't mean it.

Warren leaned back in his chair. "It doesn't really matter what you say to her as long as you start the conversation. You'll figure it out as you go along."

AJ swallowed a lump in his throat. Why was this so damn hard? He felt like a gawky teenager when his stomach fluttered.

"And what if she…?"

Warren chuckled. "You're such a pussy. She won't reject you, AJ. She loves you now just as much as she did back then. If she didn't she wouldn't have hid from you. The Jackie I remember would have walked her gorgeous body right up to you and then told you to go fuck yourself."

AJ smiled. That was the first time he'd ever heard anyone call Jackie gorgeous. Even though she always had been, no one ever commented on her beauty, not even Warren. Yet, just like AJ, he preferred women he could wrap his arms around and feel their warm, soft curves press against him.

Most of their fraternity brothers felt the same. They just never flirted with Jackie like they did with the other pretty girls that came by the house, because Jackie wasn't available. The girls his brothers flirted with flirted back and it became a game that sometimes led to sex. They knew which girlfriends they could toy with and which ones they couldn't, and Jackie was on the "Don't Toy With" list.

He never knew how to explain that to her. She had seen things differently. Jackie viewed their lack of attention as a sign that somehow she wasn't good enough, that she wasn't pretty or sexy. To her, getting their attention meant she was desirable. She didn't seem to understand she already was. Maybe that's why she believes he betrayed her. Maybe she never felt completely secure in his feelings for her.

His smile faded. He needed to talk to her. He'd waited too long for a chance to get back what they'd had to let this opportunity get away without one hell of a fight.

"Talk to her," Warren said. "You two were meant to be together."

AJ nodded his head. He knew what he had to do. Whatever Jackie needed from him he was willing to give her. She was worth it.

Susan M Baer

Twenty-Four

Friday afternoon AJ sat on the back deck at Warren's house. His brother had taken a group of holiday vacationers to his ski resort since his outdoor excursion company had expanded into winter sports. Their parents had stopped celebrating holidays years ago when they couldn't be in the same room for more than five minutes without screaming at each other, and AJ refused to choose between them. He knew spending the day alone in his condo would drive him crazy with constant thoughts of Jackie, so when Warren suggested they watch the Alabama game at his place AJ decided it was worth the risk of wearing out his welcome.

He had called Jackie twice yesterday and left messages when she hadn't answered. He assumed she had spent the Thanksgiving holiday with her mother and he hadn't wanted to intrude on their time together. She hadn't answered when he called her again this morning either, but Marie insisted he keep trying. His pride was taking a beating but if that's what it took to prove to Jackie he wasn't letting go of her this time, so be it. He would just keep calling until she answered.

AJ watched Warren play with his son in the yard. Xavier giggled each time Warren tossed him into the air. The feeling of envy he had each time he saw the father and son together was beginning to feel comfortable. The pain was cleansing, especially after a night filled with dreams of Jackie.

He heard Marie open the door behind him and step to the chair next to him.

"Does he surprise you?" She sat down and placed her drink on the table.

"Warren? No. He was always able to find the fun in anything. I'm not at all surprised how much he loves being a father." He turned to her and smiled. "I bet he's a handful for you though. It's probably like raising two children."

She laughed. "Sometimes. But I wouldn't have him any other way. His attitude is infectious. He can make me smile when all I want to do is cry."

AJ looked down at his drink to avoid exposing his aching heart. "That's because he loves you so much. It tears him apart to see you hurting."

"Is that a guy thing or a Warren thing?"

AJ looked out at Warren again. He was talking to his son as he carried him around the yard. Xavier smiled each time Warren spoke. How much he envied his best friend.

"When a man loves a woman as much as Warren

loves you her happiness becomes as vital to him as the beating of his heart." He continued to watch the father and son play.

"Have you talked to her?"

AJ looked up at the sky, then the trees, anywhere to keep him from looking at Marie. He knew the pain would be etched into his features. "She still won't answer my calls."

"Keep trying. She can't avoid you forever."

"She seems to be giving it her best shot."

"You should've gone to her place yesterday. She was planning to bring her mother home for a visit and it's harder to ignore someone who's knocking on your door, especially when your guest can hear them. You could've talked to her then."

"I don't want to pressure her."

"That's not pressuring her. That's showing her you aren't going to give up."

"I'll try calling her again later."

She sighed. "I almost forgot how stubborn you could be."

He looked at her. "And what exactly am I being stubborn about?"

She leaned forward and rested her arms on the table. "You love her and yet you're avoiding what you really need to do to make things right."

"I can't make her talk to me, Marie."

"No. But you can make her listen to you." She paused. "AJ, she loves you. She told me so herself. Go see her. She'll let you in. Then you can tell her you're sorry."

He scowled. "Why does everyone assume I have something to apologize for?"

"You men can be so thick sometimes." She crossed her arms. "You can be sorry about something even if it was completely out of your control. Tell her you're sorry you can't remember what happened, or that you couldn't find a way to fix whatever was wrong. Tell her you're sorry the two of you have been apart for so long." She leaned on the table once more. "Tell her you're sorry she's been hurting all these years. Wouldn't those be true statements?"

He rubbed his jaw and hesitated. "They're all true."

"Then tell her. And give her the chance to explain her side."

He laughed sadly. "She won't tell me what happened. She has never believed that I don't remember that night."

"That was a long time ago, AJ, and so much has happened since then. Maybe she'll believe you after all this time. She knows what kind of a man you've become. You're certainly not prone to lying. As a matter of fact, you are painfully honest most of the time." She smiled.

AJ laughed in spite of himself. "I am, aren't I?"

"Yes." Marie poked her finger into his bicep.

A few minutes of silence passed and Marie spoke again. "My guess is she's had time to think through this whole mess more than she cares to admit, and she's probably ready to talk it out too, but she's just as scared as you are." She leaned over and touched his arm. "Jackie has been hurting so long the pain has become a part of her. I don't think she knows how to let go of it. You can help her do that, AJ… Talk to her."

Warren walked up the steps from the backyard. Xavier was still giggling as he squirmed in his father's arms and Warren talked on the phone.

"I don't care if he's asking for me. Call the doctor on the schedule." He handed Xavier to Marie and sat down in the chair next to her. "A lot of people know me, Dwight, that doesn't mean I'm coming in just because they request me. I can see him on Monday."

Xavier squealed and reached for AJ. Marie kissed her son on the cheek and handed him over.

"Fine," Warren said. "I'll be there in twenty minutes." He shoved his phone in the pocket of his jacket.

Marie looked at Warren and said, "What's going on, babe?"

"A trauma patient came in and the man is asking for me personally. He is refusing to talk to anyone else and Dwight is worried if he doesn't get this guy to calm down he won't make it through the night." He paused. "His condition is critical and Dwight wants to sedate him but the man is refusing treatment."

"Well, Janet and I can change our plans. We'll find something to do here."

Warren stood and kissed her on the top of her head. "I'm sorry, baby. I'll make it up to you."

AJ held Xavier as he bounced on his knee. He turned to Warren and said, "I can stay with the X-man. I'll record the game on your DVR."

Warren turned to Marie and said, "Works for me."

"Me too," she said. "Janet won't be here for another hour or more so they won't be alone together too long."

AJ smiled devilishly. "While you're gone I'll teach my godson a few bad habits."

"That's what we're afraid of," Warren said. "So I won't be any longer than I have to be."

Marie stood and Warren cradled her face in his hands. He kissed her again, this time with a bit more passion.

AJ cleared his throat. "I said I'd watch my godson, not his parents making a sibling for him."

Warren hugged her and spoke to AJ over her shoulder.

"You're just jealous." He stepped back and looked at Marie. "I'll call you when I get home. Tell Janet I said hi."

He punched AJ on the shoulder then headed into the house.

"Later, Golden Boy."

Marie hugged her jacket tight and turned to AJ. "You really don't have to do this. Janet and I can go out another time."

"Marie, are you questioning my abilities to care for my godson?"

"Not at all. I just want him back. That young man would follow you home if he could." She smiled and took a sip of her drink. "You can make one of your own."

AJ held Xavier's wrists while the baby clung to his thumbs. "Little does your mommy know I don't want one of my own because they'll be too eager to get revenge over all the neat little tricks I'm going to teach you." He looked sideways at Marie.

"Oh, don't worry. I will get you back one way or another."

"You are a very lucky young man, X. Not everyone has a mother as smart and beautiful as yours."

"Flattery won't save you, Dr. Carrington."

"I have no idea what you're talking about."

Xavier blew raspberries and AJ closed his eyes when he was sprayed with mashed pea scented drool. Next came the burp that heralded a flow of pale green lava. He seated Xavier in his lap and pulled a handkerchief from his pocket to wipe his face.

Marie laughed hard and pulled Xavier into her arms. "It would appear karma is getting a head start on that revenge."

"Thanks."

She wiped her son's face with a napkin and said, "I'm sorry. Let's head inside. I'll get you one of Warren's shirts then I'll get the X-man into his pajamas before I leave."

AJ stepped into the half bath next to the garage and looked into the mirror as he rubbed his jacket and shirt with a wet washcloth. He smiled when he realized that Xavier was the only one who could get away with spitting up on him and not make him want to neuter the child.

He walked back into the kitchen and Marie handed him a sweatshirt.

"Give me your shirt and I'll wash it with the others."

"Others?" He pulled his shirt over his head.

"The X-man has a habit of spitting up on Daddy because Daddy likes to toss him into the air after he eats."

AJ laughed. "So that's why the two of you passed him off to me so quickly."

"You're learning." She winked at him. "I'm going to give him a quick bath and we'll be right down."

AJ watched her carry her son up the steps. She talked to him the whole way and he couldn't help but smile. Marie was an amazing mother.

When she reached the top of the steps he went back to the kitchen and grabbed a beer from the fridge. The game would be starting soon so he set the DVR and settled in for the three hour battle. The pregame show was on and he shook his head at the wild college students fighting to get on camera. Their bare chests were painted in crimson and yellow.

"Jesus, they haven't gotten any smarter." He remembered one Saturday night sitting in the fraternity house while Warren and a few others huddled under blankets, feverish and moaning like a bunch of babies because they had gotten caught in a freezing rain at the game.

AJ couldn't resist the temptation to rub it in considering the ribbing he took for refusing to attend the game half naked and painted like a circus freak.

His mind began to wander and he remembered the first time he had met Jackie. It was Homecoming. He had felt energized by all the excitement and decided to go against his better judgement and attend the game in body paint.

AJ laughed and shook his head. It was a wonder Jackie hadn't hated him. Most of his torso had crimson paint on it when he tripped going up the steps to their seats. He had landed on Jackie's lap, but not before he fell against her beautiful breasts. For an instant he was filled with complete ecstasy when he looked into her amazing blue eyes. Then the look of shock on her face yanked him back to reality and he realized he'd just smeared his crimson body paint down her sparkling white t-shirt and shorts.

She looked like she was about to kill him when laughter bubbled up and lit up her face like an angel. He had been totally entranced by her and stood there smiling like a fool. That was when Warren had elbowed him and pointed out, to his grand amusement, that AJ's mascot had morphed into a well-endowed and aroused alien of some sort.

AJ had decided to risk total annihilation of his dignity and asked her out. She had accepted and that night as he had made love to her for the first time he knew she would hold his heart forever.

His smile faded and the voices from the TV dispelled his memories. Alabama was set to kick off. The ball was sailing to the end of the field when Marie stepped into the den.

"Xavier fell asleep after his bath so I put him down for the night." She held out her phone to him. "Warren wants to talk to you. He said he needs you to come to the hospital. I'm going to call Janet and we'll stay with Xavier."

AJ took the phone from her and sat up straight.

"What's wrong?" he said.

"You need to come down here, AJ. It's Mike Hollister and he wants to talk to you. I don't have time to explain. Just get here as soon as you can."

AJ swallowed. "Yeah… sure. I'm on my way."

"Is everything okay, AJ?" Marie took her phone back from him.

"I don't know." He blew out a heavy breath. "The trauma patient is Mike Hollister. He's a fraternity brother of ours. I haven't seen him in years but… I better get going." He grabbed his keys and headed for the door.

Twenty-Five

Warren was pacing outside the doors to the ER when AJ walked into the hospital. He looked worried and AJ took a deep breath as he stepped up to him.

"How bad is he?"

Warren shook his head. "I don't know how he's still conscious."

"Then let's get in there. You said he was refusing treatment until he talked to me."

AJ stepped to the side and Warren touched his shoulder to stop him.

"AJ, I need to talk to you before you go in there."

"I think I can handle this. I've seen my fair share of gore."

"I know that. But this is going to be different. You need to know what you're walking into."

"Like I said, I've seen my—"

"AJ... That's not what I'm worried about. He has a piece to the puzzle." He sighed. "A big one."

"So your hunch was right. He was hiding something."

Warren nodded. "He was there that night at the house, the night you can't remember. He told me what happened and you're not going to like it."

AJ stood still, unable to move. "What do you mean? What..." He swallowed. "What the hell did I do?"

"You didn't do anything. They did."

"Mike?" He paused. "And who? Jesse? What did they do to her? Did they touch her?" AJ could feel the anger scorching his veins. If they touched Jackie he would... He could feel his hands shaking with the need to hit something, more like someone. He stuffed his fists into his pockets and clenched his jaw.

"No, AJ. They never touched her, not like that." Warren sighed. "Look, Mike told me he wanted to tell you himself. I think he knows he's not going to make it. Dwight was right. It's a miracle he's still alive."

AJ couldn't speak. A million scenarios were rushing through his head. If Mike and Jesse didn't touch her and he didn't do anything, what the hell did she run from?

He followed Warren through the doors and down the hall to the last room. The smell of iodine hit his senses and he felt his demeanor change. His emotions shut down and he surveyed the room. The lights had been dimmed and the only sounds were the soft beeps of the monitors. He walked to the side of the bed and looked at the man lying on it.

There wasn't a spot on his body that hadn't been marred by whatever tragedy Mike had survived. AJ made a quick mental list of the injuries he could see. A square bandage was taped to the right side of his chest and a small piece of metal protruded from underneath it that had been cut off. Obviously surgery was required to remove it safely. Below the bandage his skin was red and a long thin blister could be seen under the edge of a tented sheet that covered the lower half of his body, possibly protecting severe burns. His eyes were covered with thick cotton ovals that were kept in place with a strip of gauze that wrapped around the back of his head. His forehead was swollen on the right side and blood had saturated the top of the eye patch. The skin that was showing on his chest and right shoulder was cut, bruised, and swollen. He had two stitches on his collarbone that only closed a small portion of the laceration that ended at the base of his neck. The rest of it had been temporarily taped.

AJ sighed. There were a lot of injuries that needed attention, no doubt more were internal. But unless Mike let them sedate him, that wasn't going to happen.

A woman stood from the other side of the bed and AJ looked up at her. He hadn't noticed her when he had walked in.

She leaned over Mike and whispered, "He's here, baby. I'll be right outside." She tenderly kissed the gauze covering his eyes. "I love you."

She lightly touched the bandage on his head and

looked up at AJ. Her face was streaked with tears and pain. She tried to smile but more tears spilled from her eyes and she turned to walk out the door.

"AJ?" Mike's voice was barely audible.

"I'm here, Mike." AJ sat in the chair next to the bed and leaned closer so he could hear him.

"My wife thinks I'm going to heaven." He pushed out a ragged breath that AJ knew was an attempt at a laugh. Mike wasn't the most angelic of his fraternity brothers.

"Women can be pretty smart, Mike. Maybe she knows something you don't."

"I can't disappoint her, AJ. I need to come clean. I want to be waiting for her when she gets there."

"You will be."

"No… not without your forgiveness." His breath gurgled and he coughed.

"Mike, you need to relax. Whatever you're worried about I'm sure it's not important anymore. You played a lot of pranks on me. There are no hard feelings."

"No… I'm sorry about Jackie."

AJ could feel his heartbeat quicken. "What about Jackie, Mike?"

"I was drinking a lot that night… Me and Jesse…" He swallowed. "We thought it would be funny to spike your drink."

AJ looked at Warren who was leaning against the far wall. Warren nodded toward Mike and mouthed, "There's more."

"When did you do this Mike?"

"The night of the formal, the night Jackie left." His breath hitched. "I swear to God, AJ. I didn't mean for it to go that far."

"I don't remember a lot from that night, Mike. Can you tell me what happened? What did I do to Jackie?"

"You didn't do anything. We set her up, we set you both up." His voice cracked. "Jesse convinced me it would be funny to get you wasted." He paused. "After you passed out we put you in bed with Stacey."

"Stacey was Jackie's best friend, and Tony's girlfriend. Why would she do something like that?"

"We drugged her too. I thought it was just a joke, AJ. I swear. But Jesse started shoving me around after Jackie left the house. He wanted her, AJ. I swear I didn't know what he was doing. He was pissed because I didn't stop her from leaving." Mike's voice quivered. "That's when I saw Jackie coming back. I stopped her before she got to the house and I told her to run. AJ, I'm really sorry. Jesse was freaking me out. I thought he was going to hurt Jackie."

Mike began to weep and a soft ping emitted from the heart monitor. AJ looked at it. Mike's heartrate was rising.

"Mike, I want you to take a deep breath. Let Dr. Collins give you something to help you relax."

Mike took a breath and shook his head slowly. His heartrate was leveling off and a weak smile appeared below the bandages on his face.

"I'm not going to make it, AJ. I know that." He sucked in a sharp breath and groaned. "I have to tell you what I did or I'll never see Angie again... please."

"I'm listening, Mike."

"I told Jackie you'd been sleeping with Stacey, and that she should run. I was afraid Jesse would get to her before you woke up." He paused. "I thought she'd come back the next day and fight it out with you and..." He swallowed hard. "I thought you'd make it alright. You always made everything alright. But she didn't come back."

A dull ache settled in AJ's chest. He never thought one of his fraternity brothers would do something like this to him, even Jesse. They all knew how much Jackie meant to him.

"What about Stacey?" AJ said.

"She never knew what happened. When Tony found out what we did he flipped out. He carried Stacey to his bed and then he almost killed Jesse." His breath hitched. "He shoved his .45 in Jesse's mouth and told me if we ever talked about what we'd done he would kill us."

AJ could feel his temperature rising. It was like he was getting caught in another nightmare. No wonder no one would talk about it. The brothers who lived at the house used to joke about Tony's father being part of the mafia. Maybe there was more truth to that than anyone realized.

"What exactly did Jackie see, Mike?"

Mike's body convulsed and he sucked in a deep breath. "Please forgive me. I want to be waiting for Angie. I—I can't lose her."

"I forgive you, Mike. You're not going to lose Angie. But you have to let the nurse help you relax. Okay?"

Mike shook his head. "No. You don't

understand. You don't know what I did."

AJ motioned to the nurse to get Dr. Collins. "Mike you need to calm down. You'll have time to tell me the rest later."

"No—" Mike gasped. "You'll never forgive me. Tell Angie I'm sorry."

"I forgive you, Mike, now take a deep breath. It's okay."

"No. You can't..." His voice broke. "I almost killed you."

AJ heard a loud ping and looked up. Mike's heartrate was spiking. "Mike, I'm fine. That was a long time ago. Take a deep breath and relax."

"Tell Angie I'm sorry. I love..." His body started to quiver.

The monitors screeched and the blue strobe light in the ceiling nearly blinded AJ. Warren burst through the door to the hall.

"Angie!"

Mike's wife was at his side before AJ could move. She looked at him and his ears began to ring almost as loudly as the alarms. The pain in her face was devastating to see.

AJ backed up as the medical personnel rushed in and Warren touched him on the shoulder. He turned to follow him out into the hall. They walked in silence to the waiting room and Warren led him into the staff lounge on the other side.

They sat at the small square table in the center of the room and AJ covered his face with his hands. Now the wait would begin. For the first time in his life AJ was on the other side. He hadn't seen Mike in years but it was still personal. Personal enough that AJ didn't want to think about how he was going to feel if Mike didn't make it through this.

He dropped his hands to the table and looked at the clock on the wall. He never thought he would ever want to wish his life away, but right now he'd give anything to fast forward to the end of this ordeal.

****

AJ sat alone in the doctor's lounge. His third cup of coffee was half empty and cold, and sitting on the Formica tabletop in front of him. Warren had left an hour ago, maybe two, to check on another patient that had come in to the ER. It had been four hours since Mike went into cardiac arrest, yet it seemed more like four days. Each minute was excruciating and it was as if the world had abandoned him in this small room until he figured out where his life would go from here.

As each hour passed he gained more compassion for the many people who had endured the same. Every day a new family would sit in this hospital and wait as they hoped for the best and feared the worst. Every day a new tragedy would sentence them to reflect on what was truly important in life as they did their best to deal with the mix of emotions swirling inside them.

Relief, anger, sorrow, and guilt ran a vicious cycle in his mind. The feeling of liberation from finally knowing the truth, that he hadn't betrayed Jackie, was incredible. He felt vindicated. But then the anger set in when he thought about what had been taken from him with such cruel and selfish intentions. The pain Jackie must have felt in that moment was more than he wanted to think about. She had been left with the sting of betrayal, and the humiliation and loneliness of being abandoned by the man she loved.

Then he thought about the look of agony on Angie's face when he had walked into Mike's room. The unmistakable sorrow in her eyes had left a mark, one he was sure he would remember for a long time. He had envied Mike in that moment because Mike had what AJ had lost when Jackie walked away, a soulmate who would feel his death as deeply as if a part of her had been ripped away forever. His logical side told him he had every right to be angry, so much had been stolen from him. Yet it felt disturbing and immoral to feel anything other than empathy.

The door opened and tired footsteps approached him from behind. He looked up when Warren dropped into the seat across from him.

"Any word on Mike?" AJ said.

"I checked on my way back." Warren rubbed his eyes. "He's still in surgery."

AJ looked down and stared into the dark liquid in his cup, more waiting. In the meantime, he had some questions he wanted answers to.

"I need to know," he said. "Mike said Jesse wanted Jackie. Do you think he got to her?"

"No. Mike was bearing his soul in a desperate attempt at redemption. He was convinced he's going to die. He wouldn't have left out an important point like that." He paused. "I believe Jackie ran from a broken heart after she saw you and Stacey in bed together."

AJ kept his eyes on his reflection in the coffee. "Was I... when Jackie saw us was I... doing anything with her... I mean with Stacey?"

"I doubt it. Mike said you were both out cold. He told me they had stripped both of you naked and put one of your hands on Stacey's breast and the other between her legs. Then Jesse told Jackie you were waiting for her in your room." He scratched his jaw. "Mike said Jesse tried to grab her when she came running out into the hall but she slipped through a crowd and made it outside."

"I don't remember any of this." AJ shook his head. He couldn't believe he would let something like this happen to him.

"I'm not surprised considering what they gave the two of you. Mike couldn't remember what it was but he said Jesse made it himself." He paused. "I called Tony about an hour ago. I wanted to know exactly what it was."

"He talked to you?"

"Reluctantly. Mike was right. Stacey still doesn't know what happened that night and Tony wants to keep it that way." He tapped his fingers on the table. "I told him I couldn't make any promises but if he didn't tell me what I wanted to know I would call the police and he could answer their questions instead."

"What did he tell you?"

"Jesse gave you and Stacey a tainted version of Valium. Tony thinks he had been experimenting with different drugs to create his own wonder drug that he could sell. It was the extra ingredient in the

Valium that Tony counteracted. Apparently Jesse told Tony it was just Valium, but when Stacey started having a seizure Mike admitted he saw Jesse add something else."

AJ waited for the rest but Warren looked away. His insides started to quiver. Mike had said they almost killed him.

"What was the something else?"

Warren blew out a heavy sigh. "Hemlock."

"Jesus," AJ whispered. "He tried to kill me."

"Possibly. But if that was his intent why not just give you straight hemlock?" He paused. "Honestly, I think he decided to use the two of you as Guinea pigs for his drug when he decided to go after Jackie. Either way we now know why you were so sick that night. That's also why you can't remember anything from that day. A long term side effect of hemlock is retrograde amnesia."

AJ could feel his heartbeat in his temple. He never imagined finding out what had happened would be so disturbing. If Tony hadn't found them when he did they'd probably both be dead.

"Tony was interning at the research hospital that term," Warren said. "He used his keys to the pharmacy lab to get the ingredients. After he gave you and Stacey an injection, he and Drake beat the shit out of the two of them. Jesse, of course, got the brunt of it."

"I never did buy the story that Jesse fell down the stairs that night."

"Yeah, he looked more like he had been thrown off the roof." Warren blew out a heavy sigh. "And if Tony got his .45 out Jesse is damn lucky he survived that night at all."

AJ sat in silence and let it sink in. There had always been someone who didn't like him. He was strong and demanding, and people expected him to have all the answers. Even in college his fraternity brothers looked to him to be the leader, the one with a clear head who could make the hard decisions, and inevitably someone always took it personally. Still, he never imagined anyone would try to hurt him, but in a week's time he'd learned at least two men had wanted him dead. Ironically enough, both conflicts were over a woman rather than his decisions as a leader.

"Then Jackie thinks I slept with her best friend while I was waiting for her to come to the house?"

"Probably," Warren said, "and if she believed what Mike told her she thought it had been going on for a while."

AJ listened to the hum of the florescent lights. Fury crept into his heart as he thought about what Jackie had seen. She had been lied to and Jesse had gone to great lengths to make sure she believed it. If their roles had been reversed he would have been devastated to see her in the arms of another man, especially if that man had been his best friend. Then being told by a friend of hers that she'd been cheating for months would have killed him.

He felt like he was in a Hitchcock movie. He and Jackie had been ripped apart because a fucking psychopath wanted her. Emotional fatigue was taking over. He wanted to be angry but he didn't have the strength. And the relief of finally knowing what had happened, oddly enough, soothed his soul.

"I'm sorry, AJ."

"For what? You had nothing to do with this. You were out chasing a skirt to bring back to the party."

"That doesn't mean I can't be sorry it happened. I'm your best friend for God's sake." He sighed. "Tony should have told you what happened. He should have called the police."

AJ leaned back in his chair and rubbed the tight muscles in his neck. "He was protecting Stacey and if the police had gotten involved the fraternity would have lost their charter."

"Fuck the fraternity. You and Stacey could have died. He was protecting his own ass for pulling out that gun."

AJ felt his hand trembling and he made a fist to hide it. Finding out someone had actually poisoned you was more disturbing than he imagined.

"Maybe Tony did do the right thing. I think Stacey is better off not knowing." He looked up at Warren. "You know they celebrated their tenth anniversary this year?"

"Good for them. In the meantime you and Jackie have been miserable for the past thirteen and Jesse got away with attempted murder." He crossed his arms. "That seems fair."

"Tony did what he thought was right. If he had told me I would have told Jackie. Then Jackie would have told Stacey. It was easier for him to comfort her when her best friend disappeared without a trace."

"That's a bullshit reason and you know it."

AJ agreed but what difference did it make now?

"Tony and I weren't that close. I doubt he

wanted to talk to me about why I was fondling his girlfriend. Would you have handled it any differently if you were in his shoes?"

Warren hesitated. "I don't know. Maybe not."

A silence fell between them. AJ thought about what Jackie had been through and couldn't help wishing he could turn back time. He didn't know how he could have let his guard down around Jesse but trying to figure that out was just a waste of time. What was done was done. He needed to figure out where to go from here.

He watched Warren send Marie a text. He knew what it would say, that he'd be home as soon as he could, and without a doubt it would end with 'I love you'.

The door opened and Dr. Dwight Collins stepped through. He stopped at the end of the table and pulled off his surgical cap.

"We did everything we could but we couldn't stabilize him. I'm sorry. The damage was too extensive. I doubt he would've made it through the night anyway." He looked at Warren. "I have already spoken to his wife. I explained as much as I could at this point. Do you want me to call in one of my crisis nurses or do you want to talk to her?"

"I want to talk to her," AJ said.

"You don't have to do this." Warren stood up. "I can tell her you forgave Mike."

"No. I want to do this. I won't do to them what they did to me and Jackie, and I want Angie to hear it from me."

AJ waited for Warren's consent. As the Chief Trauma Psychologist it was his call. Warren nodded and AJ followed Dwight down the hall. He pointed to the consultation room where Mike's wife was and continued on to the ER as AJ quietly stepped into the room.

He saw Angie sitting alone on the small sofa. She held a rosary in her hands and she didn't appear to notice him come in. For an instant he thought about leaving but then she raised her head and looked at him.

Her eyes were bloodshot from all the tears she had shed and her face was drawn and tired, but she kept her gaze on him as he walked toward her. He sat in the chair across from her and reached out his hand. When she took it he gave her a comforting squeeze.

"Angie, I'm sorry. They did everything they could but his injuries were too severe."

"I know." She closed her eyes and more tears ran down the already moist skin of her face. "He was a good man, Dr. Carrington. He loves me so much I can still feel him here with me." She opened her eyes and looked at him. "Whatever he did all those years ago has haunted him every day. He wanted you to know how sorry he was." She paused. "That's what he was waiting for, you know. He couldn't move on until he made amends for his sin."

AJ kissed the back of her hand.

"Then know that he is at peace. I forgive him, Angie. He'll be waiting for you."

She looked at him and he could see the tension in her features ease. A sad smile graced her expression. "Thank you."

Susan M Baer

Twenty-Six

Monday morning Jackie stood at the window at the back of the hospital administrator's office. The space had been officially empty since Douglas' arrest nearly two weeks ago. The board had asked her to fill in as the interim administrator and last week, after they had procured Jameson's resignation, they had offered her the job.

They wanted an answer last Friday but she didn't have one. Instead she had asked for more time to think about it. She'd made several lists of pros and cons and even discussed it with Marie, but she wasn't any closer to a decision than she had been when they'd made her the offer.

She concentrated on the view outside and watched the people in the courtyard as they moved to and from the campus buildings. A few of them had chosen to take their break in the brisk temperatures as they sat on the benches that lined the walkways. A man caught her eye as he walked toward her building and her heart skipped a beat. It was AJ.

She took a step back from the edge of the window in case he looked up at her. If he saw her he might come up to her office to talk. He'd been trying to reach her since Thanksgiving, but she wasn't ready to see him. She didn't want more condemnation for what she'd done, so for now she saw little point in a conversation with him.

He stopped and looked up as someone approached him. Jackie's heart ached when she realized it wasn't AJ. She took a deep breath and blinked away the tears pooling in her eyes. Despite everything, her heart still ached for things to be right between them.

A soft knock on the open door made her look up. She recognized Daniel's reflection in the glass.

"I wanted to stop by and see if I could persuade you to accept the administrator's position."

She turned as he stepped into the office. He closed the door behind him and walked to the center of the room.

"I have a lot to consider, Daniel," she said. "It won't be easy for me to win over the department directors. Mercedes was right. Douglas did a fantastic job convincing them I'm not even qualified to type a damn memo."

"A reputation you allowed him to mold." He shoved his hand into the pockets of his trousers. "I hate to say it, Sam, but you helped Jameson make this bed you're lying in by keeping your mouth shut." He cocked his eyebrow. "But something tells me the director you're really worried about is AJ."

She stepped to the desk and tapped her fingers on the edge of the wood. She straightened her shoulders and took a deep breath.

"You're right. I'm not sure a business relationship with him would work. If he decides to accept his reinstatement I will probably decline the board's offer. I realize my deception was... wrong. I didn't think about how many people I was affecting, and I certainly never intended for AJ to discover the truth." She cleared her throat. "He'll probably never forgive me for what I've done and that will make things difficult for everyone here. It would probably be best for me to leave Central Valley if he returns."

"Sam, when was the last time you talked to him?"

"The day he found out that..." She swallowed the lump in her throat. He was so angry at her that day. How could he ever forgive her for what she'd done? "I never meant to hurt him, Daniel. Even when I saw them together I just... I always thought he would tell me it wasn't what I thought."

"Did you ever ask him about what happened? Did you ask your best friend about it?"

She huffed out a laugh to fight the tears she could feel building. "And what exactly was I supposed to ask them, Daniel? Is this really NOT what it looks like or did you both just forget you're dating other people?"

"So you took Mike Hollister's word as truth that it had been going on for some time without giving the man you loved or your best friend a chance to explain?"

"I saw them with my own eyes, Daniel. Even if it was the mistake I've always hoped it was, they were lying there together." She sucked in a deep breath. "He was holding her like he used to hold me. The most precious, sacred part of what we had together was gone. The part of him that I thought was for me only... he was sharing with her." She wiped a single tear when it dropped to her cheek and then squared her shoulders. "Mike only confirmed what I had discovered."

Daniel scratched his jaw and blew out a heavy sigh. She recognized the look. He was trying to figure out the best way to tell her something she wasn't going to like. Maybe he found out what really happened. A spark of hope ignited in her chest and despite her better judgement she couldn't help but wish he would tell her she was wrong.

"Daniel..." She hesitated then dropped her arms to her side when she realized what he had said. "How did you know what Mike said me?"

Daniel pointed to the couch next to him. "Have a seat, Sam."

Jackie sat down and waited for Daniel to answer her question. He sat with a sigh and she swallowed the nervous lump forming in her throat.

"I've never lied to you before and I'm not going to start now. You know I care about you, Sam, and I have no problem telling you when you screw up. So believe me when I tell you, this time sweetheart, you *really* screwed up."

"No. I know what I saw." She moved to the edge

of the seat and started to stand when his voice brought her movements to a halt.

"Sit down, Sam. It's time you heard the truth."

She watched his expression. He hadn't moved a muscle yet his presence was commanding. With only the tone of his voice he was able to make her comply. He wasn't angry, that much she knew, but he was going to make sure she heard what he had to say.

She slid back against the cushions and waited for Daniel to continue.

"I ran into AJ last night. He and Dr. Jackson were wrapping up a rather long day with a drink at the Red Door. They had spent the day with Mike Hollister's widow helping her with his funeral arrangements."

"His widow? I didn't realize…"

"Mr. Hollister was killed in an accident Friday night. His private plane landed hard when a strong gust sideswiped it on its approach. They were at the hospital when he died."

Jackie sat in silence. Mike Hollister was dead? A hollow feeling swept over her. She felt like she'd just lost a friend, even though he was never really *her* friend. He was one of AJ's fraternity brothers, but he'd felt like her friend because he'd shielded her from the humiliation of AJ's and Stacey's betrayal. All these years she'd felt a connection with him because he cared enough to tell her the truth.

"AJ asked me if I'd seen you lately and how you've been," he said. "I thought that was odd until he told me you've been ignoring his calls."

She frowned. "I suppose it hasn't occurred to him that maybe I've been busy."

"Actually, it has. He was using that very same excuse to explain your behavior. But, I know better than that, don't I, Sam? You've been ignoring him."

She crossed her arms. "I don't see the point in talking to him. He said it was over between us."

"What if I told you he finally knows what happened that night?"

"Of course he knows what happened. He just can't admit to me that he cheated."

"I didn't say he remembered it, I said he finally knows what happened. He was drugged, Sam. So was Stacey. From what Mike told them your friend still doesn't know anything bad happened to her that night."

Jackie could feel the thumping of her heart get stronger. Her hope was growing with each beat. "But what about all the times they were together hiding their affair from me?"

"Do you really believe that? Honestly, Sam, I think you're too smart to be fooled that easily. You would've figured it out from the start."

"Mike said—"

"Mike lied to you, Sam. He was one of the ones that drugged them. He told you that out of some twisted belief that he was protecting you from someone else." Daniel shook his head. "Look, I don't know all the players in this insane Shakespearean drama, but they do. So my guess is you do too."

She remembered Mike grabbing her arm and pulling her into the shadows in the yard of the fraternity house. He had caught her when she came back to talk to AJ. She'd wanted so much to be wrong she had convinced herself AJ would be able to explain everything and things would go back to the way they had been. But then Mike had told her AJ and Stacey had been seeing each other secretly for months.

The overwhelming feeling when her world had been ripped away and destroyed left her shaking. Mike caught her as her legs gave out and pressed her back against the cool bricks of the old house. Then Jesse had staggered onto the porch and called Mike's name, but Mike had whispered to her to keep quiet. Her need to trust someone, anyone, after losing AJ had compelled her to do as he said. When Jesse had gone back into the house, Mike had told her to run and never look back.

A tear dropped to her cheek when she realized she had done just that, and the harder AJ had tried to find her, the harder she had run.

"He thought he was protecting me from Jesse." She dropped her gaze to the floor. "Jesse was always making sleazy comments to me when AJ wasn't around. As soon as he would walk out of the room or turn his back Jesse would make some vulgar gesture. He seemed to think it was funny but I found him repulsive." She tucked a strand of hair behind her ear. "After a while it started scaring me. So much about Jesse seemed evil. The last time he did it AJ had walked into the room and was standing behind him." She looked up at Daniel. "When Jesse turned around and saw him, AJ had looked at Jesse with an expression I had never seen before. It almost scared me, but then AJ turned to me and smiled. That was the last time Jesse had spoken to me at all."

Daniel leaned forward and rubbed his chin. "Talk to him, Sam."

She shook her head. "I should have trusted him. I should have known Jesse would…"

"If AJ couldn't figure out what they'd done, how the hell could you?" He sighed. "He loves you, Sam. Talk to him."

Jackie blinked her eyes and wiped away the tears when they fell to her cheeks. She stood and straightened the hem of her jacket.

"You're right, Daniel. I've cried enough tears over what those bastards did."

"So what are you going to do about it?"

"What I should have done thirteen years ago. And this time, I'm not going to let anyone stop me."

Daniel smiled. "That's my girl."

Twenty-Seven

AJ strode slowly up the concrete walk to the steps in the front of his condo. The sound of the salt grinding under his feet couldn't penetrate his thoughts any more than the frosty temperatures of the early winter morning could penetrate the black wool overcoat he was wearing. His thoughts were locked in the few memories he had of the events that followed the night of the formal. At least they felt like memories compared to the fragmented dreams he'd had over the past thirteen years.

He remembered Jackie standing under the oak tree in the backyard of her mother's house. It hadn't been raining, like in his dreams, but she had been crying. Their conversation was a complete mystery to him and all he'd had to work with was what his dreams had conjured. He and Warren had debated dozens of times over the years about how much of it was real and how much of it was his imagination. The only thing AJ did know for certain was Jackie had walked out of his life that night and never looked back.

Learning what Mike and Jesse had done explained why she had left. It bridged the gap between having the most beautiful woman he'd ever met grace him with her love, and waking up the next day to find she had vanished without a trace.

Mike's funeral left him with a mix of emotions he was trying to sort out. AJ had forgiven Mike mostly because staying angry wasn't going to change the past. It wasn't going to bring Jackie back. He could forget the hell he'd been through for the sake of granting Mike his dying wish, and more importantly so he could finally let go of the past. Nothing more could be done about it that would make any difference, Mike was dead and Jesse was serving a twenty year sentence for a drug related murder conviction. But then there was what they had done to Jackie. Knowing what she had seen, and imagining the betrayal she would have felt, was harder to forget.

In the last few days he'd put himself in her shoes and his reaction to just the fabricated image of Jackie lying naked in another man's arms shocked him. Even after thirteen long years he couldn't bring himself to think of her as belonging to any other man. The pain and anger the thought provoked was so overwhelming he would do anything to escape it. He sighed. He knew he couldn't be angry anymore about the way she had disappeared, because he wasn't sure he wouldn't have done the same.

He slid his key into the deadbolt on his front door and his heart fluttered when his senses sprang to life. He turned around and Jackie stood on the top step, a nervous smile adorned her lips.

"Are you coming or going?" she said.

"Coming." He turned the key and swung the door open. "Can I offer you a cup of coffee?"

"Sure."

She smiled and he stepped aside. His hand ached to touch her as she passed over the threshold but he kept it at his side. She hadn't returned his calls so he was more than a little surprised to see her. Maybe she was here to tell him to stop calling and stay out of her life.

She stopped at the coat rack next to the stairs and hugged her trench coat tight around her.

"I hope you don't mind me stopping by like this."

He hesitated and waited for her to continue. When she didn't he said, "No. I don't mind." He unbuttoned his coat and slipped it off his arms.

"There's so much I want to say to you," she said.

"I've tried calling you. You won't pick up the phone."

"I was afraid."

"And now?"

She dropped her gaze to the floor. "Now I realize I have to face my fear and do what's right."

"And what's that?"

"Tell you how sorry I am… tell you that what I did was wrong. You didn't deserve what I…"

AJ hung up his coat and turned to her. If this was

going to be his last chance to talk to her, he was going to make damn sure she knew how he felt.

"I have a few things I need to say to you as well, Jackie. Things I should have said before." He reached his hand toward her. "Can I take your coat?"

"No!" Her eyes widened with fear and she pulled her collar together under her chin. "I came here because I wanted to…" She hesitated then took a step toward the door. "This was a mistake. I should go."

"What was a mistake?" He grabbed her arm and stopped her. "Jackie, don't. We need to talk. Please." He turned to face her. "Don't walk away from me this time. I never understood why you left me, but now I do. Let me explain what happened."

"I know what happened, AJ. I know they drugged you and Stacey. But I don't think I can do this." She looked away. "I know I should have done things differently and I'm sorry for the way I handled everything, but I didn't know what else to do. It just hurt so much to see you…"

"The past is gone, Jackie." He let go of her arm to wrap his hands around her shoulders and he stepped closer to her. "We can't change what happened or what we did, but we can do things differently this time." He lifted her chin with his fingertips and looked into her deep blue eyes. "Please," he whispered. "Stay for a while."

"I don't want to go."

"Then don't."

She shook her head. "I thought I could talk about all of this, but now I'm not so sure. I can't face what

I did."

"For God's sake, Jackie, you didn't do anything."

"Exactly! I didn't do anything except run away like a child. I should have trusted you. I should have given you a chance to explain."

He let go of her shoulders and ran his hands through his hair then blew out a heavy breath.

"I don't blame you for that. I understand why you ran, Jackie." He shook his head. "They took so much away from us and we didn't even know it."

"That's why I came here today. I wanted to try and get back some of what we lost."

He took her hand in his and brought it to his lips to tenderly kiss her knuckles.

"What did you have in mind?"

"I was hoping we could have that dance we never got." She smiled. "The one you promised me when you bought me that dress. Do you remember?"

"How could I forget?" He smiled back. "You always looked beautiful in red but that dress made you look incredible."

"Well, I don't have that one anymore so I was hoping this one was close enough."

She opened her coat and AJ almost whimpered. Jackie was right. It wasn't exactly the same. The one he had bought her was carved into his memory, right down to the last stitch in the hem. But the red satin dress she was wearing now was just as arresting. The way the material laid against her skin was irresistible and he couldn't stop himself from reaching out to touch the edge lying against her collarbone.

"Dance with me," she whispered.

He walked around her and pulled her coat off her shoulders. When her arms were free of the sleeves he hung it on the rack. He took her hand in his and twirled her around a full turn and a half before he wrapped his arm around her waist and pulled her body to his. Her soft breasts lay gently against his chest and he hesitated long enough to cement this moment into his memory. Then slowly he began to move and led her in a gentle sway to the rhythm playing in his mind.

"I used to dream about his moment," he said. He laid his cheek against the soft silk of her hair and let her scent penetrate his senses. "It was always so bittersweet because no matter how wonderful you felt in my arms, I knew when I woke up you'd be gone."

"I'm so sorry, AJ. I should've—"

"Shhh, I know why you left me, Jackie. I know what you saw, and I would do anything to take that away." He let go of her hand and wrapped his arms around her. He pulled her tighter and kissed the shell of her ear as he continued to lead her in the dance. "I want to erase that image from your mind. I want to make a new one for you to see when you close your eyes."

"But I shouldn't have listened to Mike. I should've given you a chance to explain." She buried her face in his chest. "I should've believed in you."

He lowered his face and kissed her neck. "What's done is done, Jackie. We can't change the past." He pulled her chin up and looked into her eyes. "But we can stop letting them keep us apart."

He kissed her petal soft lips and felt her body relax against him. Memories of their first kiss flooded his mind. He was more nervous now than he had been back then, because this time he knew what was at stake, this time he truly knew what he would lose if he pushed too hard.

Jackie broke the kiss and nuzzled her face to his neck. She wrapped her arms so tight around him he almost stumbled as he danced his way to the stairs.

He laid his cheek against her head and gently stroked her hair.

"You okay?" he whispered.

She nodded her head, but when she grabbed the back of his shirt in her fists he knew she was frightened. She'd always clung to him like this when she was scared and he loved knowing she still wanted him to protect her.

"I'm scared too, Jackie, but if you can trust me again we can work through this."

"I do trust you. I think deep down I always trusted you, because I never gave up hope that someday you would be able to tell me what I saw was a lie."

"It was a lie, all of it. I've never loved anyone but you and I've never wanted anyone but you." He picked her up and cradled her in his arms. He took the first step and buried his face in her hair to whisper into her ear.

"I love you, Jackie, and I want to show you just how much."

"I love you, too."

He ascended the stairs to the second floor and turned the corner to his room. He tucked her head under his chin and carried her over the threshold. When he reached the edge of his bed he set her on her feet and combed his fingers into her hair.

He brushed his lips across hers and exhaled a warm, soft breath against her mouth. Electricity shot through him when her hands clenched the linen covering his chest and his hands vibrated with restraint.

He touched his tongue against the seam of her lips and dipped it into the moist heat when she sighed. She inhaled sharply and he leaned into her body as the need to take her rose in him suddenly.

He heard himself moan as he deepened the kiss and when she pressed her nails into his scalp to pull him closer to her mouth he growled with need. The kiss was like nothing they had ever shared and he knew in that instant he would die if he lost her love again. The need to forge a new impenetrable bond with her was vital.

He dragged the zipper on her dress down her back. The weight of the satin pulled the red temptation off her shoulders and hung on the crook of her elbows. He slid his hands up her bare back and felt her soft warm skin all the way to her shoulders.

"Let it fall to the floor, Jackie. I want to feel your skin."

Before she had lowered her arms he ripped the two halves of his shirt apart and buttons flew in every direction. He leaned forward and kissed her again as he struggled with the closures on his slacks.

The satin hit the floor and pooled at her feet. He reached forward and slipped his finger under the red lace thong she was wearing, the last obstacle between them. She reached behind her waist and with a light snap the material fell into the palm of his hand.

He picked her up and held her against his torso, her legs wrapped around his waist. He crawled onto the bed and laid her back softly onto the comforter. He caressed her thighs then gently pressed them back against her stomach. He held himself over her and looked into her eyes with a smile.

"I can't find the words to tell you how much I love you, how much I want you." He kissed her tenderly. "How much I need you."

"Then show me," she whispered.

AJ watched a tear roll across her temple into her hair. The sparkle in her eyes made his heart thunder and her smile filled it with joy.

"My pleasure," he said.

Jackie wrapped her hands around his head and pulled him down to her. She moaned when he gently raked his teeth along her neck. He licked away the tingle his incisors left behind and slowly wandered his way to her breast.

His need to possess her was strong, but his desire to love her slowly and sensuously had taken control. If he wanted to erase the image of Stacey in his arms he had to take his time and make sure he left no doubt at all in Jackie's mind that he never loved anyone but her.

AJ circled her nipple with his tongue. The long

sensual strokes conjured memories of the first time he'd made love to her. He closed his eyes and pulled her breast into his mouth. He gently suckled her then groaned when she gripped his heavy erection in her hand.

"I want to feel you inside me," she whispered.

He released her breast and panted as he laid his forehead on her shoulder. The feel of her hand on him, stroking him, was incredible.

"I will be, Jackie. I promise."

"I want you to do it now. I need to feel you inside me and know that you're making love to me, not someone I'm pretending to be."

"I want to take it slow. I want to erase the image you saw. The lie you were led to believe all these years."

"Then do it now." She wrapped her legs around his hips and pulled herself closer to him. "Take me, AJ, like you did back then. Let me feel you inside me as you hold me tight."

He slid his fingers between her folds and felt the arousal spilling from her body. She was more than ready for him. He dragged the head of his penis between her lips and touched it lightly to her clitoris. She moaned and tilted her hips up, and he pushed into her softness.

His strokes were slow and deliberate. He wanted to give them both time to feel every inch of his possession.

She grabbed his biceps and squeezed. "Hold me tight, AJ. I need to feel your arms around me."

He thrust the last of his erection into her channel and snaked his arms under her. He held her shoulders tight to his and began a rhythmic slow dance as he moved in and out of her body.

Her soft moans increased his need and when she pushed her nails into the flesh of his back he pressed his teeth into her neck. She moaned again and combed her fingers through his hair.

"He loves me," she whispered.

The sound of her voice was so slight he almost missed it. He moved his hands to cradle her face and looked into her eyes. A glimmer of fear still remained and he smiled gently.

"Always, Jackie." He increased the speed of his movements and kissed her hard.

Her body tightened around him and she broke the kiss with a gasp. She screamed his name and arched her back as her arousal bathed his shaft. Her legs quivered with her orgasm.

He thrust twice more and exploded inside her. For a moment, time stood still as the connection he needed with her was cemented into their history. Their souls had reunited. The pain of the past was drifting away and he lowered his body to rest against hers, his weight pressed her into the soft bed beneath them.

He rolled to his back and pulled her with him. He kissed her softly as their bodies slowly cooled. When her breathing had returned to normal he cradled her face once more.

"I've loved you from the first moment I saw you. You smiled at me and my heart became your prisoner." He wiped a tear from her cheek with his thumb. "And I gladly accept the life sentence you gave me because no matter where we go from here,

Jacqueline Samantha Dean, my love will always follow you."

Epilogue

Eight Months Later

AJ sat on the end of the bed and watched Jackie get dressed. She stood in front of the full length mirror and buttoned the silk blouse she had bought last weekend while shopping with Marie and Janet. She tucked the hem into her skirt and placed her hand over her abdomen. She turned sideways and looked at him, a smile burst from her cheeks.

He smiled back and stood to hug her from behind. When she laid her head back on his chest he inhaled the soft, spicy fragrance of her perfume. He brushed her hair aside and kissed her neck. Her scent filled his lungs. It penetrated him completely and readied him with a renewed sense of strength to face the day. The bond they had repaired was getting stronger.

"I love you, Jackie," he whispered into her hair.

"You better because you're stuck with me now."

He looked up and watched her reflection in the mirror. A glow emanated from her rosy cheeks and his heart nearly burst from his chest, he knew exactly what she meant. He *was* stuck with her, or rather she was stuck with him. She had accepted his proposal on New Year's Eve, the two carat diamond he had given her sparkled when she ran her hand up his arm. On New Year's Day he had awoke to the sound of her voice. He found her sitting at the small desk she had moved into their master suite. She was making notes on her PDA while she chatted with Marie. The two women had already started the wedding plans.

The big day was still a month away, but yesterday she had given him an early wedding gift. After dinner she had quietly placed a long white jewelry box on his dessert plate and sat across from him with the best pokerfaced expression he had ever seen. Tucked inside the box was a small silver spoon engraved with the words 'Special Delivery'. Before he had even seen the miniature rattle at the end of it he knew what it meant. Jackie was pregnant with his child, a child he never imagined he would want, but now he knew he could never live without.

"That was my plan all along," he said. "I can't believe you let me trap you into marriage."

"Yes, I suppose I should have figured it out. After all, you can't seem to keep your hands off of me."

He spun her around and pulled her tight against him. She opened her mouth on a sigh and he softly traced her lips with his tongue.

"I've never heard you complain," he said.

He squeezed her firm ass and pressed his arousal against her abdomen.

"I'll never complain about this," she said.

She slid her hand underneath the waistband of his silk trousers and wrapped her fingers around his shaft.

He groaned and gently bit her neck. How he wished they weren't due in court in less than an hour.

"You are a dangerous woman. One of these days I'm going to tell the world to go to hell and tie you to that bed." He pulled her hand from his pants and kissed her forehead before he turned and headed for the closet. "But, today we need to meet with the board attorneys before the hearing. Anderson wants us to be prepared for any surprises Jameson's attorneys may be planning."

"I thought we weren't expected to testify today. They said this was a formality."

"It is, and if everything goes as smoothly as they plan this preliminary hearing shouldn't take long. But I am not willing to underestimate that man a second time." He turned and looked at her. "He hired an assassin to kill you, Jackie. I will never be so complacent with your safety again."

"He hired that assassin to kill you first, AJ." She crossed her arms under her breasts. "I just hope I can control myself long enough not to leap across the room and strangle the bastard. If I never have to see that man again I would be perfectly happy."

"Believe me I would like nothing more than to keep him as far away from you as possible, but Charles wants us there." He adjusted the knot in his tie and turned toward her. "As for keeping you in your seat, I will be at your side the whole time and Daniel and Mercedes have assigned security details to both of us. I think the *bastard* will be safe for now."

"Party pooper." She smiled. "What happened at Suzanne's hearing yesterday?"

"She was ordered to stand trial for tampering with evidence and embezzlement." He kissed her hand and led her to the stairs. "I also found out she had outstanding warrants and that is why her bond was denied. So now she is serving two years for past offenses while she waits for her trial."

"What a beautiful family." She snickered. "I wonder what their family reunions are like."

AJ took a deep breath before he opened the front door. "I don't even want to know."

****

The courtroom was packed. AJ was surprised, but somehow he knew he shouldn't have been. The board had tried to keep the embezzlement out of the papers, but the more they tried to suppress the story, the more the reporters pried. When the story broke about Douglas and his daughter, Suzanne, working together to frame AJ and Jackie, a lot of eyebrows were raised. But then the charges of Conspiracy to Commit Murder against Jameson were made public and a firestorm of gossip swept the town. In no time at all it became the favorite topic in every social circle. Therefore, it was no surprise that the date of Douglas' preliminary hearing made the front page of the Lincoln Chronicle, and it seemed as if half of the city's residents took the day off so they could attend the proceedings.

Judge Margaret McMahon had listened to testimony from four witnesses, and after what seemed like an eternity of questions from both sides, she had ruled the case be sent to trial. The instant her gavel echoed along the mahogany walls two bailiffs flanked Douglas and he was escorted out. The bright orange jumpsuit and the jingle of the shackles he was confined with drew the attention of every eye in the room.

AJ watched him shuffle across the tile floor. His head was down but the sideways glance he threw AJ's way was filled with bitterness and hatred. Obviously the very real threat of time in prison wasn't enough to give Douglas a change of heart. His distaste for AJ was just as strong as it had ever been.

The bailiffs treated Douglas with little respect for who he was when they shoved him through the door. He had hesitated long enough to take another good look at AJ and Jackie. The expression on Jameson's face was tinged with pain and frustration, and AJ wondered if he even realized that his life was never going to be the same. The career Douglas had spent more than twenty years building was gone forever. His life was in complete ruin.

AJ listened to the electronic lock engage after the door shut behind the bailiffs. Douglas' freedom had been taken away and he was locked up like the animal he had become, but the sight didn't give AJ the satisfaction he was hoping for. He wanted to feel justice was being served for what Douglas had put Jackie through, for daring to threaten her life. Instead, AJ couldn't help but feel a touch of sympathy for him. Douglas had reduced himself from the hospital administrator of the world's largest and most reputable healthcare facility, to a lost soul with no future all because he had let a small seed of jealousy grow into a colossal monster he could no longer control.

The public started their slow exit from the courtroom while security formed a wall of flesh around AJ and Jackie. They were led into a room at the end of the hall where Jake Winston was seated in a chocolate leather, wingback chair. Together the three of them would wait for the crowd to dissipate before they left the building.

Jake looked completely unaffected by what had just happened. He had endured harsh questions from Jameson's attorneys given the fact that he was the one to procure Jameson's confession. But Jake had maintained his ironclad composure, one he obviously developed from a lifetime of experience.

Jake's family was a favorite target for newsmongers and tabloids. Every misstep was scrutinized, every imperfection magnified, and his parents seemed to make things worse by their subtle alienation of their only son. Jake was rarely seen with his family and if he wasn't alone he was with someone who he wasn't particularly close with.

AJ sighed as he and Jackie sat across from Jake.

Despite all the money, power, and influence, Jake's life never appealed to him. And today he was never so glad his name wasn't Winston.

****

Jake Winston felt a muscle tighten in his jaw as he sat on the hard leather chair. The musty old office belonged to the oldest senior partner of Gibson, Moss, and Associates. The old man was annoyingly detailed, ridiculously meticulous, and left nothing uncovered, unprotected, or unaddressed. All of this made the man the epitome of exasperation. But it was also the reason Jake chose him for his legal counsel.

"Mr. Gibson, I am paying you to draw up the necessary paperwork, not to question my judgement," Jake said.

"Ordinarily I would not, but this situation is different, Jacob," Gibson said. "I suspect there is a great deal more at stake than you realize."

"Perhaps it will make you feel more at ease to know that I have given this decision more thought than it warrants, and despite my desire to have this process behind me I plan to mull over my decision while you close any loopholes. There is one consideration I want to be sure of before I put them permanently out of my misery."

"I doubt that any amount of time will completely quell my reservations about the fact that you want to forfeit the entire Winston family fortune." Mr. Gibson sat back. "But, I have been your legal counsel long enough to know that you will do what you want regardless of my advice."

Jake smiled. "Precisely."

Gibson sighed. "I will have two sets drawn up by next week, one exactly as you have asked and one with a loophole you can use if you change your mind. There are ways to make the clean break you desire without walking away empty handed. Don't you think you deserve something from your father?"

"I want nothing that man has a connection to, and that includes any assets he had prior possession of." Jake could feel the heat of his anger burning in his temples. "If you had walked in my path for even a day while living in that hellish existence as Frank and Miranda Winston's son, you would not hesitate to do this. In fact, you would be amazed I have waited this long."

"Very well. Just remember, what you are asking me to do cannot be undone unless your father initiates the reversal."

"The only concern for me would *be* a reversal." Jake stood and shook Mr. Gibson's hand. "I will see you in a week."

Gibson led Jake to the door and hesitated before he opened it.

"Jacob," he whispered. "I have known your family for many years, and yes, your father is a very difficult man. But I want you to be absolutely sure you know what you are doing. Perhaps you should talk this out with someone. Maybe Henry can help you put this in perspective."

Jake crossed his arms. "You want me to discuss my personal and financial affairs with Miranda's beck-and-call boy?"

Gibson smiled. "Henry Jensen is the best friend you have, Jacob. Talk to him. If he tells you to sign the papers I will put my reservations to rest."

Jake smiled. Jensen knew better than anyone the hell his parents had put him through. Jake had no doubt at all Jensen would tell him to sign the documents and sever his connection with the Winstons.

"Consider it done, Mr. Gibson. Let me know when the paperwork is ready. I will even bring the old man with me so he can tell you so himself."

Jake opened the door and stepped into the hall. Freedom was so close he could taste it.

ABOUT THE AUTHOR

Susan Baer grew up in western Pennsylvania as a second generation born American and currently resides in western North Dakota. She manages her husband's private practice during the day and writes romance by night. Their two children, of the four legged variety, do their best to be supportive but on occasion can't resist the urge to demand her attention.

Writing has been a passion for her since she was young. She enjoys telling stories of love and loss, and most of all, stories she hopes will inspire her readers to never settle for less than the best. Your dreams are out there if you're willing to keep looking.

<u>Other Titles by Susan M. Baer</u>

Conceit; It's All About Jake, *The Lincoln Series, Prelude*

Coming Home, *The Lincoln Series, Prelude*

Amorous, *The Lincoln Series, Book I*

Redemption, *The Lincoln Series, Book III*

Find out more about Susan Baer and her upcoming books online at www.susanbaerauthor.com